FLAMMES DE PIERRE

for John

FLAMMES DE PIERRE

Anne Sauvy

SHORT STORIES ABOUT MOUNTAINS
AND MOUNTAINEERS

Diadem Books · London

Other books by Anne Sauvy:

Le jeu de la montagne et du hasard   (Editions Montalba, 1985)
La ténèbre et l'azur   (Les Editions Arthaud, 1991)

British Library Cataloguing in Publication Data
Sauvy, Anne
    Flammes de pierre – flames of rock
    I. Title
    843[F]

ISBN 0 906371 83 X (cased edition)
ISBN 0 906371 88 0 (trade pbk edition)

First published in France in 1982
by Editions Montalba, Paris

Published in Great Britain in 1991 (in cased and tradepaper editions)
by Diadem Books, London

Trade enquiries to Hodder and Stoughton,
Mill Road, Dunton Green, Sevenoaks, Kent TN13 2YA

Typesetting by J&L Composition Ltd, Filey, North Yorkshire

Printed and bound in Great Britain by
Biddles Ltd, Guildford and King's Lynn

CONTENTS

CONTENTS

INTRODUCTION

Anne Sauvy discovered the Alps at the age of thirteen and took up mountaineering in Chamonix at seventeen. Preferring to be far away, 'high away', from the crowds, she quickly found herself drawn to the big classic ice routes and numbers among her 170 alpine ascents the north faces of the Mönch, Aletschhorn, Bionnassay and Verte as well as two routes on the Brenva Face of Mont Blanc. When in 'exile' — as she calls it — in Paris, she lectures on the history of publishing and censorship at the Sorbonne, specialising in works of the seventeenth and eighteenth centuries. She is married to Oxford don and fellow alpinist, John Wilkinson, and her father was the celebrated demographic economist, Alfred Sauvy.

She has never, she says, got over that first shock of amazement at seeing the Alps. It resurfaces constantly in her stories. From a deep love of nature, combined with a feeling for alpine tradition, she sets the stage that all can recognise for its authenticity, then upon it enjoys nothing better than to ambush her audience with the unexpected. Her range is wide, finding its finest expression in fantasy and suspense where, with nothing forbidden, wit and humour can enjoy free rein. Alike she treads the realms of dream and nightmare and she exhibits a keen edge of satire. The consistent elegance of her tales has prompted critics to see in them echoes of de Maupassant and Daudet, and also Edgar Allen Poe and Samivel. And she herself revels in literary allusion — 'La Fourche' is an ingenious improvisation on the Dr Faustus theme, while '2084' predicts a chilling Orwellian future. In the amusing parable 'Liberation!' she imagines mountains fighting against their exploitation. Turning the tables on mankind, they — like the beasts of *Animal Farm* — adopt all the destructive characteristics of their former oppressors.

Sauvy humanises her often dark plots with a sympathetic evocation of character, the result of close observation of the mountain scene over three decades. During that period she has enjoyed the confidence of the top mountaineers of the day — names like Terray, Couzy, Desmaison, Hemming, Badier, Afanassieff and Profit — and has been well placed to observe their preoccupations as well as the typical foibles and vanities that climbers are prey to.

Thus Sauvy's tales — all set around Mont Blanc — are to be enjoyed on several levels. In scope and vision, they add an important facet to wealth of comment on mountaineering today by a talented new wave of short-story writers. When *Les flammes de pierre* first appeared in 1982, it earned for the author Le Prix de l'Alpe of that year, followed by an award from the German Alpine Club and it is now the first collection of Anne Sauvy's work to appear in English*. Her other collections are *Le jeu de la montagne et du hasard* (1985) and *La ténèbre et l'azur* (1991) which recently won the Grand Prix du Ier Salon du Livre de Montagne.

Audrey Salkeld

---

* Plus two additional stories

THE COLLECTOR

Who is more fascinating than a collector? Combining the worship of a particular object or aesthetic with his need of possession, he seeks, in this ephemeral world, to reassemble fragments of space, to govern long-gone days, to discover the indiscernible, to conquer and perpetuate delicate mysteries.

Childish or sublime, the collector's dreams are inhabited by exotic butterflies and engraved pencil boxes, by Nestlé chocolate labels and Ming china, by campaign buttons and fine crystal, by gold coins and tobacco grinders, by Kandinsky canvases and cork-screws, by autographs of divas, by Fabergé snuffboxes, by jade dragons, by Isfahan rugs, by Christmas tree ornaments, and by colourful matchbooks.

A philatelist of this mould would give ten years of his life to obtain the Mauritius two-penny stamp, the Barbados one-shilling with the colour error, the imperforate vermilion Cérès, the crimson-magenta one-cent from British Guyana, the priceless inverted swan of Western Australia, or the Blue Boy of the United States.

Another collector, of the curious race of bibliophiles, fills his library with books that will never be read, thus preserving the uncut pages untouched by the centuries, the venerable olive morocco leather binding guarding pink stitching, and the barely handled, delicate Chinese paper of the item he has coveted for years. Overlooked by the printer and proof reader, the typo error on the tenth line of page 177, which distinguishes the original edition of *Dominique*, rather than shocking him, excites him. And, far from offending his eye, the marginal comments of a sixteenth-century learned man, possibly Wimpheling, fill him with unadulterated joy.

But Lucien Péridot, perhaps the most passionate, the strangest and wildest collector the earth has ever borne, had another passion: he collected mountains.

The activity itself is not so remarkable, since all alpinists yield themselves, more or less consciously, to a quest for summits and routes they would like to be exhaustive. The difference is that Lucien Péridot did more, pushing the game to an extreme no one else would have dreamed of.

Nothing in his upbringing indicated this predisposition. The only son of a small Parisian shopkeeper, he was born at the end of the nineteenth century — a time when alpinism amounted to a personal calling that touched only a few odd fellows and their dauntless guides. And Lucien's father certainly did not encourage his son to pursue the 'glory' of hazardous ascents. On the contrary, he lived solely to assure his child the education he himself had never benefited from.

Between schools and tutors, young Lucien had therefore excelled in the humanities and pursued his academic studies with a zeal that almost cost him his health. His discovery of the world of mountains occurred when his parents, duly reprimanded by the family doctor, sent him to spend several summers at Briançon — during which time he revealed some real talent as a climber. But the young man managed to keep within reasonable limits, and it was with pleasure that he went back every fall to the delights of the ablative absolute or the subtleties of deponent verbs.

At first he had intended to devote part of his life to the study of the metric clause in the work of Sulpicius Lupercus, but this ambitious project fell through because, on June 28, 1914, a man from Bosnia, of whom he had never heard, murdered in Sarajevo an Austrian archduke, of whom he also knew nothing, thus precipitating World War I. Lucien Péridot returned safe and sound from his four years in the trenches, but his life had been shattered; he understood that nothing would be the same ever again. His father and his mother had fled Paris in an ultimately futile attempt to escape the Spanish influenza epidemic. And the young and tender-hearted neighbour whom he regarded almost as his fiancée, and who, with tears in her eyes, had promised to wait for him, had long since married another man. Many of his friends had died — old-time friends or comrades in combat with whom he had shared hopes and fears, cold and discomfort, and parcels from home. Paris had changed and seemed to be sinking into a frenzy of distractions, as unbearable to Lucien as political disputes and financial speculations.

He tried to contact his cousin, Ferdinand Beaufer his only remaining relative, deciding to wait for him at the exit of the public administration office where, most likely, he still worked. The two men fell into each others arms.

'Guess what, I got married, despite my lopsided jaw!' Ferdinand burst out after the first effusions. 'I'll take you to dinner at home! You'll meet Léontine and my two children, Germaine and Yolande . . . The third one is on the way!'

'Are you happy?' asked Lucien.

'Of course! . . . Absolutely!' Ferdinand replied. 'It's really something, you know, having a home and no longer hanging around cheap, working-class cafés. Now when I get home in the evening, I find the stove hissing and supper on the fire . . . All I have to do is read my paper under the lampshade, listening to my chattering kids . . . After so many years alone, this is certainly a nice thing. . .'

'And your wife, won't she mind having an unexpected guest?'

'Bah! If she starts nagging, it won't last long. . . Come on! I'll take you there!'

Ferdinand Beaufer lived on the fifth floor of a modest property on Rue de Batignolles. As they went upstairs, he gave his cousin a few words of advice.

'I'll go in first, to let her know. . . Make sure to use the felt pads to walk on the floor. . . Most important, tell her you like her cooking. . .'

In spite of these precautions, Leontine's demeanour was measured, not to say hostile. She was a large, dark-haired woman, in whose face authority had started to form some angular wrinkles. She saw no reason to conceal her displeasure.

'Without telling me in advance! And I suppose I should say nothing . . . Look, all we have for dinner are leftovers from yesterday's stew . . . and the servings will be reduced for everybody . . . I hope you aren't too hungry!'

'I could just leave, cousin,' Lucien suggested. 'Tsk, tsk! . . . You stay!' Ferdinand cut him short, embarrassed by the incident. 'Lucien has come back from the front safe and sound,' he explained to his wife, to justify his stand.

'So much the better for him!' Léontine replied, dryly.

They sat down at the table, and it was with pleasure that Lucien, ignoring the obvious censure of the woman and the two little girls, found again the naturalness and the jesting he had shared with the companion of his youth. They evoked the past and the memory of their late friends. Over dessert, the subject of future plans was broached.

'So, what do you mean to do now?' Ferdinand asked him. 'Take up your old work? . . .'

'No . . . I don't think so . . . If I stayed here, the atmosphere of classrooms and libraries would stifle me, and I no longer want this. . . Maybe someday, anyhow, I'll end up teaching . . . For now I'm not the least tempted by that . . . And there's nothing more foreign to me than the idea of that thesis I meant to do on the metric clause in Sulpicius Lupercus . . . I need action . . .'

'But how can you make a living?'

'I've talked to my accountant . . . By selling my father's business to the manager — he wants to buy it — and with the inheritance my mother left me, I can deposit all this money and live on the interest . . .'

'Some people are born lucky!' Léontine broke in.

'Please, my dear Léo!' Ferdinand remonstrated.

Unperturbed, and fully realising that he risked not being invited again, Lucien continued revealing his projects to his cousin.

'I could rent a little house in the country . . . hire a war widow for a maid-servant; she could serve me as a cook, seamstress and housekeeper . . . I would be free, you understand, free! . . . I'd settle in the foothills of the Alps. . . . In the past, I accomplished some fine climbs . . . That would be all I'd have to do, you realise? . . . Far from the crowds, on the heights . . . Maybe I'll find again that spirit of brotherhood and human warmth I knew at the front — and which is lacking in this city . . . Sulpicius Lupercus! . . . When what I really need is fresh air, challenge, wind, snow, sunshine, clear sky . . .'

'That's it!' Léontine concluded. 'Some of us work our fingers to the bone to raise children . . . And others have nothing better to do than live on their interest and take nature walks . . . After all, nothing detains you here in Paris . . .'

Lucien held back from telling her that, in any case, *she* wasn't detaining him at all. He felt his vague inclinations grow into a firm and definite resolve to depart, and shortly he took his leave.

'Good luck, Lucien, old pal!' Ferdinand exclaimed, escorting him to the door. 'I envy you a little, you know . . . But be careful about your living costs . . . You are not used to . . . Times have changed since the war . . . Prices are rising . . . I'd hate to see you get into trouble, because I'm really happy for you . . .'

'Don't worry! I'll be all right!'

'And most important, send me your news! . . . I'll be thinking of you . . .'

The following summer Lucien took up residence at Annemasse, the town he had chosen for a base in easy reach of Switzerland, of the Mont Blanc massif, and even of the Dauphiné.

Just as he had announced, he rented a summer cottage that included a little garden, and hired a widow of respectable age as his house-keeper. Gertrude Levernois, although quite satisfied to have found such a position serving just one master who didn't seem too particular, dis-approved of his style of living, which was not in keeping with her ideas of bourgeois dignity.

In fact, once he had rid himself of all material concerns, Lucien couldn't think of anything but climbing. He gathered a network of new comrades, still without finding that carefree and friendly climate he had dreamed of. But the mountains themselves lived up to his memories — beautiful, wild, and profoundly desirable.

This is when he embarked on his first collection. Whenever possible, whenever the weather was favourable, whenever he found climbing partners, Lucien methodically travelled all over the Alps. When alone, or when the weather was dubious, he still roamed at mid-altitude, sometimes on foot, sometimes on skis.

When rain or snow fell, when the conditions were not favourable, or when he had to wait for a partner to make himself available, Lucien found again the charm of his studies — but these no longer concerned classic erudition. He had quickly put together an extensive library consecrated entirely to the mountains and the history of alpinism. Soon he added a card system, which he placed inside a series of shoe-boxes, ordered by number, on some shelves that lined the walls of his office. There one could find a myriad of index cards, cleverly arranged in topographic order correspond-ing to all the summits of the Western Alps and to all the known routes on them. On each card he wrote the particulars of the first ascent, date, first ascenders, difficulties, time taken — and some codified information that referred to the technical accounts contained in the books and magazines of his library. In some cases, cards showed the date when Lucien Péridot himself had climbed the route, and the conditions he had found; his conquest was also emphasised by a colourful, triumphant little symbol that rode the upper part of the card.

Before long he experienced almost as much delight at seeing himself enter the marks of his achievements on the cards as he did at finding his way up a new summit. He collected everything — the passes and the rock spires, the granite ridges and the ice couloirs, the 3,000-metre summits and the 4,000-metre peaks, the standard routes and the North faces. He was always ready to go, ready to climb, ready to persist, heedless of the cold or obstacles. Returning from a climb, his eyes still shining with the adventure, he had learned to ignore the complaints of Gertrude.

'Where is Monsieur coming from, in such a state? . . . If I may say, what a way of living, for somebody like you . . . running around like a bohemian . . . and getting home so worn out, so dishevelled . . . I saw it right away — that rip in your breeches . . . it will take me hours . . . Not to mention that, when you are out, I have no idea where you are or whether I should cook a meal for you . . . You told me Monday and now you come back on Wednesday . . . I'm losing my wits . . .'

'Please, Gertrude, I'm tired . . . just bring me what you have ready, when you can . . . to my office — since I have some forms to fill out . . .'

And, plunging back into his cards, Lucien had the feeling that he could preserve from the passage of time the hours of struggle and passion he had just experienced.

But soon he ran into some difficulties he had not foreseen. As a practice ground, mid-elevation mountains were nothing more for him than a transition, and the courses he had done at altitude during the first three years of his new life now made him more demanding in his choice of objectives and pushed him toward particular routes, often difficult, which didn't appeal to everybody. He suffered some distressing days of inactivity because of a lack of adequate climbing partners. Lucien preferred to climb without a guide, for he loved discovering a line and feeling himself responsible for the decision. But he suffered when he had to bear with lesser climbers who, regarding mountaineering as a mere pastime and not a passion, dragged behind, struggled with moves he judged simple, and shuddered at what was child's play for him.

He often went climbing with anonymous partners chosen at the last moment; he made few friends for himself and soon even had an enemy in a new arrival, Julien Reyssouze. Driven by alpine ambitions, this man wished to become a local star, and he couldn't help being jealous of the fact that a rival was methodically accumulating success and planning more and more.

Lucien, fervently yearning for the expansion of his collection, had taken to dreaming up specimens of a unique kind: first ascents! It must be said that in those happy times there was no need, in order to forge new territory, to force an overhang located ten metres to the left of the normally overcrowded cracks, or fourteen metres to the right of a slab smoothed by numerous users. A number of routes were still open for firsts — and what routes!

When he started to talk about them, Lucien met with nothing but indifferent scepticism. His closest companions were largely satisfied with the existing courses. And Julien Reyssouze had even awakened some doubts as to his rival's actual achievements on these.

'If he really did them,' he insinuated, 'all those routes he brags about . . . If you were to count them, you'd end up numbering them by the hundreds . . . One day the Brenva Spur! . . . Another time the Innominata! . . . The Aiguille Verte from the Grande Rocheuse! . . . The Norman-Neruda on the Lyskamm! . . . Monte Rosa from Macugnaga! . . . All routes that demand more experience than he has ever had time to gain, I assure you. Who can believe him?'

Respecting tradition, Lucien had until then taken to heart the famous principle of the Club Alpin Français, even before it was officially announced: 'Never go by yourself!' But he fretted when he saw splendid sunny days go wasted — and with them magnificent climbing opportunities.

During a clear week in June, unable to find local climbing partners, he resolved to go, alone if necessary, on a reconnaissance trip to the foot of the Triolet North Face. He thought it could be climbed, and the idea haunted him more every day. He took his gear just in case he found a mountaineer in Chamonix ready to try the adventure or to accompany him on another climb. But he was alone in Chamonix, and later in the great Argentière cirque, where he spent the night. About two in the morning, in beautiful moonlight, he left for the face, without daring formulate to himself the temptation he felt possess him.

The bergschrund presented no problems: he climbed over it and, almost without a conscious decision, found himself committed to the steeper slope above. By good or bad luck, the conditions were optimal, and he gained altitude on snow absolutely firm, yet soft enough for the tips of his boots and his crampons to bite perfectly. The slope, however, seemed extreme, and after reaching a considerable height on the face, he could no longer conceive of descending any more than he could conceive of what still lay ahead. Feeling the empty space grow hollow below, he finally chose to cut steps. Whether he found hard snow or blue ice — as in the case of a serac passage — he could no longer think of interrupting this kind of progression since, having adopted it, he found the method gave him security. So he went on for hours, cutting step after step, his muscles contracting, his arms in pain from the continuous wielding of the ice axe. When his right crampon came loose during an uphill traverse, he barely regained his balance, and shuddered nearly as much for the accident he had just avoided as for the judgments that would have followed: 'Péridot! All alone on the North Face of the Triolet! The guy must have been crazy!'

More and more carefully, he proceeded with increased attention, and it was not until late afternoon that he emerged, unbelieving, at the Col Superieur, intoxicated with air and empty space, exhausted but charged with an exaltation such as he had never known. He gained the summit, then decided to bivouac nearby, so as not to break his tie to the mountain.

In the morning he buried his small lantern deep in the snow at the place where he had finished the route. He had slipped a scrap of paper into it with his name, his route, the date, and the time. Then he started to descend toward the Couvercle, the Mer de Glace, and Chamonix. Gloomy clouds crept into the sky, and he rejoiced that the weather hadn't betrayed him during his climb. His heart throbbed, and in the midst of the deserted mountains he had an urge to trumpet his victory. He remembered right then that a meeting would take place that evening at Julien Reyssouze's. The train schedule didn't allow him to get back in time to announce his victory to the group. But he would call! The communication was difficult to establish from a small hotel he came across on the descent. Lucien insisted, argued, and finally obtained his connection.

'Julien!' he cried, 'I just did the first ascent of the North Face of the Triolet, solo . . . It's amazing, isn't it? . . . I started yesterday morning and I finished in the evening . . . I was right when I said it could be done! . . . And you fellows didn't want to believe me!'

'You must be joking, I suppose,' Reyssouze coldly replied. 'It's quite unbelievable.'

'What! I meant what I said . . . I can prove it . . . No! We're still talking, Madame! Don't cut the line, please . . . Julien! . . . I did the North Face of the Triolet! Solo! . . . You can go check my footsteps . . . And I left my lantern at the top of the route.'

'And by strange coincidence, its starting to rain here, and I suppose its snowing up there . . . My dear Péridot, you'd better think up something else . . . Nobody will believe that!'

And nobody did.

With despair in his heart, Lucien Péridot had to admit it: even his most detailed description was not enough to convince anybody. Nevertheless, when good weather returned, he persuaded a half-believer to accompany him on the standard route of the Triolet. On top, no matter how much he dug, he couldn't find his lantern; it had been swallowed by new snow.

'And even then, my friend', his companion sighed, 'who can prove that lantern of yours wasn't brought up here by the route we just did?'

They descended in silence. Lucien was haunted by the setback. He couldn't shut his eyes that night. Until then, he had hoped the truth would emerge, but now he realized there was no point in pursuing it — no point in writing to some well-known alpinists in Paris or wherever, as he had considered doing. If no witness stood up on his side — and such was the case — no one would acknowledge his feat. He felt nothing but resentment toward mankind. By early morning, Lucien Péridot had contrived a plan of action — or of revenge — that seemed to him absolutely impeccable . . .

And this is how he began his second collection of mountains, by far the more precious, since it would be entirely a collection of first ascents.

The project was at once simple and subtle. Having proved to himself what he was capable of, Lucien Péridot was going to lengthen his list of exploits, devoting all his energies to the task. He would train himself more intensively; he would improve his technique; and he would secretly harvest new climbs. Whenever possible, he would deposit in two or three keypoints of each route — in cracks in the rock — small metallic tubes containing his signature, and he would then note their exact sites. He would get additional proof by taking some evidential snapshots during his climbs. Finally, he would compile technical notes with so many details that no one would dare call them into question. And each time he would collect these pieces of evidence inside a large envelope, which he would have officially sealed and dated by a notary. The day when he would decide to make these first ascents public — after others might have done them, possibly thinking of them as firsts — that day would compensate for the humilation and unbearable scepticism to which he had been subjected. The shock would be astounding, the triumph absolute. Lucien Péridot's new passion soon took on the character of an obsession. He jealously devoted himself to the preservation of the mystery, doing most of his climbs early or late in the season, or when a place was deserted, or when a propitious fog concealed him. He wore clothes the colour of snow and rock. He stopped frequenting huts, to be closer to the mountains, to avoid people, and to bivouac near the starts of the routes.

Those who were familiar with his tanned face, with its prominent cheekbones and piercing eyes, now got used to watching his long ascetic silhouette only from a distance. They thought he wandered in the mountains without any other aim than rambling in solitude.

'Poor fellow!' they said of him. 'After all, he wasn't so bad ... he even had a sort of mad enthusiasm in collecting his routes ... who knows what he's collecting now: scree slopes? That old loony, Péridot!'

Lucien, indeed, was accomplishing marvels, launched as he was on his new path of adventure, comforted by his undeniable success and by the feeling of his own worth. The special training to which he had submitted himself daily, the climbing methods and ice techniques he had perfected, and the endurance he had developed — all brought him to a level he hadn't even envisioned, and almost matched him with the great climbers of the end of this century. Furthermore, with his natural mechanical inclination, he rapidly invented some technical devices still unheard of, ahead of the times. Forged by a local blacksmith according to Lucien's design, his crampons with fifteen points were extremely ingenious; and he was the first one who had the idea of angling an axe's pick and of deepening the notches, in order to climb the steepest ice slopes with a new technique, of which he was the true initiator.

Hardened to any weather, capable of rapidly progressing on difficult or unstable terrain, ready to bivouac anywhere and in any conditions, heedless of any taboos as to the inaccessibility of some mountains and to the defences they could confront him with, Lucien Peridot soared from conquest to conquest.

He proceeded, however, very methodically, studying maps, taking photographs of the walls, reviewing possible passages with binoculars, and then he went out, ready to conquer. How many routes of which we think we know the first ascenders were actually mastered by this astonishing pioneer! Though this period between the wars was called the *Golden Age of Alpinism*, it would have been more proper to define it as the *Golden Age of Lucien Péridot*.

Do you believe that the Nant Blanc, the arête of the Grands Montets, the Couturier on the Verte, the Ailefroide North Face, the direct route on the south-east wall of the Écrins, the Gervasutti Couloir, the Major, the Sentinelle, the Pear, the North faces of the Dolent, of the Grosshorn, of the Obergabelhorn, or of the Grand Combin de Valsorey — do you believe these routes were first climbed by the names reported in your guidebooks? No! They were first climbed by Lucien Péridot, as solo ascents.

He certainly had some great rivals, whom he couldn't help but admire, and who sometimes beat him to a climb. What a disappointment when he saw himself robbed of the Sans Nom on the Verte or the North Arête of the Dent Blanche! But the traverse of the Aiguilles du Diable was his; the North-West Wall of the Olan was his; the North Face of the Grands Charmoz was his! For he had an advantage over his competitors: he had consecrated his entire life to the goals he had set for himself, sacrificing all family joys, all concerns for material goods, and all social responsibilities. He sometimes spent weeks without coming down to his village, and every time he returned to the world of the lowlands he was more and more like a stranger — and more anxious to find again the solitude of his mountains.

'My God! Here you are, finally!' his old housekeeper sighed. 'I didn't know what to think anymore. Is this any way to live, I wonder?'

'Well, I'll tell you once and for all, Gertrude, that this is my life. You don't have the slightest idea of the satisfaction I find in it, or of the work I'm accomplishing. If you only knew!'

'I only know one thing: Monsieur is going to make himself ill.' She sighed as she left the room. 'He has such a wild look,' she muttered to herself. 'When I think he even hinted that he may not come back . . . Isn't it crazy?'

It was true that, conscious of the risks he was running, Lucien had taken all the necessary steps just in case an accident happened. He had written a will that left his cousin, Ferdinand Beaufer, a fair part of his small estate — or what was left after the years had eaten away most of it. The remainder would go to Gertrude, who had been told of the paperwork she would have to take care of, and who knew his cousin's address — where she had to send any bad news. She also knew above all, the place where she would find the carefully sealed letter she'd have to forward to Ferdinand.

But Lucien Péridot counted on the good luck that had never abandoned him, and as the alpinists of the time did, he started dreaming of the last, great problems the Alps offered. The North Face of the Matterhorn? He had the good fortune of doing it in one day, well before the Schmidt brothers, thanks to snow conditions that allowed him to ascend quickly part of the route with his crampons, while the cold and the ice held back the rockfall. The North Face of the Grandes Jorasses gave him, to tell the truth, much more trouble. He made several attempts, using different starts, and it was not until the beginning of June 1935 when he managed to overcome the Croz Spur. It was just in time! The second and third ascents occurred in the month that followed. The Walker Spur eluded him. As for the North Face of the Eiger, that was quite an adventure.

Lucien was eager to do this route, but exposed as it was to observation by telescope, it presented him with the double challenge of the climb itself and of keeping the secrecy. Elsewhere it may have happened that somebody saw him on a route, but when that was the case the observers must have thought it was an abortive attempt; since no news was divulged about it, no one ever gave it much thought. But on the Eiger it was a different story. The competition was intense, the observers watchful. In 1936 occurred a great tragedy, when Kurz perished almost within reach of his rescuers. Since he was often in that vicinity, Lucien knew where the route must go. The following summer he took advantage of a prolonged spell of fog to make his ascent, quite slowly because of conditions he himself judged extremely dangerous. He luckily succeeded, a year before Heckmair and his friends.

At this point he questioned himself on what he ought to do next. It seemed that the moment of truth had come. But still, he postponed his revelations, contriving some reasons in his mind and resolving to add yet more routes to his outstanding collection. The North Face of the Droites, maybe? He didn't dare admit to himself that, once the curtain was lifted and his exploits made public, his life would no longer have the same flavour — it would, in fact, lose all its spice, all its meaning.

Lucien Péridot didn't have to question himself much longer, for he died foolishly in the middle of the next winter. This man, who had mastered his fate so many times, had climbed ice slopes as smooth as mirrors, had leaped up to catch a hold and force a passage, had avoided rockfalls, had found his way back in stormy weather — this man now met his destiny where he least expected it.

It was February. Extensive snowfall had prevented him from going out, but when the hint of a lull appeared in the sky, Lucien, with his skis and sealskins, took a bus for Abondance. He intended to cross the Col d'Ubine, the Pas de la Bosse, and the Col de Bise, then to return via Saint-Gingolph.

While he was climbing up a hanging valley toward the Col d'Ubine, he suddenly saw a powder-snow avalanche break loose from above, where the wind had piled much snow, and roar down the narrow slope separating him from Mont Chauffé. He barely had time to turn around on his skis before he saw that the slope on his left was also starting to slide. He was overthrown and swept away. At first he couldn't believe it, but in spite of his struggling, he soon found himself overpowered by a force greater than his — and then he slowly submerged. The mass of cold, light snow into which he had flown a few instants earlier hardened around him with the consistency of cement. He didn't feel pain, but he thought his spine must be fractured because he had no feeling in his legs. The snow covered him entirely, he didn't know to what height. Prone and trapped in the solid mass, he couldn't move his arms at all. An air pocket that had formed in front of his face allowed him at least to avoid immediate suffocation.

He had a glimmer of hope that some ski-tourers might have seen the accident and would possibly rescue him. But nothing came about. Not a sound. Not a cry.

'This is it.' he thought.

Cold invaded him. Still, with the vigour of his forty-odd years, and strong because of the hardships he had endured, he held out for a long time, reviewing his life. After all, wasn't the task he had taken upon himself accomplished? And wasn't it better to end like this instead of becoming an ordinary, sick old man, beholden to other people? Wasn't he leaving the essence of his existence with the records of his ascents? Ferdinand would be informed of everything in the letter addressed to him. He would find, in his office desk, all the envelopes attesting to the success of his ventures. Ferdinand would entrust them, as instructed, to the presidents of the Club Alpin Français and the Groupe de Haute Montagne, and they would open them in front of many witnesses and a notary. Even in his desperate situation, such an image made Lucien smile.

Then he felt overtaken by a wave of inner cold and by an immense desire to sleep. And he let himself go. That's how he died, peacefully and, in a certain way, fulfilled.

Lucien Péridot had announced a two-day trip and, in fact, had to be back the third day, a Thursday, to meet with his landlord and renew his lease. The man had considered taking back his house for one of his daughters, but he had eventually yielded to Lucien's request to keep it, since he had been a good tenant and he had known him for a long time. The two of them had to discuss some new conditions and check out the leaking roof.

That's why Gertrude was very surprised when her master didn't show up, and she had to turn away the landlord, who had inconvenienced himself for nothing. Friday, Saturday, and Sunday passed. Accustomed to his long absences, the housekeeper nevertheless knew that Péridot kept his appointments on the few occasions he made them. She sensed that something was wrong.

The following week she consulted the local notary, who suggested that she inform Ferdinand. Since nobody had the slightest idea of the itinerary the alpinist had had in mind, they could do nothing but wait. But the landlord was upset. If the lease was not renewed, he wished to reclaim his house.

Lucien Péridot's corpse was found after some time. Two skiers touring near the Col d'Ubine noticed a ski pole sticking out of the snow. They approached it and realized that there was also a man . . .

When the news was reported, the notary sent a telegram to Ferdinand Beaufer asking him to come immediately for the funeral, if he could make it, and to decide about the furniture and the personal effects contained in the house before the lease expired.

As misfortune had it, on the previous day Cousin Beaufer had felt ill and had to stay in bed. The doctor who visited him the same day the telegram arrived diagnosed a catarrhal jaundice, which made his patient quite unfit to travel. So it was Léontine, who, leaving to her daughter Yolande responsibility of the house, of the ill father and of the two young brothers, was given all the power of attorney forms, and who left with Germaine, her elder daughter, so as to speed the probate proceedings.

'Your father's cousin,' she grumbled in the train, addressing her daughter, 'he couldn't act like everybody else . . . Not even dying . . . Do you think I'm having fun, having to go to the country while your father is in that state? And buying these two round-trip tickets . . . Even in third class, you know how much they cost us! . . . If it were not for the inheritance — and it seems we have to share it with the maid — I can tell you that we certainly would not have gone to the trouble . . . Luckily we still have the mourning veils from Aunt Marie . . . I certainly wouldn't have had them made for him . . . It's as if he did it on purpose, dying right at the expiration of his lease . . . I met him just once, but that was enough for me to judge him . . . An artistic temperament, if you know what I mean . . .'

Germaine, who was just like her mother, disapproved of Lucien's free-and-easy behaviour even more than her mother did, if that were possible.

The relationship the two women established with Gertrude, whom they regarded as a schemer, was marked by bluntness. But all three agreed at least in recognizing that the adventurous life Lucien Péridot had led was highly reprehensible.

'He could have been so happy!' the housekeeper exclaimed. 'Getting a job, marrying, filling the house with children . . . But the mountains had a hold on him . . . That was all he had in his head . . . He seemed possessed . . . There were months when I hardly saw him . . . just barely the time to stop by here, to dry out his climbing gear, his woollen cap, and his torn gloves, then plunge into his office to examine some books, scribble on sheets of paper, and he was soon off again . . . Oh, by the way, here's a letter for Monsieur Beaufer!'

Léontine carefully put it in her bag. She went to see the notary, found out the exact terms of Lucien's will, magnanimously paid for a crown of artificial pearls, which would last a long time at the graveside, and finally took upon herself the task of unloading the house. She only had two days for this.

After choosing some furniture she wanted to keep, she called a dealer to get rid of the rest. He grudgingly agreed to take Lucien's books and sell them to a colleague. Once the price was settled, they still had to find an old-clothes dealer. Then Léontine and Germaine set to work on the papers, watching for important documents and especially for share certificates.

'Thousands of index cards! Léontine exclaimed. 'And not even for serious work! . . . Nothing but names of mountains and rock peaks! . . . Take all these boxes to the kitchen, Germaine, and have them burned!'

Gertrude, though sincerely sorry for her master, was not displeased to see those papers consumed by the furnace, since they represented, for her, the folly that had carried him away.

When Léontine opened the desk that contained the stacks of envelopes referring to Lucien's first ascents, she believed for a moment she had found a treasure. But she was soon disappointed. The notations on the outside of the envelopes about the 'Aiguille Verte by the North-North-West Arête,' or the 'Winter ascent of the Barre des Ecrins' were all too explicit. She broke the seal of one at random, and out fell pictures and some papers covered with Lucien's tiny handwriting.

'All that to the furnace!' she ordered Germaine.

And that was how the records of the most fantastic alpine adventures were lost forever. And when the convalescing Ferdinand read his cousin's letter and asked his wife what had happened to the papers in the desk, he had to take her reply philosophically. After all, those mountain stories couldn't be that important . . .

Just like most collectors, Lucien Péridot had piled up nothing but leaves for the wind. Still, it was for the wind that lightly grazes shining snowfields, for the wind that whistles in the nooks of boulderfields and hisses at night through mountain gaps, for the wind that carves cornices above the chasms, for the wind that pushes dishevelled clouds along the crests and wails over lost summits, for the wind that wrests starry spindrifts from white powder, for the peculiar wind of high altitudes.

Translated by Franco Gaudiano and published in collaboration
with Ascent and Sierra Club Books

TIME REVERSAL

'Ah, papers everywhere ... what *are* these bits of newspapers? You're collecting clippings now? Come on, father, give me all that. There is enough of a mess around you as it is.'

'No, Odette, no! Wait a second! Don't throw away that one especially. And that one also. I am saving it!'

'But it's a date! Do you want to save a date, cut from a newspaper? And afterwards, everyone is astonished that there is a mess here! You're not reasonable! Oh, all right. I'll throw away the rest of the paper and tonight I'll straighten up. But, for God's sake, don't start cutting up newspapers again. I have enough to do without that. And don't look at me like that. I don't need your complaining on top of everything else. I have to go now. I am going to be late for work. Don't try to move by yourself. Don't try to go to the toilet by yourself. Wait for the nurse. And don't forget to take your drops.'

My daughter gives me a peck on the forehead and disappears. They say I am the one that talks drivel. But she's the one who repeats the same things every day. I wait to hear the outside door close as she leaves. I was able to save the clipping from the newspaper — and even the date. I am tired. I let my head loll on the pillow fixed to the back of my armchair. Outside the window I can see three chestnut trees. I know them well. They are old friends. Their leaves are already beginning to turn even though it is just the beginning of October. I ask myself, how awful, if I will still be here in the spring to see them blossom. It isn't nice to be old — not nice at all. I could often die of boredom. I wait for the nurse to come, and later, my daughter and her husband. Of course it's good of them to have taken me into their home. They could have put me into an Old People's Home. It's just that they treat me like a child ... and I know what they say behind my back: that I am going senile, ga-ga. It isn't true! It is absolutely not true! There are things I remember very well ... above all, my youth ... oh, what good times. They have taken away almost all my things — my books, my notes, my photos — but they can't take my memories.

It's unfortunate! I was beginning to fall down at home. At first I tried to keep it secret, but one day they found me on the floor, since I was not able to get up by myself. Pity! I could no longer live alone and my daughter has taken me in. Fall! I didn't fall when I used to climb. It was out of the question to fall!

All right . . . where was I? What was I thinking about just now? Something nice. Ah yes . . . that little newspaper item I saved. Hardly an article. If my daughter had not been late for work she would have thrown it away with the rest. Now, maybe I can hide it in a book. And the date, too. It was a little silly to have cut off the date. But there's no doubt about it, I found the item in yesterday's newspaper, alongside all the articles about Euromissiles, assassinations, inflation, new taxes, trade deficits, opinion polls about the government, etc., etc. What a carry on.

But what matters is that little news item. I have it in front of me and read it and reread it. I can't — or don't want to — understand. It has brought everything back afresh . . . as if it happened yesterday. To think back on it is my best distraction. I am alone. I race past days and seasons. I reverse the flow of time . . . and above all, there is *that* memory! My God, that was sixty years ago!

It was the last day of September and the weather was superb . . . with a light that was both golden and shimmering. The sky was infinitely blue. We were not much over twenty. The whole of life offered itself as an immense promise. And the present was a thing of joy because we had just succeeded in doing the Charmoz-Grépon traverse which at that time still had a reputation, and still does in my old eyes. The Mummery Crack . . . the Virè a Bicyclettes . . . the Râteau de Chèvre . . . old names . . . famous names . . . dreams of our winters . . . now at last ours; goodness how happy we were. I was with Charles Maisoncelle and we were climbing without a guide. From the beginning we were very anxious because that same evening we had to catch a train back to Paris. In order to be on time we left the hotel Montenvers in the middle of the night. The fog obscured the night sky. The air was cold. The timid glow from our lanterns barely lit our steps. But the higher we climbed, the more the fog dissipated. And little by little we could see the stars scintillate against a beautiful background of black velvet. Sleep still weighed on us. In the night the mountains we could make out seemed far off and inaccessible. We arrived too early in the morning at the base of the rock, and used the time to eat. The sky gradually whitened and the stars went out one by one. With the growing daylight our confidence returned.

As we started up, the surrounding mountains stood out in full detail. The rock was inviting . . . solid. Our muscles responded with strength and elasticity. Ah, what marvellous climbing! We were warmed up before the sun reached us. We moved both rapidly and safely and quickly reached the summit of the Charmoz. Our happiness was tinged with a feeling of anxiety about what was to follow but, at the summit of the Grépon, all that was over.

I will never forget the look on Charles' face and his yell of pure joy. What a panorama — a feast for the eyes! Without a word we shook hands. It was truly an unforgettable moment. No wonder those memories have remained fixed forever in my mind. Oh what a route . . . had we been slower and had to go back down to leave our great ambition to next year . . . but we had succeeded, and faster than we dared to hope. So we rested a while after a bite to eat, lingering in the joy of a victory that I cannot describe, bathed in that special light of early autumn . . . palpable, enveloping, moist. But as the wind started to rise we began the descent, and soon we found ourselves back on the glacier. The snow, which had been hard in the morning when we climbed it, was now soft and deep despite the lateness of the season. We leapt down the slope in great bounds, not bothering about the hemp rope, which dragged in the snow between us, soaking up water. There would be plenty of time to dry it later. We were just two young idiots driven crazy by our enthusiasm for life. Before 3 o'clock, we were at the Rognon des Nantillons. Plenty of time to get back to the valley and even visit that climbers' haven, the Patisserie des Alpes.

But . . . man proposes and God disposes. Just as we reached the rognon we heard the thunderous sound of a terrible rockfall. It was in the direction of the Grands Charmoz. An immense block had detached itself and smashed at the foot of the mountain producing a boiling cloud of grey dust. The earth trembled even where we were. It was a terrifying spectacle. We stood transfixed until the mountain once again became silent and then . . . and then we thought we heard a cry.

We all but ran down the rognon to see if someone had been trapped in that furious rockfall. Soon we saw him, half-seated on a rock, wounded, signalling to us desperately with his arms above his head. His two friends had been killed. Charles went across to make sure nothing could be done for them. He had been thrown to the ground under a large block — the one on which he was now resting — and it had shielded his body — a miracle. At first, because of his curious clothing and alpine equipment, I took him for a foreigner. But when he began to speak, it was clear he was French. He had many cuts and bruises, but most seriously a broken leg.

Fortunately, my companion, Charles Maisoncelle, was an intern just finishing his medical studies in the Cochin hospital. He was able to put the stranger's leg in a makeshift splint, but when we tried to move him, it caused him such pain, we had to stop. He said that there was no need to stay with him while we went for help, and we promised to get back down to the valley and give the alert as soon as possible. We helped him to swallow a little of the drink we always carried and left him the flask. Since he had no heavy sweater, I left him the new Tyrolean loden jacket I had bought at the beginning of the summer. We didn't hang around or go into what he and his friends were doing in the spot where we found him — well off the usual route. I did ask his name — Xavier Berthiand — a courageous young man for whom we felt the greatest sympathy. I promised I would learn what happened to him afterwards.

Despite our fatigue we decided to take the shortcut through the Alpages de Blaitière, which leads directly down to Chamonix. It would have been easier to go via the Montenvers but it was slower and the time it would have taken to wait for the old steam train and descend by the cog railway would have been lost; the season was too advanced to hope to find any guides at the hotel who might mount a rescue. So we raced down the snowfields, moraines and finally the trail as quickly as we could and were soon back in Chamonix. My flannel shirt was drenched in sweat when I got to the Bureau des Guides and found Ulysse à Valancogne whom I had got to know particularly well as a result of doing some routes with him the year before. Still in a state of shock, I told about the avalanche and the accident. He promised that he would organise a caravan of eight guides that same evening and go to the Montenvers, and that at dawn they would go to the injured man and also, if possible, bring down the bodies of his friends. I asked the guide to keep me posted and also to recover my loden jacket.

Eight days later I got a letter. It was so strange that I kept it and have it still. It read, 'Monsieur, as I promised, we put together a caravan of guides to look for the young man who was injured. We slept at the Montenvers that night, and the next morning went to the base of the Grands Charmoz. What I am now going to tell you will probably surprise you as much as it did us. We found no one. We looked everywhere — even in the crevasses near the bottom. If the young man had been able to leave by himself, how could he have carried the bodies of his friends? And who could have helped him, especially this late in the season when the mountains are almost deserted? Living or dead, we saw no one. If I had not known you I might have thought you were playing a bad joke, and it would have been, for eight of us spent two days searching the mountain for nothing. Naturally I could not find your climbing jacket. Hoping to see you next year in our mountains. I respectfully send you and your wife my best wishes.'

There was a postscript: 'As for the avalanche you spoke of, it did not seem to have been as substantial as you thought. There were a few rocks here and there that probably fell recently from the wall — but that need cause no surprise, for even a small rockfall can appear impressive. But I simply can't explain what happened to the bodies.'

I have often thought about this since, and just as often wondered about what happened to Xavier Berthiand. Was he rescued? The mountains have their mysteries. But for all I thought about it I can find no logical explanation. My friend Charles Maisoncelle frequently talked about it, and our discussion with Ulysse the following summer got us nowhere. Time moved on, and about ten years later poor Charles was killed on the Weisshorn, and it's now quite a time since the worthy Ulysse died. I have aged, but to escape the moods of my daughter and the tantrums of my grandchildren, the problems of cholesterol, rheumatism, and a failing mind. I bring back images of our youth in the mountains . . . those little climbing huts with smoking stoves . . . the sparks that our hob-nailed boots gave off on the rock . . . summits swept by the wind . . . and sometimes I ask myself about that injured young man, without finding any clue to the puzzle. I would so much love to talk it over with someone . . . why is nobody interested in what I have to say . . . it is the same for those who fought in the war. No one cares about them or understands why they need to share with others moments which were the most outstanding or terrible in their lives. So it is with me with that business on the Charmoz, which remains such a bizarre mountain experience but is always cut short by that same reply: 'yes, yes grandpa . . . we know it by heart . . . we all know they found nobody . . .' So I just mull it over by myself . . . but I think about it time and again.

And then yesterday, that strange item in the newspaper. Strange, that is, only to me. For anyone else it would be a dry — perhaps sad — banality. The newspaper was dated the 2nd of October — the dispatch was sent on the 1st — and what is described took place on the 30th of September. The article was entitled 'Another Mountaineering Accident'. It said: 'Yesterday at about 2.30 p.m., a giant rockfall took place on the flanks of the Aiguille des Grands Charmoz in the Mont Blanc range. A rope of three climbers who had just rappelled down the Cordier Pillar, was swept off by the rockfall. Almost by a miracle one of them, Xavier Berthiand, a twenty-four year-old native of

Blois, escaped the catastrophe suffering only some bruises and a broken leg. Some climbers were descending the Nantillons glacier and were able to offer first aid.'

'The two companions of the wounded man, whose names we do not know, died in the avalanche. The wounded man was able to give a Y signal to the helicopter of the Protection Civile, which was returning from a reconnaissance of the Aiguille du Peigne. It landed immediately. That evening, Mr. Berthiand was evacuated to the Chamonix hospital and the bodies of his comrades were also brought down to the valley. This accident has brought to thirty-nine the number of deaths in the Mont Blanc massif during this summer's climbing season.'

In the days after I found the clipping, I was in a state of constant turmoil. I needed proof. I needed to know that I was not totally mad. I wrote to the hospital in Chamonix giving my name and address, but, of course, not my age.

This morning, someone knocked on the door of my room. Despite all the warnings, I got up and opened it. I did very well and did not fall. It was the mail . . . a package for me! I went to my chair and opened it. Inside was my Tyrolean loden climbing jacket. In a pocket I found one of the handkerchiefs my sister had embroidered for my twentieth birthday. In the pocket, too, was a modern drawing of the route the injured man had taken before the accident. He must have taken it from his pocket to put in mine. A note from the hospital said that after the severe shock of the accident, Xavier Berthiand was now doing well and wanted to send his warmest thanks to my friend and me.

My old climbing jacket! I put it across my knees so that my gnarled fingers could caress the thick waterproof loden of which I was so proud. I can already hear my daughter . . . 'Where did you dig out that old rag?' I will laugh silently. For now I know.

Translated by Jeremy Bernstein and John Wilkinson

LA FOURCHE

In Chamonix there's an old saying which goes: 'Every conceivable sign is a sign of bad weather, and worst of all is the absence of signs. . . .'

There is something in this. For the *habitué* the Chamonix valley, which enjoys quite unusually heavy rainfall, is a veritable compendium of weather signs all indicative of storm and rain: west wind; red sky in the morning; pale or watery sun in late afternoon; halo round the sun; stars particularly brilliant; pall of smoke lying flat along the valley; tap-water flowing milky; mountains looking very close; cotton-wool clouds or, worse yet, clouds in long trailing reddish fronds; long plume of cloud on Mont Blanc; hat on the Verte. . . . True *cognoscenti* turn to the animal kingdom as well; trouble is on the way if flies are unusually aggressive; if bees hover around the hives; if slugs take to the road or spiders take shelter; if swallows swoop along the ground; or if the cows are lying down (this last phenomenon unfortunately has become more difficult to observe over the years as more and more holiday flats leave less and less room for cows . . .). At high altitude there are other signs to alarm the alpinist, such as humming ice-axes; hair rising gently on the scalp; or a faint sound of crackling. And absurd as it may seem, a few alpinists (no doubt for uncomfortably Freudian reasons) attach some importance to the movements of the barometer and the *obiter dicta* of the weather forecast. . . .

The weather-signs are legion then, but at one time one sign was universally recognised as infallible: the arrival in the Chamonix Valley of the unfortunate Georges Faustin.

No sooner was his tent up, indeed sometimes no sooner had he set foot in the valley, than the cloudless blue sky would turn a livid grey, heavy clouds would mass on the horizon, and rain would begin to drip dispiritedly on the larch trees and chalet roofs. These premonitory signs were followed, invariably, by a prolonged depression which settled over the Alps and whose dampest days were those which Faustin chose to walk up to a hut.

At first it was just a joke. Every year the phenomenon provided some of the best laughs of the season, and indeed one year, when Faustin was known to be on his way and when the forecasts, predictably, were growing progressively more gloomy, a group of climbers paraded on the square with a banner reading: 'Save Our Season! Faustin Out!' But the joke soon wore thin, and there came a time when more prudent climbers would discover the dates of Faustin's holiday before laying their own plans.

Faustin himself was never discouraged. He became a walking catalogue of species of Chamonix rain: Scotch mist, drizzle, driving, freezing, thunderstorm, cloudburst. . . . Over thirty years of experience, he built up an impressive alpine list comprising all varieties of hut-bashes-in-pouring-rain, descents-in-white-out, hurried-retreat-in-blizzard — all adventures which may have had their heroic moments, but which scarcely added up to glory. In all those years, he had achieved only a short list of climbs and the quality of those fell well short of his dreams. In spite of appearances, he was perhaps not so bad a climber; but his career was necessarily a modest one, and it was allied with an unhappy reputation for bringing bad luck.

Everybody knew him. He was always around, hovering on the fringe: every Thursday evening in winter at the Club Alpin headquarters in the Rue La Boetie, and in summer occasionally in a hut, but more often in whatever bar was currently 'in': the Potinière, the Drug-Store, the Choucas. There he would be, with his long thin nose and his mournful doggy brown eyes, battening on other people's stories and other people's jokes; on occasion he would try and get in some anecdote of his own, but he would soon find that no one was listening, and he would fall silent in favour of some other speaker who was better able to please the crowd.

But nothing dimmed his enthusiasm. The mountains were his life, and his life contained precious little else. He lived alone. Very few people remembered that he had, once, almost got married, and that the engagement had been abruptly broken off when his fiancée unwisely asked him to choose between the mountains and herself. Faustin, unhesitatingly, had chosen the mountains. In professional terms his life was no more successful; when young he had spent his time climbing rather than studying, so that now, at over fifty, he held a mediocre post in a rather second-rate laboratory, where he still spent much of his time dreaming of the mountains like an adolescent. Every inch of every wall of his little flat was papered with superb photos of soaring ridges, plunging faces, sparkling snows. He had the complete range of Vallot Guides, Kurz Guides, topo-guides, and spent every winter evening planning every detail of every route for the following summer — the one that would be *the* summer, *his* summer. This time he would be one of a remarkable team doing the most sensational routes — and the following autumn he would come back to Paris the uncrowned king of the Alps. *La Montagne* would phone to ask him to write articles: *North Faces*

Across the Oberland; Five 4,000: A two-day Solo Epic. That would teach them to call him 'poor old Faustin'! But then, invariably, inexorably, the grey drizzle would set in as his season started.

Surprisingly, he seemed reasonably content with his lot, and with the very modest place he held in alpine circles. But as he grew older, the climbers he had known in his youth drifted away, and the younger generation, while perfectly polite, rarely wanted to climb with him. True, he had never found it easy to find partners, but he had scarcely admitted this even to himself. To save face he would refer, sadly, to the death of one of his first climbing friends, Paul, killed many years before on the Meije. When asked with whom he was going to climb the next summer, he would always say:

'You know, since Paul died, I've never really had a regular climbing partner. . . .'

In point of fact, even with Paul he had never really climbed very much, but this had been his nearest approach to a team.

And then it finally happened. For once the summer was perfect: the weather was totally reliable and all the routes were in condition. There was never the slightest need to send an 'apprentice' staggering sleepily out at two in the morning to check on the weather: always, invariably, it was good. The nights were just cold enough to ensure that there was snow in the couloirs; the days were just warm enough so the rock was always dry. The dream season.

Faustin was by now older and slower and gloomier and apt to get breathless, and no one was interested in climbing with him. Days went past. From down in the valley he gazed up; at the dazzling sky, the sunshine flooding over white snow and red granite. He put up a little notice in the Club Alpin, and was contacted by a shaggy, self-confident student. They set off together to do the Papillons Ridge: the young man fell off twice, and when things got awkward he had an unfortunate tendency to call out for his mother, but on easy ground he soon outdistanced his companion and stood waiting with ostentatious patience. Their first expedition together was their last.

Another week of perfect weather went past. Faustin hung around the valley, not daring to go off even for a low-level walk in case he missed a possible climb. And every evening he would go down to the Guides' Bureau where everyone met to look at the weather forecast (it was always the same: 'Continuing good weather. Outlook settled') and to listen to triumphant accounts of other people's routes.

'How about you, old man?'

'Oh well, you know. . . .'

He was more and more miserable. He had planned his season so carefully, praying that *this* time the weather would finally be favourable. Well, the weather was favourable, but. . . . And then there came the first glimmering of a possible partner, a young lad called Claude Auxy, not a bad climber. It turned out that neither of them had ever done the Old Brenva, and as it happened Claude was stuck in the valley because his usual partner had pulled a tendon.

Georges Faustin was filled with child-like excitement as he went into the supermarket to stock up on food for the route. He chose the items with a sense of almost paternal solicitude: 'A bit of ham — he's young, he'll need proper food — chocolate, yes, young people like that, I'll get some good stuff, Swiss. . . .' Claude Auxy, simultaneously and in the same super-market, was doing his own shopping, not realising that his future partner was just on the other side of a display-shelf. He met Jean-Pierre and explained his plans.

'You're joking!' exclaimed Jean-Pierre, 'You're never going to climb with that old has-been! He was never up to much at the best of times, but he's completely past it now. And besides, he's real bad luck. No kidding, if you set foot on the Old Brenva with him today, by tomorrow morning it'll be peeing with rain. Forget it! Otherwise. . . .'

Faustin didn't stay to listen to the rest. When Claude Auxy got back to his tent a little later, he found a note to say that Georges had thought better of it — and he was profoundly relieved: now he could forget the web of Machiavellian excuses he'd been dreaming up to get out of it.

Georges Faustin, however, had come to a decision. He would show them he wasn't finished: one last flamboyant gesture if it killed him. Before his inner eye passed the depressing vista of the years: a catalogue of petty failures, minor humiliations, broken dreams. Alone, if need be, he would take on the Italian side of Mont Blanc, the Old Brenva, even the Sentinelle. He would fight to the end and return victorious. And come to that, if he didn't return, would it matter? He wallowed in a great sea of bitterness.

He would allow himself two days' respite, one to get fit, one to rest and organise his gear. He was living in a nightmare. He was tortured by the thought of how he must have seemed to everyone all those years, and by the thought of the lonely, friendless old age that lay ahead. And deep within him the fear was growing: the fear of the Old Brenva solo. And yet he could not give in: he clung to this plan, his last remaining illusion, with an ageing man's febrile pig-headedness. . . . All round him the sun shone; in him was nothing but a flat, leaden sense of despair. From time to time he was shaken by a wish for revenge: if he was killed, Claude, Jean-Pierre and the rest of them would be sorry. They'd see what they'd done!

This welter of feelings and motives was whirling in his mind as he stepped off the téléphérique at the Col du Géant into the vast solitude of the mountains. Somewhere there was still a faint hope that someone would see him and stop him, give him a fatherly lecture on the dangers of solo climbing, beg him to come back. But no one took the slightest notice of him. He set off, very slowly, down the Vallée Blanche and then up towards the Tour Ronde. Oddly there was not a soul about, and late afternoon sun flooded over a deserted glacier. He had made up his mind to spend the night in the old hut at La Fourche; true it would mean an awkward start the following morning, but the way up to the new hut at Le Trident involved crossing a difficult bergschrund. And besides, there would be other climbers in the hut who would be bound to let him use their abseil to the glacier on the other side.

Faustin trudged doggedly on, bent under his rucksack. Every time he stopped for a breather, he shivered with cold and apprehension. The curved bowl of the Combe Maudite seemed positively menacing. For the first time he registered the real meaning of the word *maudit*: 'accursed'. And as he climbed, the word *maudit* beat in his mind — and around him crowded the Mont Maudit and the Aiguilles du Diable, the Fourche, the Trident. . . . What on earth had possessed them to give mountains names like *Accursed Mountain*, the *Devil's Needles*, the *Pitchfork*, the *Trident*? He felt increasingly apprehensive, increasingly threatened.

At last he came to the foot of the couloir leading to the hut, and as the shadows lengthened he made his way painfully up. He forced himself to concentrate on every step, and visualised his arrival in the hut. It might well be crowded; in fact he might well have to sleep on the floor; but at least he'd be among friends. He'd step through the door: 'Oh God, not another party! Alone? Fantastic! You must be pretty good, I guess, you don't get many solo climbers over this way. Where are you heading? Us too! Fantastic! We're a rope of three. I don't suppose. . . . You wouldn't consider joining us, would you?' He savoured the scene and improved on it as he struggled up, aching and breathless.

His disappointment was all the more acute, therefore, when he found the hut empty. Empty! Unheard of in good weather at the height of the season.

Perhaps everyone who wanted to had already done the Old Brenva? Perhaps the weather had been so good that all the climbers had given up out of sheer exhaustion? Still, it was not too late — he needn't give up hope. But no one came. The light faded. The great Brenva Face of Mont Blanc loomed larger in the grey twilight, cold and hostile. He tried not to think about it.

It was a depressing evening. It would have taken very little to make poor old Georges burst into tears. He was terrified: terrified of the ordeal which awaited him the next morning, and which was now unavoidable since he could not bear to go tamely, defeated, back to the valley. The nightmare grew bleaker and more hopeless. The hut was cold and damp and not very clean, and the blankets smelt musty. By the light of a single flickering candle he ate what might well be his last meal. He picked at his food, with a queasy memory of all the other last meals that must have been eaten here. He went out, huddled his duvet round him and made his way up to the col. It was pitch-dark and the absolute silence was broken only by the occasional clatter of a falling stone, or creak as the glacier settled. Sheet lightning flared suddenly behind the Aiguilles du Diable, and they strode black and menacing across the horizon. Faustin's spirits plummeted. He went back into the hut, took a sleeping pill, pulled a couple of blankets over his ears, listened fearfully to the whispering wind and then finally, thankfully, receded into sleep.

It was the light which woke him up. He was vaguely surprised not to have heard the climbers coming in, and faintly irritated to be woken up. 'To hell with them!' he thought, 'Fancy turning up like this in the middle of the night!' and he snuggled down further under his blankets. But then a further thought struck him: how quiet everything was! Faustin peered sleepily out and saw a man by himself. Another solo climber? Or was there a second who had already gone to bed? Faustin woke up and took a closer look. The man was sitting in the corner in the candlelight, and he was studying a sheet of paper which he must have brought with him. His face was nondescript: not particularly handsome, not particularly plain, just the sort of face that Faustin liked, friendly and pleasant but with none of the showy good looks of the self-confident young. Faustin was delighted not to be alone; he went on watching. The man looked to be a little above average height, well-built. He had on grey wool climbing breeches, climbing boots, a red V-neck sweater. His face was clean cut and very brown (this couldn't be his first route of the season), and he had thick black curly hair. He was sitting with his chin in one hand, holding the paper with the other, and he was so still, so dramatically lit that Faustin thought at once of a portrait by Georges de la Tour.

But there was something odd about him, something Faustin couldn't quite pinpoint but which left him faintly uneasy. He stared at him again more closely, and it was then that he noticed, sticking out of the thick black curly hair, two neat little shining horns.

Faustin jerked suddenly and completely awake. Out of his subconscious swam scraps of stories, bits and pieces of legend — how he regretted having dismissed them so lightly! — which led him to suppose that his companion could only be the Evil One.

However sceptical or cynical you are, however often you have disclaimed the supernatural; even if you are so world-weary as to undertake a route way outside your capabilities with few expectations of surviving it, it is nevertheless an appalling experience to find yourself with no warning, at midnight, in a lonely hut, three thousand metres up, and face to face with the Devil. Faustin was duly appalled.

His companion was still motionless. He sat with his chin on his hand, apparently lost in thought. And an idea struck Faustin: did the Devil realise that he was not alone? That there was someone in the hut? And come to think of it, what *were* the Devil's powers? A bit late to think of that! If only, he felt, he'd spent a bit more time on the supernatural, he'd have had some idea of what to do, but as it was he lay absolutely still, trying to stifle his breathing. He even shut his eyes in case they caught the reflection of the candle — then decided it was worse not to see what was going on, and opened them again the merest slit.

A few endless minutes crawled past. And then Satan spoke:

'Well, now, old chap,' he said, his voice pleasant and surprisingly human, 'your life hasn't been up to much, has it?'

And gently but inexorably he set out the failures, the disappointments, the absurdities, which had so far constituted Faustin's life. He relayed a number of telling remarks made about him by acquaintances. He listed the opportunities Faustin had let slip. None of it seemed meant unkindly — indeed he sounded sympathetic — but it was said with ruthless clarity, and stripped away all the half-truths which usually enable one to conceal unpleasant memories. Faustin's life was, in short, a wash-out. He had started with certain undeniable advantages, he had achieved nothing, he had contributed nothing. Nothing whatever.

When the Devil drew to a close, Faustin was no longer able to conceal the fat tears which came rolling down his face and splashed damply on to his bunk. How could he have made so little of life? How could he now be declining empty-handed into old age?

'And yet you know,' the Devil went on, 'it's not as though the rest have missed out on everything like you. You've had a pretty bad deal. Happiness isn't just a myth, you know. For every woman you've met who's looked happy and fulfilled, there's been a man. Everything you've bought has been invented and manufactured by someone like you. Every advance in science has been pioneered by someone like you. Every book you've read has been written by someone like you. Nothing's impossible. And take you, for instance: Hell knows there are enough climbers who've been on expeditions to the Himalayas or South America, who've had routes named after them! There's always a few who turn their dreams into reality. You're just about the only one I can think of who's never had as much as a taste of what he wanted. And you can take my word for it, too. . . .'

Silence fell again. The silence of despair. Never had Faustin seen himself with such awful clarity.

'Yet . . .' said the Evil One, 'Yet . . . It's not too late. You *can* still have everything you ever wanted. Everything. . . . You can start all over again. All you've got to do is sign this little sheet of paper, and tomorrow morning you can have it all. A penthouse like you see in the films. . . . That Maserati you used to yearn after, the white one. . . . And the girls to go with it. . . . Actually you won't need the Maserati — one glance and they'll fall into your arms. And just think: muscles like iron, absolute fitness, a superb sense of balance, perfect eye for a route. . . . First ascents everywhere. . . . Full-scale expeditions. . . . Lectures in the biggest halls in Paris if that's what you'd like. First winter ascents. . . . And if I'm emphasising the climbing side, it's only because I know that's what you're interested in, but really you could do anything — the Académie Française — Nobel Prize for Physics — President of the Republic. . . . Just imagine. . . . And look, more than likely you're going to get killed tomorrow, and if you do, it's suicide as near as damn it, and then I'll have your soul anyway. So all you're doing really is signing away a soul you've pretty well mortgaged already, and that's it — for the next twenty-four years!'

He was persuasive, and he had picked his moment. He took out a little Opinel penknife and a goose-feather quill, and waited. Georges Faustin didn't hesitate; not a murmur came from his conscience. Admittedly the document when he came to look at it seemed a little more sulphurous than was necessary in the twentieth century, but if you treat with the devil you treat with him, and he swallowed the text without quibble or qualm.

'Oh great Mephistopheles!' it read, 'Lord and Master, I, Georges René Faustin, recognise you for my God, and renounce Christ and Mary and all the Saints and the Holy, Roman Catholic and Apostolic Church. You undertake to provide all worldly advantage for me for the next twenty-four years, in return for which at the expiry of that time you will be sole master of my body, my soul and my life. Written at La Fourche, on the Mont Maudit, in the seen and unseen presence of Satan, Beelzebub, Asmodeus, Moloch, Lucifer, Pan Lord of the Incubi, Lilith Lady of the Succubi, and all other Infernal Powers. In witness whereof, I sign with my blood.'

Faustin took the little penknife, pressed the point into his left palm, caught the drop of blood on the quill, and then, with never a backward glance, he signed the pact.

Everything had vanished. Faustin was alone in the little hut, vaguely aware that he had been dreaming. The effects of the sleeping-pill had not quite worn off; he yawned and crept further under the blankets.

A few hours later, his alarm-watch woke him. For a moment or two he did not know where he was, and he smiled wryly at his nightmare. Then he stretched out a hand for his headtorch and pressed the button. He stared, rigid with shock: those long, slender hands! He was breathless. There was no mirror in the hut and of course he hadn't brought one. He was so dumbfounded that he fell back on a sequence of simple mechanical acts; he lit the stove, he set the billy of water on it, he had some tea. . . . And then he got his gear and set out — to discover now, with joy and astonishment, that his body was transformed and renewed. His every movement was supple, rhythmical, powerful. He felt no sense of strain as he strode down the steep slope to the Brenva Glacier. In the starlight his senses were preternaturally acute: he could make out every minute hold, judge the quality of every scrap of snow or ice. His legs were firm and muscular, his arms strong and agile. Effort brought not pain but happiness — and when he came to the Col Moore, he turned not right towards the Brenva Spur, but quite deliberately left, towards the North Face of the Aiguille Blanche de Peuterey. . . .

The climbers sprawled on the terrace of the Potinière on that warm early evening would long remember the advent of Yann Faustin on the Chamonix scene. The first manifestation was the long, low, white Maserati which slipped smoothly into the parking space which fell empty, quite by chance, just as he pulled up. A radiantly smiling young man leapt out, in perfectly faded jeans and a spotless, freshly laundered, white T-shirt. His tan was impeccable and his tousled fair hair blew becomingly in the breeze. With a carefree laugh he flung himself into a chair.

'Hi, Gros Louis!' he said. Gros Louis, who was very short-sighted but preferred not to wear his glasses in public, replied with every sign of confidence:

'Hi, old man!'

The newcomer's eye fell on Jules and Gilbert, and he reminded them that he'd been in the Argentière Hut a year ago when they were trying to decide whether to do the Tournier Spur. Within seconds, everyone felt that he must be the only one around who didn't know this striking young man, and the conversation picked up again. Gilbert, all southern verve, was just describing how that morning he'd done the Old Brenva, from the Trident Hut, and seen someone soloing up the North Face of the Blanche, straight up and over the seracs.

'And he didn't even hesitate, mates, just straight up and over the seracs! And you know how it's bulging there at the moment! And then he went on up towards the Peuterey Ridge. Must have been on the summit of Mont Blanc by twelve at the latest!'

'Half past eleven,' said Yann, with a light laugh.

It took them a moment to realise that he was talking about himself. But the way he told his story, gripping but self-deprecating, held everyone's attention. He'd been on the seracs when a great ice-block, the size of a wardrobe, had come thundering down and smashed on the glacier just beside him. He'd been lucky: when it shattered, all the bits had missed him. But his ice-axe had been knocked out of his hand, and he'd only managed to rescue his rucksack with a frantic grab for one strap. He'd had to finish off the route with an ice-dagger and an ice-screw. But even so, what an amazing route! He still couldn't get over it! But he was pretty glad to be back, he could tell them! He laughed and paid for a round of drinks.

It was the beginning of a marvellous life. Even the speed with which his former self was forgotten did nothing to dampen his spirits. He took down his tent early one morning when everyone was asleep — and no one bothered to ask questions later. He sold his old Renault down at Sallanches, where no one knew him. He wrote to his employer and his landlady and told them he'd been offered a very promising job abroad and was leaving immediately, and asked the landlady to dispose of his furniture and effects and keep the proceeds to defray expenses. Only one person was likely to ask awkward questions: the tax inspector. Faustin sent off a polite letter and a substantial cheque: conscious of his duties as a citizen he apologised for not filling in his tax-return, asked the inspector to use the cheque to sort the matter out and to give the residue to the Widows' and Orphans' (Tax Division) Benefit Fund. Surprised and touched by this unusually elegant and beneficent act, the inspectorate did, with earnest rectitude, precisely what it had been asked to do.

Clearing up took exactly forty-eight hours. By then everything was sorted out, Georges had disappeared for ever, and no one gave him a thought. Much later he was to know a second's resurrection. A friend asked Yann:

'You're no relation of an old bloke we sometimes see here, are you? He's called Faustin, too — Georges.'

'Never heard of him,' said Yann with a smile.

It was all the obituary that Georges was to get.

There is little need to go into the details of the next few years. Very soon Yann was recognised as the best climber in France, the best in Europe, the best in the world. . . . And moreover the best-known newspapers snatched at every morsel he told them about his earlier life. He'd been born in Iceland, where his father was consul, then brought up all over the world wherever his parents were posted. His upbringing had left him very cosmopolitan, and with a remarkable knowledge of languages. He'd been orphaned early, but he'd been left an apparently inexhaustible fortune which grew effortlessly under his control. He dreamt up ingenious and profitable climbing-aids; he lent his name to a range of sportswear, then to leisure wear in general; he set up his own factories, and then devised a distribution network which soon had worldwide coverage. Everything he touched turned to gold.

But fame and fortune did nothing to diminish his charm and good nature. He never sought publicity. In fact he remained natural, unspoilt, hail-fellow-well-met, and was always ready to give due weight to his seconds and his team-mates. Everyone liked him. He was a highly successful and efficient businessman, but he was always quite ready to fly back from New York or Tokyo so as not to miss a planned ski-trip. And once back he was the driving force, never tired, never down-hearted, always good-tempered and cheerful.

For the mountains remained his consuming passion, and no wealth, no fame, no love-affair (and they were legion) ever distracted him for long. He did all the great alpine routes with consummate ease. Weather and conditions were nearly always right for him; he became known as a lucky beggar. He did the aspirant guides' course and the guides' course (a pointless formality really, but one cannot buck the system) and graduated from both in first place, with the highest marks ever awarded. He took part in a number of expeditions, national and international, in the Andes, the Caucasus, and of course the Himalayas. His was the rope that did the first ascent of the North-West Face of Nuptse (until then thought to be unclimbable) and of the Fifth Ridge of Ama Dablam. The whole world gasped when it learnt he'd done the first winter ascent of Everest, solo and without oxygen. He took part in a number of dramatic rescues; on one occasion, single-handed, he saved eight of the world's best climbers who had been stranded on the North Face of the Eiger by appalling weather conditions.

Yann never got tired of success. He'd spent so many frustrating years in part one of his existence that he could only savour every second of existence number two. And so, carefree and triumphant, the years slipped away. . . .

It was Margot's death that seemed to dim Yann Faustin's zest for life. Scarcely surprising, of course: few alpine tragedies have ever combined such drama and such romance.

Yann had had countless affairs — a modern Don Juan, his every appearance was greeted by a bevy of frenzied and nubile young women. But not one of his conquests had he ever taken seriously. Margot Buthiers was different. She was neither one of the liberated tomboys who haunt alpine circles, nor one of the beautiful clothes-horses who hang on the arms of celebrities the world over. Margot was young and lovely and pure. Yann fell deeply in love with her at first sight; he took her climbing, and she turned out to be a natural. Gossip-columns followed every phase of their courtship, every route they did.

It was not long before there was talk of marriage. Yann was getting on for thirty-two, still young enough not to give too much thought to the fate that awaited him. It hung on the horizon, of course, and occasionally flickered across his consciousness — a faint but very distant menace, so distant that Yann could ignore it and think only of his happiness with Margot.

It was then that he decided that Margot should do the North Face of the

Jorasses. It was in excellent condition; the Walker was fully pegged up, the weather forecast was good. Margot was very fit and should have no trouble, especially since she would not need to do any de-pegging. And in any case, Yann would be beside her all the way, ready to look after her.

The bad weather came down out of a clear sky just above the Black Slabs. They were already too high to retreat. Yann knew they would have to go on up, although he would probably have to help his companion on the more awkward pitches. The wind rose and howled round them, hurling flurries of stinging hail. Verglas formed on every hold. The cold became ever more bitter, but the terrain was delicate and they had to climb bare-handed. The wind and the cold sapped the girl's strength surprisingly quickly. At first, Yann remained quietly confident and simply redoubled his own efforts. He swarmed up every pitch, belayed himself, then fixed a rope down to Margot and came down to show her the holds and give her moral support. She still had a remnant of will-power, but she was visibly flagging and she whimpered like a child as the storm tugged at her.

Yann was still convinced he could save her, at whatever cost to himself, but he suffered agonies with her. For the first time in twelve years he was at a loss. Should he call on God, or on the Devil? Too late. . . .

When night fell they were still well below the summit. They would have to bivouac on a narrow, sloping, snow-covered ledge. To save time, next day, Yann was tempted to solo the next few pitches and fix the ropes, but Margot could not do without him. He settled her in the least uncomfortable corner of the ledge, belayed her securely, wrapped both duvets and all the spare clothing round her, tucked her into a bivouac sack and spent the whole night melting snow to make cups of hot tea; she sipped them with difficulty. Every so often he abandoned the stove to massage her feet and hands; as the circulation was restored she could not control her moans.

Never had any bivouac seemed so endless! But things were not improved the following morning. The face was thick with verglas and every hold was iced up. The wind still whined around them and the cold was just as intense. They were in thick cloud: no hope of a rescue helicopter. They could only go on. The summit was a mere three hundred metres away, but in conditions like these, that meant several hours of desperate climbing. And below them, hidden in the cloud, were a thousand metres of impossible descent.

Yann tied Margot's rope for her, got her ready, conjured up a little watery smile from her, gave her a sip of coffee and a bite to eat, and went on. It was even worse than the previous day. He could not climb fast enough to prevent

Margot, back on the belay-ledge, from being overcome by cold and exhaustion, and every time Yann came sliding back down the abseil rope, he would find her lolling on the peg, her eyes closed. He had to wake her up, shake her, bully her into climbing again.

At two o'clock that afternoon, he realised that Margot's hands in the mittens he'd given her were horribly swollen with frost-bite. They could go no further. He spent the few remaining hours of daylight rigging up another bivouac. She was weakening rapidly. In the middle of the night she was delirious. Meaningless words and phrases tumbled out, punctuated by whimpers:

'The forest — the field — we won't climb again, will we, Yann? — Shall we get married, Yann? — Look at that lovely little chalet. . . .'

She died as the first faint light crept across the sky. A few hours later the weather began to lift. A few scraps of blue appeared through the heavy clouds. No one ever knew how Yann had managed to haul her lifeless body to the summit of the Jorasses, or how he brought her safe down the snow-covered slopes of the South Face. He stumbled into the Boccalatte Hut as pale as death, his face haunted, with what remained of his intended wife close against his heart.

He never got over it. Life resumed its course, and the mountains their accustomed place — but the vital, eager Yann Faustin was no more. Everyone assumed they knew the reason why; the only puzzling thing was that Yann's grief seemed to grow with the years, rather than diminish.

In point of fact, of course, Yann's preoccupation was two-fold. On the one hand there was his real and heartfelt grief; on the other, a new sense of disquiet, until now masked by his self-confident happiness. His brush with death, its snatching away the person nearest to him, when as usual he had remained invulnerable, had been a terrible blow.

Not a night now passed but he spent it meditating on life and death and after-life. Others could at least shelter behind doubt or ambiguity. He alone *knew*. No longer could he doubt the existence of his immortal soul, since he had sold it for the aptly named mess of potage, no longer could he doubt the existence of the Devil and therefore of God. He might have wondered if he'd dreamt that night in the Fourche Hut — but he had proof positive in his transformation from the grey Georges Faustin into the flamboyant Yann Faustin. In any case it was pointless to rack his brain for rational explanations: it had all been decided, once and for all, on that strange night in La Fourche.

The twentieth century had paid little attention to the Devil; hoping that earlier ages might have been more specific and more helpful, Yann threw himself into avid research. He bought books on philosophy and theology and metaphysics; he haunted libraries and second-hand bookshops. His sources agreed on one thing: in any lifetime there came moments of decision, anodyne and innocent on the surface perhaps, but fundamentally irrevocable. And none of his readings gave any clue as to how to dodge the consequences of decision.

One day in Paris he walked past a church. He made up his mind suddenly: he would act as so far he had hesitated to do, consult a priest and find out what remedy the Church might suggest. He was close to the end of his tether; he had drunk a little too much the previous evening, he had been unable to sleep, and the only recourse, he felt, was to a specialist. Until that moment his contacts with the Church had been infrequent and perfunctory: a few duty funerals or weddings. And since that night at La Fourche, he had felt a certain reluctance. . . . But childhood memories conjured up a vision of a priesthood which knew all about heaven and hell. Only to a priest could he admit the true cause of his distress.

In the sacristy he found a little notice telling him to apply to the reception office across the street. He found this faintly annoying: the setting would be out of kilter. An elderly lady sitting behind a desk asked him to wait while she contacted a priest. She did not, to his chagrin, seem to recognise him. . . .

The priest was an anonymous figure, in jacket and slacks; he ushered him into a little modern office. The setting made Yann's predicament even more outlandish.

'Father . . .' he began. He stumbled over the unfamiliar words and choked to a halt.

'Well?' said the priest. 'I've got this dreadful problem . . . I . . . well, I . . . I hardly know how to put it. I've . . . sold my soul to the Devil.'

The priest stared at him, then started on a long and practised speech. Man, he said, was always free, and no choice he could make would condemn him utterly; true, 'Evil' (the Devil if Yann preferred) was always present in the world and in ourselves, but until the very last moment it was never too late, and in the sight of God, if the sinner truly repented. . . .

'But it is too late,' cried Yann, 'I've seen the Devil himself, and he's got horns just like in the stories!'

'Now listen . . .'

'No!' Yann was shouting, 'And to prove it, I've been given another life!'

'Now calm down,' said the priest, visibly flustered, 'you'd better make another appointment and we'll talk about the whole thing properly when you're feeling less upset. But first. . . .'

When Yann came out into the street, he had in his pocket a sheet of paper with the name, address and telephone number of an eminent psychiatrist. He had promised to ring for an appointment and then to come back to see the priest. He tore it up and never went back. He had had such high hopes — might there be some sort of miracle? — and all he had got were doubts about his sanity. He must bear his burden alone, and every day the burden became heavier.

And yet life went on. Yann continued to make money, effortlessly and mechanically. He led clients on routes, did some high-class climbing of his own, took part in rescues, gave slide-lectures, introduced his own films, signed his own books. But it was all routine, all curiously joyless. He started drinking. The lines etched themselves deeper and deeper into his face. Younger men came noisily on to the climbing scene and began to oust him, but he scarcely cared. Yann no longer looked outwards; his life had narrowed to a long, dark tunnel.

At long last, summer came round again: the twenty-fourth summer. And the actual anniversary of the pact crept nearer. On the very day, Yann packed his rucksack and set off for La Fourche. He would see the Devil, and offer him anything, anything at all, if he would only release him from the pact. . . .

When it became known in the valley that Faustin had disappeared, no one had any clear idea where to look for him. The weather was bad, so there could be no helicopter search. When a mechanic in the téléphérique station said he had seen Yann setting off alone with his gear, a rescue team was sent up to search the Vallée Blanche and Combe Maudite. Almost by chance they stumbled on his body crumpled at the foot of the path up to the Fourche Hut. The rescuers put the remains in a bag; nobody seemed eager to say very much. The official report spoke of 'multiple injuries'. One of the guides who had been in the rescue team was less discreet; the body, he said, looked as if it had been clawed to pieces. . . .

Translated by Jane Taylor

THE ABSEIL

Noel Gille took off his rucksack and got the rope out. A long, thin one-hundred-metre rope for the major abseil that was to follow. It was for this purpose that his sack had been laden during the whole climb. He uncoiled it, checked that it would run properly without knotting and threw the ends out into space. It sizzled through the air, vibrating as it unrolled.

He had done the climb. A fine climb. A hell of a climb. The first solo of the great South Face of the Pico de los Maleficios! A proud summit that did not cede easily. What was more, his solo was only the second ascent. Noel Gille had been lucky and made good time: only two bivies, in a hammock, the second not far from the summit. Fine weather all the way until today, when a sort of fog had formed. Jacques Merlin, who had made the first ascent, had carefully described the route to him. He had followed it without any mistake and now the descent seemed to be going correctly.

'Below the summit,' Jacques had explained, 'you will find a sort of steep staircase of broken rock. Follow it trending slightly left until you come to a wide ledge hanging over nothing. I left a peg there with abseil tat. It's below a sort of obvious reddish slab. From it you make the big fifty-metre abseil: you'll need a long rope. We had to tie our two ropes together. After that it's straightforward.'

Noel Gille slipped his sack back on, clipped into his descendeur, stepped over the edge and pushed off into space. Because of the fog he could only see a few metres below him. It was an impressive abseil, straight down a wall of smooth, compact rock. He descended it in a series of free bounds. At this rate he would soon be back in the valley. A long abseil can be tiring, but he had never felt it like this before. Doubtless it was the result of the fatigue that must have accumulated, imperceptibly, over the last two days. Fifty metres! It was never-ending. It must be an effect of the fog. Even when driving, a familiar road can appear interminable when there is no visibility. . . .

Noel Gille realised that he had slowed and was now only descending gently, carefully and tiredly. It was ridiculous. He could see far enough below him to know when he reached the end of his rope. He had to take a grip and get on with it. He breathed in deeply and once again started leaping down the cliff.

Really! Was he going mad or what? He blocked his descendeur and tried to take a hold of the situation. He looked at his watch. Ten to eleven. He had an impression it was a bit after ten when he had got the rope out. On the other hand, he would have taken time to set up the abseil. So what was he thinking of? This fog was getting on his nerves and he must be more tired than he thought. But that was not enough, he still had to reach the end of the abseil which could not be far now. Keeping his eyes skimmed below, he set off down the rock again, furious. Interminably.

He stopped once more and looked at his watch. After eleven. He broke into a sweat. It was purely as a test that he did another five minutes of abseiling. What had happened, he could not understand, but one thing began to impress him, he had to get back up, to the ledge, the peg, the abseil tat, to find the normal world again and then look for another way down, by the overhangs of the South Face if necessary.

It was fortunate that he had his jumars with him. With a bit of manoeuvring he managed to get them out of his sack, drank some tea from his flask and prepared to reascend. If it was as nutty up as down then he had two or three hundred metres in front of him.

For hours Noel Gille jumared. For hours and hours. He knew it would be long and forbade himself from looking at his watch or from thinking more than the minimum about this ludicrous situation. Strong as he was, his arms began to give the first spasms of cramp. He could feel his harness cutting more and more into his thighs. But he carried on, he carried on. . . .

In the end he had to stop. God, how the time had passed. It was mad. And still no ledge. He must have gone down further than he thought before. How could he tell?

Suddenly a bright idea came to him. Noel Gille undid one of his shoulder straps and slid the rucksack round in front of him so as to dig out the altimeter he remembered bringing with him. Scrabbling around, he eventually found it at the bottom. His head spun and he had to look again, scrutinise time and again the figures he saw, before believing them: he was now two hundred metres higher than the Pico de los Maleficios.

It was mad, stark staring mad. A terrible nightmare. Except it wasn't. Aching muscles, cramps, parched throat, shoulders bruised by the sack, every inch of his body told him this was reality.

What should he do? Surely not go on ascending to the clouds above the level of the summits! So he had to descend. Calmly, Noel Gille replaced the jumars with his descendeur. Then in a series of bounds he started off down again. . . .

Translated by John Wilkinson

THE PENANCE

Father Jayat was an excellent priest. A man of faith and zeal, he had in no way been shaken by the post-conciliar crisis, nor been tempted to query his calling. Unrivalled as a youth team-leader, as the organiser of a prayer group, or as an enthusiast for the renewal of the liturgy, he had even published some articles of exegesis that were distinguished for their deep and original theological perception.

Virtually a saint? Not at all, for Father Jayat had one great weakness, climbing. Considered as one of the best alpinists of his time, he spent whole summers in the Alps, cleverly combining his vacations with organising youth holidays and scout groups. Thus, as soon as conditions were suitable, he was in a position to attack the most renowned faces and difficult ridges with one or more friends. His immense satisfaction in climbing them was in no way lessened by awareness of his own strength, technique, daring and stamina, whilst the delight of recounting his exploits and playing to an audience was not the least part of his satisfaction. Undoubtedly, when it came to climbing, Father Jayat fell into the gravest of sins, pride.

He was aware of it, and admitted it to his aged confessor, Father Neyrolle, who knew nothing about climbing and only half listened to this admission, which seemed to him rather attractive.

'No harm has ever come from love of a sport. Perhaps, if what you tell me is true, you should try and talk rather less about it and, of course, avoid what might be construed as boasting . . . Do you, in fact, confine yourself to the truth or do you embellish it a bit?'

'Oh, the truth is quite sufficient because . . .'

'All right. Then just try and talk a bit less about your sporting successes, and let others get a look in. Now, with respect to other matters . . .'

It was mere coincidence which caused Father Neyrolle and two friends on the way to Rome to stop over at Chamonix, which they had never been to before. Since Father Jayat was camping there with a youth group, they left it to him to find somewhere to stay. Thus, one fine afternoon in July, the travellers found themselves contemplating with an uninstructed eye the array of peaks, aiguilles, snowfields and ice which dominates the Chamonix valley. They had arranged to meet at the bottom of the Aiguille du Midi téléphérique and it was over a round of half-pints that Father Jayat met up with his guests and had the pleasure of pointing out the sights to them.

'How I envy you spending all your summers in this valley,' confided Father Neyrolle. 'How it must help your spiritual awareness to have nature's splendours before your eyes, day after day.'

Father Jayat did not have time to reply, for just at that moment a load of tourists and climbers spilled out from a cable car, seeking refreshment on the terrace. Someone called out, with a jocularity tinged with respect.

'Jayat, old mate, good to see you again!'

It came from a fairly young guide, whose even younger client looked at Father Jayat with an expression of pious admiration.

'We've just done your route on the Capucin,' the guide went on. 'May I introduce Cyrille, a climber of great promise . . . Whew, what a route! I'd heard it was good, but even so . . . And with virtually no pegs. What a line! You never cease to amaze me . . .'

'It's not bad,' agreed Jayat, with a deprecating half-smile.

'And they say you had to finish it in bad weather. How on earth did you do it? This youth never stopped talking about you on the way down. Tell us a bit about it.'

'Oh, I'm not a magician, you know. True, I was particularly fit at the time, and I had to pull the stops out as Laferté had problems with his eyes and I had to lead it all . . . That was an especially fine pitch on the slabs, very thin didn't you find? Apparently Lespinasse couldn't do it the other day and had to rap off . . . It's where Wilkinson failed too when he tried to open the route before us.'

'Wilkinson couldn't do it,' muttered the youth beside him.

'No. Still, someone had to do it sooner or later . . . It just happened to be me . . . And I must admit that when the sleet started it did not simplify matters.

A respectful silence followed, eventually broken by the guide.

'You've also put a new route up on the East Face of the Jorasses, I believe. It's an area I don't know. Any special hints you can give me?'

'Look in at the camp,' replied Jayat, 'I'll show you the notes I based the route description on. It's a fine route. You'll manage OK, but I wouldn't say that to everyone. Tell me what you think of the overhanging crack-pitch . . . And I've never seen anything like the corner at the start . . . We only took seven hours for the whole thing, but I should allow more than that . . . I don't know what it was that day . . . Inspired we were, like gods . . .'

A discreet cough reminded him of Father Neyrolle, whom he had for a moment forgotten in his enthusiasm. The party broke up cordially, and Father Jayat devoted himself to showing his guests around.

The youth group was installed near an old farm, their blue tents lined up in a clearing. The visitors were lodged in simple but pleasant rooms in the building itself, and pronounced themselves delighted with their accommodation and the setting; the grass was young and green, the bright sun filtered through the pine branches, the air smelt fresh and resinous, and beyond, above all, was the sparkle of the eternal snows.

The evening passed splendidly. They dined outside around a camp-fire, and the carefully composed menu, which included chanterelles, bilberries, strawberries and raspberries collected in the forest, received unanimous accolades. Then, as it became cooler, they moved indoors into the barn where they sung, until a new temptation arose, offered by a piping voice demanding: 'Father Jayat, you still haven't told us about your last route.'

'Oh do please, Father, do,' the other voices chipped in.

This time, Father Jayat felt a little warning premonition, which he quickly put behind him. After all, it was not boasting to tell them about this really exceptional route. Quite the opposite. It was only a mark of courtesy to his guests, who knew nothing about climbing, to give them some idea of what big mountaineering was about. It was simply a matter of making his account brief and even modest.

These good intentions were quickly forgotten as Father Jayat felt the thrill of the story take a grip of him. Encouraged by the eyes shining with excitement and, occasionally, with fright, he related the climb with all its many incidents at far greater length than he had intended. His voice plumbed the depths of despair when he explained how his partner, Alain, one of the best of the new generation of climbers, could not force the key section.

'Come on down,' Jayat had cried, 'come back, it's too dangerous.'

Anxiously he had watched Alain's slow retreat as he did his best to belay him from the little ledge on which he was precariously perched.

'Your foot, put it over there on that flattening. No, lower!' he yelled.

Alain had eventually rejoined him at the stance, shaken and discouraged.

'It's mad to try that wall,' he had panted. 'It will never go. We'll have to go back down, we'll never make it.'

'Yes we will,' Jayat had replied shortly. 'Let me have a go.'

And it had gone. True, it was perhaps the hardest piece of steep slab-climbing he had ever done in the mountains . . . So the day went on . . . The bivy that night was freezing . . .

The audience drank in his words, and his account of the arrival on the summit was received with a burst of applause. Father Jayat smiled comfortably, and it was with an overflowing heart that he intoned the final evening prayer.

'Fascinating, quite fascinating,' Father Neyrolle said to him a few moments later. 'Really, I had no idea what mountaineering was about . . . A fine adventure . . . But I wondered . . . Since I am going to be away some time, I would like to take the chance of this short visit here to have a little chat with you . . . Shall we say tomorrow morning?'

This time Father Neyrolle had understood, and when Father Jayat asked to receive the sacrament of reconciliation he dwelt on the dangers of the vainglory which the exploits of climbing might bring.

'As a penance,' he thoughtfully concluded, 'As a penance . . . tell me, if I understand correctly, one generally climbs in a team, but there is nothing to stop a good mountaineer climbing alone?'

'Certainly not, I might say . . .'

'Fine,' Father Neyrolle cut in, 'in that case, as a penance I ask you to do a route alone, difficult enough to satisfy you, and tell no one about it, either before, or after.'

'But . . .' Father Jayat could not help exclaiming.

'Prepare now to receive absolution in a spirit of humility . . . May the Lord God show you his forgiveness. . .'

After the visitors had left, Father Jayat felt uncomfortable. What a pointless penance. Wasn't Father Neyrolle getting a bit gaga? To throw him into a route, solo, just like that, simply to oblige him to say nothing afterwards. There was no sense in it . . . And if he, Jayat, should smash himself up soloing, what would Father Neyrolle look like then! No! . . . God would not let that happen to a penitent . . . Certainly not . . . Still, what a stupid idea . . . It could only come from someone who knew nothing about mountaineering, nor about how one organised one's climbing season around partners . . . And yet, he had not even tried to argue, nor to explain the stupidity of the step he was being asked to take . . . What was more, if the penance were to be valid he would have to ensure that no one else was doing the route . . . And that, nowadays, was asking the near-impossible. Might as well expect him to do a first ascent.

It was at that moment, like a flash of light, that the idea came to him, to try, solo, the first ascent of the North Couloir on the Strabhorn. Twelve hundred metres high, it was a sort of cleft of cascading black ice, broken by smooth, more or less over hanging verglassed rock-steps. The North Face of the Strabhorn itself had been climbed, both to the left and the right by several routes, none very elegant or direct, and it was now considered as done. But with the new ice-climbing techniques, the goulot might go. And what a route . . .

'And what a penance!' he said to himself with a quizzical smile.

Conveniently, the camp was about to finish and he would be free.

It would be the first attempt on the North Couloir of the Strabhorn. Father Jayat made his preparations carefully, even foreseeing the possibility of an accident and the need for a rescue . . . Of course, he would play the game and warn no one, but he would leave a letter for Alain, to be opened after four days should he not have returned. Even without knowing his objective, he could not help thinking, Alain would know he was on to something big, and soloing it. But Providence was surely working with Father Neyrolle.

'Alain's not here,' his mother stated when Father Jayat went round to his friend's chalet. 'He's just left for the Oisans for four days with a client . . .'

'OK', said Jayat, slightly disappointed. 'Would you be kind enough to give him this letter when he comes back.'

He left the next morning. He had to get to Switzerland and do a long hut slog starting low in the valley. On his arrival, he did not tell the hut warden his objective and he was not asked. He set his alarm so as to get up on his own, but as, unusually for him, he crept off into the night without a chorus of good-wishes, he was comforted by the thought that the North Face of the Strabhorn was partly visible from the little hut and a rope might see his headtorch moving up the first snow-slope. Later it would not be possible to see because the couloir was too enclosed . . . In the event, he had to do the approach in a fine mist which hung about all morning, a sea of cloud trapped in the cold valley bottom, and it was through it that he saw the rising sun break through to light up the summits of the Oberland like tall, isolated islands.

In the Strabhorn Couloir, the sun never shone and the route was worse, far worse, than anything Father Jayat had imagined or feared. The ice was glassy, like polished steel, the exposure extreme and resting places virtually nil. The rock-pitches made him look forward to the ice. Progress was very slow, and the heavy sack made balance difficult. On the first evening, seeing how little he had climbed, Jayat nearly gave up and considered how he might organise a retreat. But he forced himself to continue.

Those were not bivouacs on the North Face of the Strabhorn, at best unpleasant periods spent waiting for daylight. Jayat had to endure two of them . . . The second, after a day of frightening climbing, was particularly horrid. No question of being able to find a place for the stove and make a warm drink, but he did eventually succeed in digging out a bit of salami from his sack and stolidly munched this, along with a few sweets. His legs shook with fatigue, but he had no support except a couple of slings hung from pegs. Far away, in the black night, the stars came out. This bivouac was if anything colder than the first. He had to stop himself from continuously looking at the luminous hands of his watch . . . He forced himself to wait so as to get a pleasant surprise . . . And then only a quarter of an hour, or at best twenty minutes, had passed . . . The cold became penetrating and, shocked at the chattering of his teeth, Father Jayat felt a sudden mounting resentment against Father Neyrolle, however much he recognised, deep down, that it was deliberately, and through pride, that he had chosen such an excessive course. Vanity had no place on this North Face of the Strabhorn where man found himself for what he really was, vulnerable, overwhelmed by nature, fragile, alone. So he could only offer his suffering, admit his weakness and go on letting his teeth chatter until, at last, the greying east announced a new day.

The accumulation of fatigue, suffering and cold made this third day even worse than the others. About midday, whilst Jayat was trying to make a delicate traverse on his frontpoints and ice picks, a boulder, large as a grand piano, broke off and started rolling down directly towards him. There was no way of avoiding it, just time to abandon himself to Providence: hypnotised, Jayat awaited the impact. Less than twenty metres above him the block broke on a rocky outcrop. The pieces smashed past him and he thought he would be carried away by the blast. The avalanche bounded interminably down the whole couloir. Silence returned and Jayat was safe. With palpitating heart, he recovered his breath and then smiled, thinking that clearly Father Neyrolle enjoyed considerable influence up there. He carried on more cheerfully. The exit was now only a matter of a few hours . . .

He arrived on the summit in the full glory of the setting sun. Mentally exhausted but happy, he only stopped a moment to eat a bit of chocolate and think about his victory. What a fight it had been! . . . And so close to the end, that rock-fall which still made him tremble! . . . A real epic . . . Already the words were beginning to shape themselves to recount his story . . . But then, of course, there would be no story . . .

He had to get through a bad section of ice-fall before night fell, in order to find somewhere safe to sleep. But like an automaton he continued by torchlight to the first of the moraines where he slept deeply, despite the cold.

In the morning he felt relatively fresh. He was hungry and heated a proper panful of soup; it seemed the best thing he had ever eaten. Then he continued on down the screes and grassy tracks that brought him back into civilisation. He knew that he had just lived the greatest adventure of his alpine career and felt replete with happiness.

He found his motorbike and loaded his rucksack. It was now four days, or even a bit more, since he had left his letter for Alain, proof that he had underestimated the difficulties of the route at the start. He ought to have allowed five days . . . However, he would see how things were.

He stopped at his tent to drop off his gear, took the time for a shower and even to shave, and then set off for Alain's. He too had just got back and greeted him enthusiastically. No, he had not yet read the letter, but if it was a matter of doing a route together, he was ready to set off the next day.

'Not me, mate,' said Jayat. 'I need a real sleep . . .'

'Me too,' cut in Alain. 'We climbed all four days, ending with the Traverse of the Meije. A marvellous route. Nothing really difficult of course, but long and superb. And do you know, when we arrived on the ridge . . .'

Father Jayat put in his pocket the letter that had remained unread on the sideboard, and tried to appear interested in the recital of incidents that had marked the Traverse of the Meije. To know that with one sentence he could plunge his friend into stupefaction, share with him the harvest of memory, of deeds, of fears, of joys ... It was a hard battle. Certainly, Father Neyrolle had put his finger on the sensitive spot in his penitent's conscience.

But this was simply the first of many trials. The temptation never left him and continued all the rest of that summer. All the more so since the weather went bad, putting the mountain out and leaving conversation as the sole alternative for climbers.

'In fact, you have not got much done this summer,' one of Jayat's friends remarked one day.

'No,' he replied, choking on the word.

'That's the way it is! You can't have a big season every year, and even someone like you failed to profit fully from the spell of fine weather. I am delighted we got the North Face of the Droites done. I have been wanting to do it for ages; you know what happened to Paul on it . . .'

There was no choice but to listen patiently to what happened to Paul . . . Father Jayat had an insatiable itch, a crying need to talk about his great first . . . He was able to contain himself, knowing that at least there was someone who had to listen to him . . .

'I have an account to settle with you,' he began smilingly, 'over that penance you asked me to make in July . . . It so happened that I thought about . . .'

'Shh . . .,' said Father Neyrolle. 'I am sure that you are going to tell me that you have settled everything properly. I believe you. Now let's move on to other things, please . . .'

A real temptation of Tantalus, that's what it was. And when he rejoined his lads and they asked him for his climbing exploits, Father Jayat was only half-hearted in telling them about his other routes, so eclipsed were they by the savage, hard and magnificent North Couloir of the Strabhorn.

So the year passed and the summer returned. One day in August came the extraordinary news:

'The Chalopin brothers have made the first direct ascent of the North Face of the Strabhorn, via the couloir. Yeah, it's true. They are at the *Cheval Rouge* talking about it. It seems to have been an unbelievable ascent ... Go and listen to them, it's worth it. I've got to leave for a dental appointment, I'm already late . . .'

The Chalopin brothers were lording it over a group of admirers. They were taking it in turns to tell, time and again, the details of their achievement, batting impressions and quips back and forth between them like a ball. Old hams, the Chalopins, unbelievably pretentious . . .

'It'll be a long time before there's a second ascent,' one was saying.

'To be honest,' the other replied, 'I cannot see any other pair able to do it . . . There's no one like my brother on steep and overhanging hard ice. He could teach the Scots a thing or two . . . And I'm not exactly a laggard on icy rock . . . Believe me, you bastards . . .'

Father Jayat listened in silence. This time he could not take it. He would burst if he did not speak. He had to spill it out. With just one phrase he could restore the situation. A thousand ways of doing so occurred to him. He could say:

'Well, it might surprise you to learn that last year . . .'

Or more subtly:

'Tell me, on that last rock-bar, you didn't come across a nut I got jammed . . .?'

Or more viciously:

'So what it adds up to is that as a pair you took three hours longer than me solo . . .'

Ah, what a stir that would cause! . . . First the shock and then growing comprehension. All it needed was for him to open his mouth and make some such remark, and then they'd know about the true, the only first ascent of the great North Couloir of the Strabhorn.

The Chalopin brothers continued to bullshit and laugh, foolish, vulgar. True, they were good, but they were neither likeable nor very clever . . . And how they went on, laughing, complacent, smug, proper idiots . . .

Father Jayat opened his mouth . . .

It was at that moment he realised that he could not destroy their happiness. That same happiness he had felt when he had made the real first last year . . . An overwhelming joy which he could still almost feel, a joy mixed with a sort of exultation born of fatigue, of jubilation ... With one word he could cut down those poor lads to size, and yet they were only expressing in their own way, the pleasure of the exploit they had accomplished.

Father Jayat knew now he would never breathe a word about his first. And as he moved slowly away through the crowded streets, a deep peace began to take hold of him.

Translated by John Wilkinson

2084

It was a bright, cold day in April. Boris and Michel reached the last pitch and could feel on their faces the touch of the west wind from which they had been sheltered while on the climb; it would be blustery on the summit. If Frédéric had managed to do as they'd arranged and come with a snack, it would be much healthier, in all senses of the word, to be up there in the keen wind.

Boris reached the last stance and brought up Michel who soon joined him, climbing as smoothly and as competently as he had done on the rest of the route. Together they emerged on to the summit platform, where the wind was enough to make them reel slightly. And by a stroke of good luck, there indeed was Frédéric, with a broad smile under his shock of white hair. All of them realised that they were doing something dangerous, but this was a choice they'd made, and come what may Boris and Michel were determined to find out about climbing in the old days: Frédéric must be the only person alive who still remembered anything except, of course, for the Higher Authorities — and it was no use expecting any information from them.

And what Frédéric had to say was more amazing than anything they could ever have imagined. Back in the pre-industrial age of climbing there had been some two hundred years of nothing but green valleys, meadows and pine forests, wooden chalets and rushing streams — and wild and empty mountains, which were at first thought to be accursed and were soon to be explored and conquered by rugged individualists: no forward planning, no organisation, just imagination and enthusiasm. Nobody, even Frédéric, knew very much about this period: it was lost in the dawn of time.

It had been around the end of the nineteen-sixties that some of the more far-sighted authorities had begun imposing much needed order on anarchy and egotism: the first climbing competitions were organised in the Crimea and Georgia, on prescribed routes with points allocated for speed and style. Gradually the whole of Europe adopted this pleasingly uniform system; the Anglo-Americans held out longer than most, in the interests of what they insisted on calling *purism*, but after a while, overtaken by events, they had no alternative but to bow to the new alpine code of conduct.

It was the French government that first had the brilliant idea of climbing permits, so sophisticated technically that they were twenty years ahead of their time. They took the form of plastic cards each imprinted with the chromosome print of its bearer: the release at the bottom of each route could be activated only by feeding in the card itself and a drop of the bearer's blood. The permit classified climbs into twenty-four different categories, each sub-divided according to the precise technique required. The qualifying tests were rigorous, and where on bank holidays, for instance, certain routes had formerly been overcrowded, now they were almost deserted. Very few climbers attempted to break the regulations: the police helicopters had orders to shoot anyone contravening the system, and they took their orders seriously. When eventually international climbing permits were introduced, things seemed set fair for the future.

Unfortunately, this happy state of affairs was complicated by a new parallel policy of recruiting from the masses. Governments screened their populations for particularly able candidates, and then compelled them to develop their aptitudes to the maximum. Very soon the routes were overcrowded again, and commissions of enquiry were set up to look for a way forward.

It was at about this time that selective breeding programmes became the vogue. Like the Dog-Breeders' Association, the Climber-Breeders' Association sought out blood-lines, dams and sires who seemed likely to produce the optimum climbing specimens. There was just one problem: any tangible results would only show themselves long-term, and several generations at least would be needed before the success or failure of the scheme could be assessed.

While waiting for the golden age, climbing had gone on much as before. Some of the variations over this period were worth recalling, even if they were sometimes short-lived and only footnotes, as it were, to the history of climbing as a whole. There was, for instance, the First Ascents Affair.

So frustrated had climbers become by the lack of potential new routes that, unlikely as it might seem, they had got permission to dynamite some of the classic routes so as to create new lines. Public opinion was at first indulgent and became alarmed only when it looked as though these new methods were shrinking the peaks at a startling rate . . . But results had been most satisfactory: no fewer than twenty-nine first ascents of the South Face of the Dibona were recorded, each totally acceptable even for the most exigent purist, and it had been most unfortunate that, just as the charges were being primed for the thirtieth first ascent, the whole Aiguille should have crumpled and collapsed.

This incident had, however, inspired a quite different activity: the Last Ascents Affair. This had had all the hall-marks of true originality, and it demanded the greatest technical competence of all the participants. The rock was pre-charged with dynamite, and the point of the exercise was to see who could set off last, do the 'Last Ascent' and get off the route before it went up in smoke. It was an amusing initiative for anyone looking for excitement, and it was extremely successful with the younger generation of climbers. But there were heavy losses in terms of human lives and of available rock, and in the final resort both First Ascents and Last Ascents had to be banned.

The Robot-Guides Affair had also characterised a considerable period. The Federation of Alpine Guides, realising that the majority of its members spent their days doing a limited repertoire of routes virtually on automatic pilot, decided to invest heavily in the cybernetic technologies. A Robot-Guide had been produced, looking more or less like a normal guide, with two arms, two legs and a head, all in stainless steel and specially reinforced to withstand stone-fall. The Federation's insignia was enamelled in jewel-colours on its chest, and round about where its navel would have been was an extensible rope, which let itself out and reeled itself in as necessary. A Robot-Guide was naturally not available for every possible route: even to programme it for a limited repertoire had required feeding in a series of highly complex moves in sequence. Normally speaking, any alpine centre would have Robot-Guides for only four or five routes, and it took some time, for instance, before the Federation of Guides in Zermatt acquired a programme for the 1200 metres of the Hörnli Ridge on the Matterhorn; for many years, indeed, this represented the summit of programming achievement. In Chamonix, Charlets 1, 2, 3, 4 and 5, the Balmats and the Payots (all similarly numbered) were generally programmed for the N.N.E. Ridge of the M, the Couzy Route, the Papillons Ridge, the Rébuffat Route on the Aiguille du Midi, the Arête des Cosmiques and the Pyramide du Tacul. On each belay-ledge, the Robot-Guide would stand firmly planted on his steel feet in his thick rubber boots and take in the rope as required. The remarkable degree of mechanical sophistication typical of Chamonix even produced Robot-Guides able to lend colour with a few choice phrases at suitable moments. These ranged from general remarks about the weather:

'Nippy this morning! Better get a move on . . .'

Or (in a force 7 gale):

'Stop wingeing . . . Just enjoy the fresh air!'

To helpful suggestions in the climbing line:

'It's a bit spooky here, watch out!'
'C'mon! I've got you! I could hold an elephant!'
'Don't worry . . . Just climb!'
'I'll show you how to get your arse into gear!'
'Are you planning to bivouac, slow coach!'
'Get back on the mountain, for Chris' sake!'
Invariably crowned on the summit by:
'There you are! . . . Fun wasn't it?'

The Robot-Guides were extremely popular, but two constitutional faults brought about their demise. The first was indirect: a surprisingly large number of their lady clients fell desperately in love with them, finding their conversation unusually polite and patient compared with that of the flesh-and-blood guides with whom they normally came in contact. Unfortunately the Robot-Guides had never been programmed for emotional response, and things became very complicated: a sizeable proportion of the female clients went so far as to abandon all thought of climbing in the Mont Blanc massif.

The other weakness was inbuilt and decisive. Ravanel 14, having been programmed that day for the Rébuffat Route on the Aiguille du Midi suddenly switched over halfway to the Papillons Ridge. In the ensuing accident, three Robot-Guides and five clients were seriously hurt. When the Minister for Alpine Affairs heard the news, he had simply issued a decree forbidding all such mechanical aids — with all the more satisfaction in that a lady had recently left him for a Robot . . .

Next came the Ecological Period, short-lived but draconian while it lasted, which followed on the election of a 'Green' member to the European Parliament. A law was immediately promulgated, forbidding skiing unless the skier dragged a 'track-eliminator' behind him, so that each skier could achieve his birthright, skiing in untouched powder. The apparatus was expensive and heavy, so much so that within a very short time skiing became impossible except on artificial slopes . . . In climbing terms, the dynamite period was left far behind. Ecological ingenuity was carried to extremes. Only rigorously natural methods were permitted. No pegs, no nuts: the emphasis was on the Joe Brown system, which allowed at most jamming small pebbles into cracks. Progressively, more and more modern sophistication was eliminated: no ropes, then no crampons or ice-axes, then no boots or socks . . . There was no knowing how far things might have gone, had the Green Member not been carried off prematurely by a smoking-related disease.

No sooner had this lamentable event occurred than a quite new venture developed, the fruit of years of arduous and patient research. For many years it seemed the ultimate in organisational climbing. The material investment required was on an astonishing scale, but the results made the outlay worthwhile. Two thousand routes were selected in each massif, and at mathematically calculated intervals each route was fitted with heat-sensitive sensors, linked to a central computer and able to detect changing weather conditions or, more importantly, every passing climber. Each climber was then given headphones and an individual waveband, and would next be instructed in detail as to the course he was to follow: 'Rope 13, route 1619: slow down, rope 12 is on rotten ice and risks knocking down stones. Wait until they are off it. Proceed to the ledge seven metres left, I repeat seven metres left, and rest . . .' 'Rope 12, move faster, you are holding up ropes 13 through 18. Keep going, you are only 374 metres from the summit which you are scheduled to reach at precisely 11.43 . . .' 'Rope 13, do not leave the ledge and please note that this has not been designated a convenience area . . .' 'Rope 5, you are embarking on the narrow cracks — still some danger of verglas. You are two minutes ahead of the specified pitch-timetable, congratulations.' 'Rope 13, you have five minutes to prepare for departure, by the dièdre on your right, I repeat right . . .' 'Attention all ropes: temperature on the face dropping, risk of snow at about 13:30. I repeat . . .'

The system worked superbly. Every day, with no route-finding problems, no waiting at the crux, no hanging about, no tension, and accompanied every step of the way by that reassuring human voice, thousands of ropes advanced in total safety, knowing that they would be made aware of any coming change in the weather, any potential danger, any mistake they might have made — later it even became possible to install sound-sensitive sensors which would give advance warning of stone-falls. On the best equipped and most popular routes even greater refinements were introduced: a coin fed into a slot on certain ledges would produce a cup of tea, a sanitary towel, a roll of film — or even better, a half-hour's use of a belay peg. Alpine life was transformed.

The worst disaster in alpine history occurred on 3 August 2052, however. The computer broke down. This was a theoretical impossibility, but even so elaborate a system could not absorb the series of problems which, by coincidence, all happened at the same moment. The main computer link-up had no fewer than two back-up systems, all as reliable as technology could make them. But by a most unfortunate combination of circumstances, just as the main system had been powered down for maintenance, the second noted unusual temperature swings on sensor 122674 (something to do with unmentionable activities by jackdaws on the North Face . . .). The second back-up system was still searching its memory banks to account for this unforeseen circumstance, so that the third system was in effect operating alone, when a young climber started up a pitch *feet first* — some sort of ridiculous bet. Such a possibility had never been envisaged at the system design stage, and caused a software error. This, in turn, was detected by the over-ride, which made a vain attempt to transfer control from system 3 to system 2, but again, this had not been allowed for in the specification, and there was an immediate shut-down, destroying several megabytes of memory. Everything, in short, blew . . .

When frenzied efforts restored function, it was found that there had been 829 deaths and an incalculable number of injured. Lost, helpless, groping in a wilderness of silence and danger, thousands of climbers deprived of their support-system had had no idea how to take responsibility for themselves.

It was this accident that led the Higher Authorities (by then in charge of world affairs) to forbid mountaineering: on the one hand it was difficult to provide controlled conditions, and on the other it encouraged the development of an individual spirit of initiative which could be dangerous. (After all, more than half of those marooned by the systems' failure had, surprisingly, managed to make their way safely to the top and down.) And to prevent nonconforming and possibly rebellious tendencies, it was decided to conceal any mountainous terrain behind translucent barriers, whose hazy blue suggested a seascape.

Some substitute was, however, essential: there were the Olympic Games to think of. Fortunately, climbing simulators had reached a degree of sophistication which offered enormous possibilities. For many years they had been used only for training for certain specific problems: the Knubel Crack, the Fissure Brown on the Blaitière, the diagonal abseil on the American Direct, the upper pitch on the forty-metre wall on the Cap, and so on. But now a stage of technical development had been reached where a climb could well be reproduced in its entirety. Micro-processors were used to co-ordinate a continuous loop of flexible plastic, which could be set to move more or less quickly according to the capacities of the climber, and which moulded itself as it moved into the shapes of the holds and moves on every pitch of a climb. Climbers were thus able to enjoy all the pleasures of solo climbing without any of the risks, and could even choose what weather to have. They had only to sign up a few days in advance for a Walker-Spur-in-storm-conditions, or a Mustagh-Tower-in-June, or a Fitzroy-with-no-wind . . .

Only the general economic recession spoiled things, otherwise climbers would doubtless have been perfectly happy for ever with the new systems. But the Higher Authorities felt that in current economic circumstances, all this complex machinery had become expensive to maintain and to run . . .

'And now you know why, in 2084, you're reduced to climbing on buildings,' said Frédéric. 'They've been building tower-blocks at such a rate over the last century that at least we're not short of *them.* 'When I saw you on the North-East Face of Original Building 114, it brought back all my own youth. And there's only one thing that I really regret: this Memory-Pooling Scheme that the Higher Authorities have introduced so that all individual possessions, even memory, can be eliminated. I don't know how I've managed to avoid getting caught so long myself . . . They must have mislaid my identity file somewhere, so that when I get into the Memory-Pooling Chamber, I just have to pretend I've forgotten . . . If I'd told them about the error, I'd have been suspect anyway . . . So far I've managed to avoid all the random checks, or I'd have been found out. And that's how I've managed to hang on to my memories. Then I decided to trust you lads, and I was pretty sure that on an old route like this one there wouldn't be any Subversive Memory Recorders. So when we got formal permission to come here, I thought I'd pass on all I knew about alpine history. A year from now, of course, it'll all be fed back out of your memories into the Central Memory Pool, along with all the rest . . .'

'But look,' Michel interrupted, 'am I right in thinking that on the other side of that blue screen behind the tower-blocks there are *real* hills?'

'Real hills?' Frédéric sighed, 'Lad, you're looking at what used to be the Chamonix Valley!'

Boris was lost in thought.

'If we could only get through the screens! There'd be real live mountains! Just for us . . . no Higher Authorities!'

Frédéric shook his head, looking dubious.

'I wouldn't risk it myself,' he said, 'I'm much too old now. And it's only a matter of luck that they haven't had my memory drained. But you lads . . . who knows? Still, come on, we'd better get on down. It'll look suspicious if we spend too long perched on this ledge.'

He put the food-box back in the rucksack, and dislodged the water-bottle in the process. It bounced on the plastic coating over the concrete, and a little black disk slipped out of its mouth, rolled to the edge of the platform and down.

The three men fell silent. Oddly enough, when they came to look at it, the water-bottle seemed quite whole and undamaged.

'Suppose it was a bug?' whispered Boris, voicing what they all feared.

'Come on, let's get out of here!' said Michel.

The lift was slow in coming. It clanked and groaned up to them, filthy, scratched, scrawled with illegible graffiti. It was quite empty. There was a long, anxious descent, in a silence broken only by the clattering of the old lift. They reached the ground floor: the door opened; a serried rank of brown uniforms was waiting.

'The Memory Police!' groaned Frédéric.

Translated by Jane Taylor

MONTENVERS

The rain hurled against the grey walls of the mountain hotel, with all the force of a thunderstorm, all the tenacity of a winter drizzle. It whipped and scudded against the windows, hammered on the tin roof, gurgled and splashed along the gutters and the drainpipes. Raindrops splattered and hissed on the ground, and streamed off the hillsides, carving out new channels in the mud.

There was a startling contrast between the lashing rain outside and the peace of the dining-room and lounges inside the hotel; by this time, late in the evening, everywhere was nearly deserted. The little group of guides sitting round the big oval table looked like a tableau, so still were they against the dark panelling of the walls and the red curtains swagged back with white tassels. The lamps cast a soft light. A great fire burnt in the hearth, and in front of it a cat slept peacefully, curled up on the wooden floor. The windows set deep in the thickness of the stone walls kept the storm at bay. On an old tiled stove with polished copper doors was a stoneware jar filled with a blaze of chrysanthemums. They fanned out, gracefully, against the pine-clad walls.

Outside was a world of water and mist, and it was only just possible to make out the dark shapes of the nearest pine trees, the rain dripping and pouring off their drooping branches. Everything else was invisible, almost as though the whole world had vanished, drowned, leaving nothing but the sheeting rain.

An unfastened shutter creaked, but the sound which penetrated everywhere, into the very interior of each person, stifling conversation and blotting out even the drumming of the rain, was the sobs of the woman who lay upstairs in a room on the upper floor. Distance and the doors in between did nothing to muffle the sound. The guides sitting downstairs felt that they had never before heard anybody really cry. There were long moans and painful whimpers, broken by gulps of despair and grief. Every now and again would come a moment's silence, but almost immediately the sobs would break out again, endless and agonising: wails, rasping sighs, breath catching in a throat, keening like a soul in torment . . .

It would have seemed uncivilised, heartless, to talk about the weather, the alpine season, the mountains, or even the accident itself, with such a grief so close at hand.

The manager of the hotel was stoking the fire. One of the guides puffed meditatively on his pipe. Another made periodic trips into the glassed-in terrace outside, pressed his face to a window and stared out at the drowned landscape: sometimes it was clearly visible, almost tangible, and then at other times the rain seemed to make it distant and mysterious. The brown pine trunks looked solid and sturdy against the delicate tracery of their branches, hung with raindrops and veiled in mist; the trees looked faint and ghostly, unkempt, like great beckoning ghosts in a Gothic imagination. A goat grazed peacefully, resignedly, on the few tender blades of grass. Down towards the valley, the willow-herb tossed and shook under the onslaught of the storm.

Suddenly, high up, for a moment, the cloud swirled apart, and the watchers caught a glimpse of the Aiguille des Grands Charmoz, immensely tall, slender, plastered with fresh snow. And then the mist and the rain flowed back again, and the mountain vanished.

When dinner-time arrived, it seemed almost indecent to sit down to table, when upstairs the sobs continued unabated — and the guides ate hurriedly and in silence, every mouthful uncomfortable and awkward.

Conditions had been like this for several days. There was no question of a helicopter taking off in this, and a rescue-team had been sent out; they would set off the following morning at dawn. The bodies must be on the Thendia Glacier, which meant they would not be too far away. Just as well . . .

It had been that morning that the sole surviving member of the party had brought the alarm, dragging himself into the Montenvers Hotel in such a state that they had wondered how he had managed to get so far: his arm was broken, his knee twisted and swollen; he was covered with bruises and cuts, and his face was puffy. He'd wept as he staggered into that very room, wept with pain and exhaustion, with grief for his dead companions, with light-headed relief at finding himself still alive.

Haltingly, he'd explained what happened. A week earlier he and his friends Robert Nanteau, Yves Rumont and Bernard Javille had made up their minds to do the North Face of the Grands Charmoz. From the very beginning things had gone badly. Bernard had wasted two days of perfect weather trying to sort out a problem to do with work, and then he'd had to go back to Lyons. They'd been unable to find another climbing partner, and had been reduced to going as a rope of three, which was bound to slow everything up. Only one of them, Yves, had had anyone with him who'd be able to give the alarm if anything went wrong: Sylvie, his wife. But Yves had always refused to set deadlines for himself if he'd known he was embarking on a serious, high-quality route where he might be delayed by conditions on the face, or by the weather, or by the competence of his companions. And Yves Rumont was not someone whose wishes could be easily gainsaid. He was a superb climber, of course, and not imprudent, but he was touchy and authoritarian, and liked to impose his will on people and conditions alike. And everything and everybody bowed to him. His wife was afraid of him and would never have dared to disobey his instructions. And in any case, she was so used to seeing him stalk down quite unharmed, cuttingly scornful of her fears, after being held up on a route by several days of bad weather, or after sitting out a storm in a crevasse. That must have been why no one raised the alarm, even though it was two days since the accident.

They'd set off, then, the previous Saturday; today was Wednesday. They'd bivouacked on a moraine beyond the Montenvers, and then started up the face on Sunday morning. The weather had looked good, but the season was drawing to a close and conditions were doubtful: the ice was green and solid, the rock was covered with verglas. In spite of this and in spite of some complicated and time-consuming rope manoeuvres, the party had moved well, and they'd got as far as the top of the hanging glacier when the storm overtook them. A wild and terrifying storm. Lightning played around them, their hair crackled, their ironmongery hummed ... Huge hailstones ricocheted off the face. They'd had no warning — the storm had swept in from the west. For an hour they'd clung there, expecting any moment to be struck by lightning and swept off the little ice-platform where they were huddled insecurely together. Then the storm moved away, and the snow came, gently at first, soon thick and steady. There was no question of cutting up the two bulges of black ice that blocked the couloir higher up; even in good weather, they'd have been extremely difficult. The only hope was to go down, and even that was fraught with so many dangers that it seemed unlikely they'd make it.

Darkness had fallen, and they passed a miserable night. The following morning, painfully, they started down, fighting the cold, fighting the drifting, swirling snow that crept insidiously into every chink in their clothing, stung their eyes, made route-finding impossible. They'd had to abseil, now from dubious flakes or loose boulders, now from a peg or an ice-screw. Over and over again they'd gone through the same series of rash moves, aware of course of the risks they were taking, but with no alternative.

There had been snow-slides, little avalanches, which threatened to dislodge them from the face. Their clothes were soaked and frozen stiff. They were near to exhaustion. Even so, over the hours, they'd managed to lose a lot of height. Things had looked less desperate, and it became possible to dare imagine that they might after all complete the hopeless descent. And it was just as they were beginning to allow themselves to hope that it happened: a piece of wind-slab broke away under the leader's feet, and the rope snatched each of them in turn off his stance and down into the long fall.

That was all he could remember. When he came to he was lying in a heap of avalanche debris, and there was a severed end of rope on his harness. No sign of his companions. The snow fell on and on. He was in great pain. He'd waited, waited. And then, realising that help would not come, he'd dragged himself agonisingly down towards the valley, had spent another night on the moraine, had staggered on to the Montenvers, to help and hospital.

Night was falling. The guides went up to bed, and as they passed the room which still echoed to her sobs, each of them thought:

'How she must have loved him!'

They were quite wrong. The Rumonts had not been happily married. Yves had been so used to having his own way that it had never occurred to him to listen to his wife. He was very demanding and never satisfied. He was determined to be master, and would fly into a rage if Sylvie made any timid move towards independence.

After a while, she had opted for peace. She'd given in, often unwillingly — she had sighed, she had aged more than her twenty-eight years. She no longer enjoyed life, she simply tried to ensure that time passed as peaceably as possible.

The previous week, however, finally, she'd rebelled — and all because of the North Face of the Grands Charmoz. For years there had been vague talk of her going with Yves to her parents' house in the Jura for the last week of the holidays. The Rumonts had no children — Yves didn't want any — and Sylvie's affection was reserved for her father and mother, who were getting on a bit, and because they saw her so rarely imagined she was happy. After so many years of broken promises, so many years when a visit had been put off because of some climb or other, this time everything had been settled and confirmed in a series of letters: they were to spend the last week of August in the Jura. And then the North Face of the Grands Charmoz had unsettled everything.

'But last year you promised! You promised me!' Sylvie wept.

'Well then, this year I've changed my mind,' retorted Yves.

'But they're expecting us!'

'Then give them a ring and tell them to stop expecting us.'

'You've done quite enough routes this season! I've scarcely set eyes on you . . . I always have to do what you want. This year I'd really set my heart on it. And my parents will be terribly disappointed!'

'Your bloody parents — they're a pain in the neck! I didn't marry your parents!'

'But . . .'

'Now what? These are my holidays, and I do what I want with my holidays.'

'Yves . . . please . . . !'

'Oh, shut up . . . !'

They had not made it up. Yves was in a bad mood anyway, principally because Bernard's problems were holding everything up. And Sylvie was still hoping that the problems, or something else perhaps, would mean that the climb would be called off. But on the Saturday, Yves had hurried in, put a few last-minute items in his rucksack, and gone out without a word, slamming the door behind him.

And it was at that point that Sylvie had finally rebelled. If that was how he wanted it, she'd go and see her parents alone. When Yves came back, he'd realise she wasn't just a slave who had to put up with his unreliability and his bad temper. She told the landlady, left a forwarding address and a short note: 'Going to the Jura, join us when you get back.'

And she left.

In her home village, everything was calm and peaceful. Sylvie felt herself again. She let her mother spoil her a little, chatted to her father, met old friends. She was astonished at the way she'd let herself be dominated by Yves, and was only mildly surprised, not at all disappointed, as the days went past with no sign of him. He'd be annoyed, of course, but it would do him good. One of these days he'd turn up, to pick her up on the way back to Paris.

But no: on the Wednesday morning, a telephone call shocked the entire family:

'Madame, your husband has disappeared on the Grands Charmoz. Conditions are pretty bad here . . . Yes, you'll need all your courage . . . Yes, we're afraid the worst may have happened . . .'

The journey was a nightmare. Sylvie was racked by doubts and questions. No one had noticed the party was missing. Four days! If she'd stayed, she could have given the alarm. Whatever Yves had said, she'd never have let things ride so long! There might have been a chance of finding one of them alive. Perhaps Yves, or Robert, had been lying there, badly hurt, dying, hoping for rescue . . . And it was all her fault! Why had she left? How could she have left? It served her right . . . Now it was the others who were paying for her thoughtlessness with their lives . . . and she could have saved their lives if she'd stayed to give the alarm . . .

When she got back to their room and saw her note and Yves' things lying around — his jacket, his lighter, his book face-down — when she realised how terrible conditions had been, Sylvie broke down completely. She was already sobbing uncontrollably on the last train to the Montenvers when she went up with the rescue-team. She had insisted on going. She had refused sleeping-pills, food. She felt an overpowering need to atone, and could not bear the thought of finding artificial solace when she was haunted by the idea of Yves' body, broken and lifeless, lying out under its shroud of snow.

They'd guided her steps through the dining-room, up the wooden stairs, where a 1900s beauty, with a cascade of waved hair woven with poppies, daisies and ears of corn, raised an uncaring pint-mug, on an old poster advertising Meuse beers, oblivious of the grief-stricken woman stumbling past. They'd found her a bedroom, clean and peaceful as a cell in a nunnery. But she'd been quite unconscious of her surroundings and now, lying face-down on the counterpane, she was crying as she had done for hours, unable to stop, unwilling to stop, almost drunk with grief. Her sobs gasped and panted, wailed in an endless litany. On and on she cried, with no change in rhythm or intensity. Yves had often made her cry, of course, but she'd made an effort not to show it, whereas now she was out of control, giving free rein to the churning emotions she felt. The accident had come as a cruel blow just as she was beginning to relax, and she was horrified to think they'd left each other so bad-temperedly, after seven years together. Her despair, her tears were a part of an ill-defined hysteria she made no attempt to overcome.

It lasted for hours, and even when she became calmer, she didn't sleep. She lay there alone, in the dark, dazed with emotion, with no conscious thought, and only an occasional gulp or sob.

Her head was spinning. Why did things have to happen like this? Why death? Why life? How had it happened that she who was usually such a worrier had managed to stay calm and happy during those days when the accident was happening? How appalling that they should never have said goodbye to each other. The words they had exchanged echoed and re-echoed in her brain. Suppose she had been there, what would she have done? Would she really have done anything different this time? Because Yves had been so cold and cruel, would she really have been readier to disobey his instructions? The night was endless ... Time seemed to have stopped ... She was totally exhausted, but her head was clear and she couldn't sleep. The thoughts chased endlessly, senselessly, round her brain. The hotel was utterly silent. Had the world come to an end while the hours of waiting dragged past? She shifted on the bed and the springs creaked: things seemed real again. More time passed. The rescue-team set off, tiptoeing past her door. There were whispers:

'Shh! She's dropped off finally.'

'Poor little soul!'

She had no feelings left. Time crept on again. She could not imagine why anyone should feel sorry for her. After all, she's always known that, sooner or later, just this would happen ...

Around five o'clock, she saw the pale light of dawn through the window. Sylvie lay there, her eyes wide open. It seemed an eternity since she'd heard about the accident, answered the telephone call. The wild emotions she'd felt over the last hours had left her numbed, drained, empty of tears. Idly, her thoughts drifted to the future. Today would be very bad, and so would the next few days. But then? She'd probably have to go back to her old job — medical secretary — which she'd given up reluctantly, on Yves' instructions. She'd be quite glad to get back to work, to be busy again, to find life a bit of a struggle. She'd have to leave the Paris apartment — it would be too big and too expensive to run now she was on her own. She'd have to find a little one-bedroomed flat, in a part of the city she liked ... A bright, sun-filled flat that she could furnish and decorate as she liked ... It wouldn't be too bad ... And faintly, through her distress, she felt a first stirring of well-being: she'd have to get organised, find a job, get in touch with friends ...

As daylight grew, Sylvie became aware of the room; she hadn't noticed it the night before. The walls were panelled in pine, there was a wooden bed with a white counterpane, a carved chimney-piece, a wicker chair ... A stone window-sill, crimson curtains. There was a sense of peace and harmony which answered her own calm after the paroxysms of her grief.

Outside it was still raining, but without conviction. She could see the bright green of the pines, the curves of the glacier, and beyond it the silver threads of streams racing down off the rocky terrace above. The rain ceased. Over towards the Flammes de Pierre, the mist shredded away and revealed a ridge spiky against the heavy, grey sky. Rain still dripped dispiritedly off the roof.

Suddenly the door opened, and the hotel manager's son, a little boy of four or five, slipped surreptitiously into the room on tiptoe. He crept up to the bed and whispered:

'You're the lady who keeps on crying . . .'

He came a step or two nearer, pushed aside a lock of hair clinging damply to Sylvie's forehead, and stared at her. She tried to smile, but tears gathered in her eyes again and spilled silently down her cheeks. The little boy fled, closing the door softly behind him. Sylvie was always sad when she saw a child. Yves hadn't wanted any. When they were first married she'd tried to change his mind, but she'd realised that he was adamant. She'd even thought of leaving him. But it would have needed more courage than Sylvie had possessed. Knowing how the matter annoyed him, she'd given in, reluctantly, always feeling a little jolt of envy at other people's children. And again she said to herself that she'd never see a grubby little face, like the one she'd just seen, look up at her with love. But wait . . . Was she so sure she'd never have children? She couldn't imagine marrying again . . . She'd loved Yves, once, but her disappointment had left her with no illusions about marriage. They'd made such a mess of everything, life, happiness, even their last moments together, what with the quarrel and their lack of goodbyes. But she was only twenty-eight . . . Was it so ridiculous to think that she might, perhaps, not always be alone? Could she, dare she, possibly think of children one day . . .?

She blamed herself for allowing such thought, but she couldn't help vague visions floating into her mind, visions of rest, or hope. In any case, she had a deep sense of peace. It was years since she had felt so peaceful.

The sun was coming out, and it fell bright on the worn, scrubbed floor. The light played behind the rocky ridge on the horizon. The air was clear as crystal.

Feet hurried up the stairs. A deep voice cried:

'He's alive! Mme Rumont! He's been found! He's alive!'

Translated by Jane Taylor

THE BISHORN GHOST

Raymond Crapin's execrable character was notorious and Luc was wondering gloomily how he could have fallen into the trap and set off on a route with such an irascible companion. Certainly Crapin was a very skilful climber, but his consistent sullenness and his violent tempers were such that it was becoming more and more difficult for him to find seconds. There was much raillery in climbing circles, after a good fondue, about his Homeric outbursts echoing round the mountains. It was said, with some element of truth, that those who had done more than one climb with Crapin were masochists, but were at least able to acquire a good leader without having to pay a professional. It was also said, with only a touch of exaggeration, that among his former friends, one had given up mountaineering for good on returning from a particularly stormy trip, another had taken to drugs and a third, formerly known as the king of bon viveurs, had become a hermit in Lozère.

Luc was the first to laugh at such tales, the details of which he now recalled with bitterness, thinking that if only Jacques, his usual companion, had not stupidly sprained his ankle the other day on the path to the Temple-Ecrins, he would not be climbing with such a thoroughly unbearable individual as Raymond Crapin.

'Savate, eh! Pauvre pomme! Cul d'oignon! Bougre d'enfoiré!' Crapin bawled out in his own delicate language . . .

'Get a move on, you wimp!' he went on. 'You're doing it on purpose, aren't you, just to make me hang about on this stance? Get your arse in gear for Christ's sake! Pathetic! You scared or what? Hey, admit it, you're scared! A four year old would find it easy, but Monsieur hangs back! . . . Perhaps you think I am enjoying myself? Shit! I'll untie and leave you if you don't get going. Hurry up! Now what? My belay isn't big enough? So what? Wait until I've gone before installing yourself. If you need comfort on top of everything, go to the Hilton! . . . Give me your ice-axe! . . . I've never seen such an incompetent! Pass me the rope! No! The other one! Idiot!'

The entire face of the Bishorn had been resounding for a good hour with the most furious swearing it had ever echoed. Luc forced himself to crampon as quickly as he could up this treacherous slope of ice coated with fresh snow. On any other occasion he would have thought he was going well, even elegantly for such conditions, but he was living a double nightmare; that of a tiring and dangerous climb, and that of a resounding flood of insults. Never, never had he felt so unhappy in the mountains and he was also becoming ever more aware that it had been crass stupidity to have got on to this route.

At dawn a violent argument had broken out over the layer of powder that had fallen during the night and made the already tricky conditions even more dangerous. However, Crapin wanted to do the face and Luc, after having been called 'a coward, a little boy who should have stayed with mummy, a pathetic fellow shaking in his pants' and the like, had decided to attempt his first climb with Crapin, a decision which he had immediately regretted.

He regretted it even more when the wind slab covering the upper part of the face broke off. Everything happened suddenly. Moving together, the two mountaineers were unable to resist and were swept down by the snowslide.

The accident was witnessed by a couple of Englishmen who, on seeing the men starting up the slope, had also decided to try the climb. This second pair had just reached the wall of seracs over on the left and were on the rising traverse that led to below the summit. It was for this reason that they were not themselves swept away by the avalanche. One of them, fluent in French, had been periodically translating Crapin's choicer remarks for his friend. He could not help himself from interpreting the last insults yelled by Crapin as he fell.

'F...ing b... ...! You did that on purpose! Stupid c... Sh...!'

The drop over the serac wall put an end to Crapin's effing and blinding. The last rivulets of snow swished down the face and gloomily, the British climbers went back to see whether by some miracle they could still bring help to the victims.

The miracle had happened. Luc was in a state of shock, but alive. The rope, coiled around his shoulders, showed that his bad-tempered leader must have carried out his threat to untie and that it would be all the more difficult to find his body. As carefully as they could, the Englishmen carried Luc out of the avalanche cone, settled him in a sleeping-bag and, while one of them hurried to the Tracuit Hut to alert the rescue, the other remained on the spot looking for any traces of the lost man, but had neither sight nor sound of him. The fact that one of the two men had survived the fall was already the outcome of an amazing chain of coincidences. The Englishman took out his stove and set about making a brew for the injured man and himself.

As for Raymond Crapin, he was finding it difficult to understand where he was. In a weird way he was aware of being in a strange and downright disagreeable environment. A cirque. A cirque of rocks. Amazingly high, for he could not see their tops, and fluted like organ-pipes. And it was of organs that those mighty, vast, overpowering voices also reminded him. Yet how could he hear them? His ears were in a pit of silence, but still those senseless voices filled his whole being. Good God, what could it mean? He felt paralysed and torn by rage at having no one to blame. Never had he experienced such an unpleasant feeling. He was forced . . . forced to listen to those overwhelming voices . . . but it was all mad! Absolutely mad!

'We are the Supreme Tribunal,' said the voices. 'The Supreme Tribunal for Climbers Killed in the Mountains. We are examining your past . . . We are probing your last moments . . . We are examining your life and the manner of your death. Justice will be meted out . . . We are the Supreme Tribunal for Climbers Killed in the Mountains. We examine your every gesture, your slightest word, the least of your thoughts so that perfect justice be rendered to you as it is to each after death . . . The Supreme Tribunal deplores what it has learnt of your life. Like most climbers, you have enjoyed through the vastness of time and space, life-conditions propitious to happiness . . . You have never experienced famine nor epidemics, neither war nor misery, nor imprisonment, nothing that is the common fate of most of humanity, and yet throughout this good fortune which should have been perfect, you have been filled with resentment, you have spread unhappiness and sown discord. You have scorned love . . . Raymond Crapin! We, the Supreme Tribunal, condemn you to roam these mountains forever. Your punishment will only be lifted if one day, you can accomplish an act of love.'

'Crazy! I've gone crazy!' thought Raymond Crapin, who never beat about the bush.

He forced himself to think calmly and to begin with, tried to recall his last sensible thoughts. Let's see . . . He had set off to climb the Bishorn North Face with that useless Luc . . . He well remembered the drive in which he had been so irritated by the crowds of idiots on the roads . . . Then the hut walk, the unsettled weather, the dormitory . . . That was it! He was, quite simply, having a nightmare from which he must force himself awake. He had to get back to reality, check the time, set off early for the climb . . . But they had set off! He could remember leaving by headlamp and that fool questioning the wisdom of the climb . . . The bergschrund . . . The slope . . . The wind-slab . . . Ah! The fall! Then those voices. Those voices . . . Right, it was obvious; there had been an accident and he, Raymond, was in a coma, haunted by strange hallucinations which he had to shake off . . . He summoned all his will-power to wake up and was overcome by a great rage as he became aware of his helplessness.

For an eternity, Crapin struggled to deny a truth which seemed too absurd. Then came a day when finally he had to accept the fact; he was dead and if the ridiculous sentence of wandering the hills in the guise of a forlorn soul seemed quite unbelievable, the cruellest in the world, it was the only truth that remained. He thought deeply about the situation and felt indignant to the very depths of his being. He spent a while cursing the Supreme Tribunal in the most virulent terms he could conjure up, which brought some definite but temporary relief and then, later still, the solution seemed as clear as spring water before the advent of pollution. Like Zazie who wished to become a teacher 'in order to give hell to the kids', he, Raymond Crapin, would be a ghost, since this was the only choice left to him, but in order to make life unpleasant for living climbers.

So he began the second part of his existence, entirely devoted to making a pastime, already difficult enough without his help, even harder. First he had to draw up a methodical and accurate inventory of the range and limitations of a ghost's condition, which he worked out with meticulous care.

He thus learnt that ghosts — in this case, himself — were invisible, even to themselves, but given some effort could materialise. Two factors affected the apparition and upkeep of bodily form; altitude and duration. Thus, a half-hour appearance at mountain-hut altitude required less concentration than a few minutes over 4,000 metres. This was an important point which had to be taken into account for successful operations.

Crapin on the other hand, visible or not, had a body that performed just as it did at the time of the accident, and subject to the same restrictions. He could ascend a steep slope, cross a col, descend a gully, climb a rock-face, only by using the same amount of effort as before. There was no question of going through a rock-face or passing instantaneously from one point to another and Crapin would have loved to get hold of the idiots who imagined that ghosts had such gifts. He also suffered the same discomforts as a living climber. He could feel cold or too hot, he could bang against a rock, hurt his fingers and feel knocks, even during a fall, for he found he could fall and that the experience was still as unpleasant as ever. The only advantage was that his body was not permanently harmed by wounds or frost-bite. Only the gash on his forehead which he must have received when he fell on the Bishorn remained, oozing blood from under his helmet.

When Crapin at last accepted the situation, he was still located at the foot of the Bishorn North Face and at first thought he would be unable to move to another range: for whenever he tried to drop below high mountain level something always drove him upwards. But with the onset of winter, he noticed that he could move down into certain valleys thanks to the snow and thus roam the whole Alps. So he chose the Mont Blanc range as his main centre of activity, for he knew it well and the over-crowding would offer a particularly suitable field for action.

It took him somewhat longer to know what effect he could have on the living, as he had to wait for the spring skiing season. His first attempts were modest and purely experimental, but the results were satisfying; he was visible to men when he materialised and by forcing his voice, which had become rather weak, he could be heard. On the other hand, he found that he had practically no power over objects — moving a bit of gravel was exhausting work. This did not matter, for it never occurred to him to cause an accident, but simply to spoil the pleasure of the greatest possible number of climbers.

During that period, Crapin often wondered what could have urged him to climb. His new state did not give him any sort of pleasure. The most flamboyant of sunsets left him as cold as a serac. Climbing a peak without being able to add it to his list seemed totally devoid of interest and he did it cantankerously, simply to shake off the creeping boredom of the long hours spent huddled up, shivering in the precarious shelter of a crevasse. He felt desperately envious of his colleagues, those deformed creatures who haunted old manor houses furnished with sofas, creaking wardrobes, four-posters, carpets, curtains and perhaps equipped with central heating and God knows what else.

How those waits in the mountains were long! God, how long! And desolate, forsaken! From October to March there was scarcely any human presence. Just one or two climbers after new winter ascents. But they were so rare, and they usually tackled such extreme routes and it was so cold up there that Crapin did not always choose, nor was fit enough, to follow them. He was satisfied just to sneer, watching them from below. 'You fools! You constipated, pitiful idiots! You must be mad to leave your warm rooms to crawl up this icy wall and risk your necks. And if you are killed I hope the Supreme Tribunal won't be lenient with you! ... Ah, those pigs of the Supreme Tribunal! . . . If only I could get at them!'

From April, spring skiing was in full swing. It had certain satisfactions and whetted his appetite for the summer. Summer was the real time for triumph, exhilaration and even exhaustion, especially the months of July and August. Never had Crapin watched the weather so keenly, even when he had been most active as a climber, for bad weather, of course, reduced his clientele, whereas fine weather . . .

He soon devised quite a collection of tricks. The most satisfactory exploited the inherent irritability of the human race and was purely verbal. All he had to do was to place himself between two partners when the rope was well run out, one on the stance, the other struggling in the lead (it was even more successful if a ridge, an overhang, or a bergschrund prevented the climbers from seeing each other). Crapin would then bellow in his most deafening and angry voice: 'Can't you got a move on, man', or 'for f...'s sake, watch the rope?', or more subtly, 'Sure you are on route?' or some similar 'pleasantry' suggested by the circumstances, his own verbal imagination, or from experience gained by observing the reaction of his victims. The result was practically guaranteed. In the tension of the moment and the irritability resulting from effort, it was rare that one or other of the climbers, or even both, did not think the insult came from his companion and would angrily retort, 'Get stuffed!' . . . 'Wait and see how you manage!' . . . 'Just shut your mouth and let me get on with it!' Once the tone was set it was unusual for relations not to go from bad to worse. So the ascent would continue under tension and in particularly successful cases, the climbers would go back down. Once, the quarrel had nearly ended in an ice-axe duel on a ridge. And who got the last laugh? Raymond Crapin, of course!

A happy variation of this procedure needed unsettled weather. Between the two climbers Crapin would shout anxiously: 'Hey! It's clouding over. Better not go on.' Relieved that the suggestion had been made by the other, each climber could face retreat more easily. 'You're right. I was just thinking it was beginning to look a bit threatening.' 'Right, let's go back down.'

That ploy was especially good if the weather went fine again.

At other times, Crapin would use purely visual effects, as on certain climbs where the route was not obvious. The best results could be achieved on the traverse of the Drus, on the Requin slabs and on the Mer de Glace face of the Grépon. There, it sufficed for Crapin to leave ahead of the first climbers, or to bivouac on the face and, when he saw a party beginning to lose the way, to materialise a little above them in a cleverly chosen place, guaranteed to confuse. It did not take him long to find the most suitable spots.

'That's it! I can see where it goes!' one of the climbers would exclaim. 'Look at that guy up there!'

Like sheep, the climbers trustingly followed, getting more and more off route, rarely able to recover the situation until finally forced to turn back without even thinking the half-seen climber, who rapidly disappeared, responsible.

'Pity! If only we could have kept up with that guy in the red anorak, we wouldn't have lost the way . . .'

The same trick had once been used under quite different circumstances but with the most satisfactory result. Crapin had noticed two of his former friends, always after 'firsts', arriving with an air of mystery at the little hut close by where he happened to be. Their surreptitious glances towards a nearby face soon showed what they were after, as did the following scrap of conversation which Crapin overheard:

'It'll go OK! Can you see that crack system? It's like the photograph showed. We can follow it up to the terrace without much trouble. After that we'll take the small *dièdre* over on the left and then straight up the slabs. The weather is all right, it's in the bag. A seven-hundred-metre route which no one has yet spotted!'

Crapin had to move fast. He rushed up the approach, exited from the cracks after dark, bivouacked extremely uncomfortably on the terrace which turned out to be a narrow, sloping ledge, set off again early to tackle the fiendish *dièdre* capped by an overhang where he very nearly fell, and finally at last reached the slabs where he materialised as high up as he could. The result was up to expectations. A resounding oath echoed around the face:

'It can't be! What sodding luck! Someone has got there first!' yelled one of the climbers.

'But where, for Christ's sake, did he come from?' protested the other. 'We didn't even see him at the hut last night!'

'He must have bivouacked! It's enough to make one puke. Come on, let's go back down, I'm too pissed off . . . We missed it by just one day, one sodding day.'

It was easy for Raymond to imagine what followed. His friends awaiting the announcement of the new route, curious to know who had done it, would be flabbergasted to learn that it had been done by three climbers, a full month after their own attempt.

Another trick that also never failed was the faked accident. At the foot of the route, usually near the bergschrund, frequently actually in it, Crapin would collapse on a snow-bridge and materialise when he heard climbers approaching. This inevitably led to their giving up.

'Eh! D'you see that body!'

'What body, where? Oh!'

'Poor chap, he must be dead. He can't be reached without a winch. Come on, let's get down and call the rescue . . . It's a shame though, with such good weather . . .'

The rescue-team naturally found no one. Presumably the snow-bridge had collapsed. Searching the depths of the crevasse revealed nothing. It was a perfect trick, but could not be used too often.

Once, while performing it, Crapin thought he would explode of indignation. As usual, he was pretending to be dead, near the Innominata, at a point where six Austrian climbers were about to pass. With no risk of being recognised, he had simply lain on his back, displaying the wound on his forehead, his mouth agape and his eyes staring into space. Some exclamations in German were heard, which he was sorry not to understand.

'Ach! Da liegt doch einer, tot . . .'

'Wahrscheinlich ist er allein, man sieht kein Seil.'

'Dann ist er selber Schuld!'

'Also, dann schnell weiter . . . Wir konnen ihm sowieso nicht mehr helfen!'

(Hey, a stiff . . . He was probably alone, he has no rope . . . He was asking for it! . . . All right, let's go on, there's nothing we can do for him now!)

Crapin, who, already pleased by his initial success, was trying not to let a victorious smirk appear on his face, could not restrain his fury when he found himself left alone in his hole, as the footsteps and voices carried on upwards as though nothing had happened.

Certain techniques belonged more to the classic arsenal of the traditional ghost. Simple tricks, like at night, pressing his grimacing face against the hut window. The first sleepless climber who saw him would sit up in fright, blink and then see nothing, but shaken and fearing it was some premonition, was liable to give up in the morning. In the same vein belonged an array of strange noises — sighs, moans, scratchings on the hut's tin roof which, well-handled, obviously did trouble the climbers' dreams, for a higher proportion than usual did not leave at the agreed time.

It was also necessary to know how to exploit conditions and circumstances as they presented themselves. During the long winter months, Crapin always recalled with relish the affair of the small hut backing direct on to the mountain, far from any water-supply. A sort of plastic pipe had been rigged up which drew water from a fairly inaccessible source. It ran towards the hut and passing over the roof, came down near the terrace. Where this pipe bent sharply, it had started to crack and the small leak was evaporating on the roof. On the day Crapin passed by, eight climbers were in the hut, happy with a forecast of splendid weather. The last of them turned in at nine o'clock and Crapin knew that they would get up at 2 a.m. With his little ability to handle matter, he found it exhausting to soften, fold, crumple and enlarge the split, but an hour and a half later the job was done. Suddenly a jet of water spurted on to the tin roof and rebounded down outside the small window.

Tired but delighted, Crapin pressed his ear to the door. At five to two, an alarm-watch rang.

'Bloody hell, it's raining!' someone groaned.

'Pouring!' remarked another.

'Oh well, good night,' said another philosophically.

No one enjoys getting up at sparrows' fart and, however disappointed one may be at missing a climb, one is never entirely displeased to snuggle back into warm blankets. But in the morning what a hue and cry there was when the door was at last opened!

'It's a glorious day! What the . . . ah, that's it! It's the bloody pipe!'

'Oh no! . . .'

'Eight in one go,' recalled Crapin. 'Ah, their faces!'

Thus time passed, so coldly and so slowly in the winter, but so rich in vengeance in the climbing season. Never did Raymond Crapin think of changing his ways. His only regret was not to be able to multiply himself *ad infinitum* . . . To ruin the ascents of all climbers, that would have been perfection!

But after three or four years, malevolence became too much of a habit, a routine of hate which was difficult to keep up. Fortunately an incident occurred which plunged Crapin into unutterable fury.

The year before his death, Crapin had fallen deeply in love with a young woman. She was nineteen and was a climber called Corinne. He had taken her on the Frontier Ridge of Mont Maudit and during the whole trip he had been patience and gentleness personified. He knew, that little by little, summer would draw them closer . . . and as he was used to getting what he wanted, he was certain that she would be his wife one day. But right from the second climb his bad temper had resurfaced. Nothing very important. He only pointed out she was not cramponing properly, that she was moving awkwardly on the rock: he had refused to stop when she asked him to, because after all, mountains were not made for weaklings. Nothing to get upset about. In fact, he was simply doing her a service by correcting her faults. However, the idiot of a woman had got uptight and told him she would never climb again with a menace like him. A menace! A menace, she'd said! And back in the valley she had avoided him. He had humbled himself so far as to suggest another climb and she had laughed in his face. That was Corinne! A harpy, a conceited female, a pretentious child! If there was anyone he hated, it was her.

Now, one day as he lingered on the path to the Couvercle watching groups of climbers go by, he saw her, Corinne! She was as pretty as ever, perhaps even more beautiful. Her face had lost the softness of childhood making her yet more striking. She had her hair cut short now, like a small fair halo. She moved strongly. She looked happy, laughing. The bitch! Crapin did not think immediately of sizing up the companion, he had eyes for Corinne only and he wished he could have struck her down with his look. But when at last he managed to wrench his eyes away from her, his anger knew no bounds. She might have been with some old guide, with a group of friends, or with anyone, but no, she was with just one young man, handsome, calm, smiling — and what a warm, tender smile he had for her! It was unbearable. There would be no need to find any other victim for the next day ... Crapin would ruin their season, would wreck their love of mountains, would make them fall out with one another ...

He did not have to intervene immediately as bad weather took over and Jean-Pierre (his name was Jean-Pierre, that friend!) and Corinne walked back to the valley the next morning. One sentence however made Crapin's future course of action clear: 'As soon as the weather turns good, we'll come back up again,' the boy had said. 'You'll see, the Droites, a marvellous mountain!'

Raymond Crapin only had to wait. He even lost interest in the few climbers who chanced going up to the hut during the poor conditions that followed. He worked out a thousand plans and finally chose one which, although it involved a downright nasty part for him, was faultless.

Fine weather returned and there they were walking up to the hut again, that dreadful Corinne with her Jean-Pierre. Crapin left immediately. He knew the way fairly well and helped by the light of the moon, he climbed at night and reached the summit early.

The Droites are not often climbed and on that morning only one group was heading for the ascent. Crapin was ready, his heart beating somewhat since he had never before tried such an experiment. The climbers stopped below the bergschrund, checked their gear and put on their helmets. Crapin waited until they looked upwards, ready to climb and then he jumped. He simply threw himself into the void, spread-eagled, trying to keep off the rocks, but soon crashing into them, every bounce catching a different part of his body, breaking, rebounding, sliding, tumbling, suffering beyond imagination. Crapin dropped nearly a thousand metres and disappeared into the bergschrund.

He was no longer in a state to see the result of his stratagem, but as he had foreseen, his goal had been achieved.

'Oh God, oh God, how horrible!' sobbed Corinne.

Jean-Pierre had rested his hand on her shoulder. His face was ashen. 'One knows accidents and death do happen, but it's awful to witness one. Hush, my little Corinne, keep calm, we must get down quickly to report it . . .'

'But . . . is there nothing we can do for him . . . ?'

'No Corinne. After such a fall, there's nothing one needs . . . except prayers. Suffering is over for him.'

However, Crapin's suffering was not over. Battered, torn and reeling, he finally managed to get up and painfully peer over the crevasse. Far away he saw the climbers reaching the Couvercle and he collapsed in the snow desperately in need of some form of rest.

He was sure that after such an event, it would be a long time before Jean-Pierre and Corinne would climb again, but he also feared that once they had recovered from the shock, Jean-Pierre would insist on wiping out the traumatic memory with a new climb where they would both rediscover the beauties of the mountains. It was for that reason that as soon as Crapin was fit to drag himself along, he made for the Aiguille de l'M. He could not go down much lower, but he had keen sight and thought that he might be able to watch the chalet where Corinne's parents used to holiday, near Les Moussoux. Doubtless they were still there and from time to time, he saw a small white car arriving which he guessed was Jean-Pierre's. Eventually, one morning he realised that something was up. He saw the car early and managed to follow its passage to the Aiguille du Midi station. To reach the

Plan de l'Aiguille posed no particular problem for him. He arrived on the glacier overlooking it just in time to see that Corinne and Jean-Pierre were taking the path to the Grands-Mulets.

'Curious idea', he thought. 'You go down that way rather than up, but that pair, in any case, will not be going up . . .'

Hobbling, he followed them through crevasses and seracs towards the hut, brewing up various Machiavellian plots. He arrived there late and pulled himself up towards an open window. The proximity of humans and inhabited places were repugnant to him. There emerged from mountain huts a smell of life which was truly nauseating, but he had to face such trials occasionally and now more than ever.

Just at that moment, Jean-Pierre was talking with the warden . . .

'You certainly are the only ones to come up,' said the latter. 'Hardly anyone sleeps here now, except those getting down late from Mont Blanc or who are too tired to go on. However, this Pitchner Ridge . . . It's a lovely climb . . . Two o'clock call, all right?'

'Let's say half past one,' Jean-Pierre answered. 'If the going is good, we'll push on from the Dôme to Mont Blanc. Best to leave early.'

He would have to find a solution quickly. It came easily enough. At dusk Crapin noticed that the warden kept his bedroom window open and that a big alarm-clock was ticking away on the table within arm's reach. When all were asleep, he managed to reach the casement and turn off the alarm button.

It was already late when Jean-Pierre and the warden appeared on the doorstep. The keeper was deeply distressed.

'I know I wound it up! I know!' he moaned. 'I remember . . . I even remember thinking that it wasn't particularly cold when I put it back on my table by the window . . . I can't understand it. I've never before failed to wake up clients . . . I am so sorry!'

Cirrus clouds gradually covered the sky and Jean-Pierre and Corinne set off valleywards, disappointed yes, but not sufficiently; obviously they were simply happy to be together, even enjoying walking through this boring icescape which Crapin could no longer stand . . . But he laughs best who laughs last . . .

Stormy weather followed. A little rain was better for Crapin than the sight of all those idiots daily cluttering up the Aiguille de l'M, where he was back on watch. Besides, the season was drawing to a close, the high mountains were plastered in fresh snow and when the good weather settled in again,

Crapin was not surprised to see the little white car drive by Les Moussoux and then park near the Aiguille du Midi cable-station in time for the first lift. The only question was: would Jean-Pierre take Corinne to the North-North-East Ridge of the M or to the Couzy or perhaps the Ménégaux? Not that it mattered anyway, for they would not get as far as starting the climb. Crapin went to meet them ready to use any means, dispensing with ethical subtleties, to settle once and for all with those two.

When Corinne and Jean-Pierre began to cross the lower part of the Nantillons glacier, Crapin, still invisible, threw himself before Corinne's feet with the abandon of a rugby player tackling an opponent. He had never tried such direct action before, but it was definitely successful as Corinne stumbled and thrust her hands forward to break her fall. When she looked at them a moment later, the palms were bruised, bleeding and encrusted with tiny bits of gravel. How she tried to stay stoical, that hussy! She didn't shed a tear, her thoughts were only for Jean-Pierre. Just as well that Crapin had been there once more to upset matters . . .

'I am so sorry,' she sighed. 'I am going to make you miss your climb again . . . How stupid! . . . It's my fault!'

'Show me your hands.' Jean-Pierre replied without any signs of annoyance. 'Poor Corinne! You are unlucky . . . You can't go on with hands like that . . . Are they hurting? Wait, I'll clean them.' 'Bla, bla, bla and bla, bla, bla . . .' Crapin mocked indignantly. What a wet that Jean-Pierre is! Can he really like climbing, poor drip, if he gives up like that. To put up with all this without even grumbling, just for the eyes of a stupid cow . . . Anyway, that's it this time. I hope they have got the message!'

The winter was long and cold. Crapin reviewed the previous season and decided he had wasted his time on that flimsy, dull creature who didn't even exist, so insignificant was she — a mere trollop on whom he had spent far too much effort. He decided that only worthy matters would deserve his attention the following year.

So when summer came round again, he returned to his malevolent routine, without much enthusiasm it must be admitted. The *belle époque* was over. Leaving aside his own role, he had seen so much stupidity, so many mistakes and accidents occur, that in the end the sight of paltry little humans tackling the high mountains was beginning to sicken him. One day, out of habit, he set off for the Brenva Col sensing that bad weather was coming in. Inevitably the storm would catch climbers at the exit from the Italian side of

Mont Blanc. Formerly he had been quite entertained by seeing these poor, exhausted, worried creatures who could not find the way, missing the correct passage by so little, no longer able to go on, afraid to die and who sometimes did die. Now, he only went up there to pass the time and treat himself to further justification for his contempt.

Arriving at the Brenva Col, he continued up the slope above. In fact, the place wasn't exactly crowded that day and the weather was quite awful. The temperature had dropped to −20 degrees. You couldn't see more than a few metres ahead, the wind was punishing and powdery snow lashed your face . . . Not the weather for a poor ghost out of doors!

Suddenly he caught sight of climbers exiting from the Old Brenva. That lot weren't out of trouble yet . . . Crapin came closer. Two figures fought against the storm, so dreadfully frail amidst the unleashed elements and one of them, a woman it seemed, a woman at the end of her tether. All tracks had vanished. It would be the dickens of a miracle if those two survived!

'Keep going! Courage, Corinne!' said the man's voice. Raymond Crapin shuddered. It was Corinne and Jean-Pierre who were about to die.

'Good!' he thought to himself. 'That'll teach them.'

However, when he saw the fragile figure of Corinne, completely done in, struggling for dear life; when he saw the ice-covered strands of hair poking out from her anorak hood, when he heard her painful breathing, he found he could no longer rejoice. But at least he would not add to her troubles, the mountain was doing enough already . . .

Uneasy, he followed the climbers. There were three possible routes for the descent and he would soon know which one Jean-Pierre would choose. Now he would see that boy in action! Naturally, he ignored the usual way over the summit of Mont Blanc, for Corinne in her present state would be most unlikely to make it; it would mean having to keep going on up and with such wind on the ridge she would never hold out. The second way, the most direct in fact, was via the Corridor, a passage rarely used: Crapin knew it would not go at present because it was obstructed by huge, impassable crevasses. So he sensed an odd feeling of relief, when he realised that Jean-Pierre was taking the third alternative, also long and tiring, but the most sensible choice; down to the Brenva Col, then crossing the slopes of Mont Maudit and Mont Blanc du Tacul to reach the Cosmiques Hut. Only there, and it was a long way away, would the climbers be safe.

What was Jean-Pierre doing? The fool! He was lost! He had his altimeter, compass, map, and yet he was drifting too much to the right! The slope he should be descending was steep, but not as steep as that! Didn't he realise? He was moving back down the South Face where, inexorably, they would die.

Ah! Now he's got it. Jean-Pierre made Corinne stop and climb back up. Good God, what emotion! The weather and conditions were bad enough without going off route as well! . . . There they were, back again and starting down the correct slope . . . The correct slope? No, not quite . . . Very slowly, they were bearing left. That was as bad as before. True it led downwards, but to the Rochers Rouges Inférieurs, unpassable. Oh, it was too frustrating! . . .

Jean-Pierre was looking at his compass again. He was hesitating, worried.

'I am not sure any more, Corinne, but I think we must go up again. Come on!

She gave him a blank look, almost uncaring, like a faulty automaton, turned round and again staggered up the slope she had just climbed down. Once more, she passed close to Crapin and when he saw her so near, that pitiful face contorted with cold, when he noticed the frozen tears on her eyelids, her lips white with exhaustion, a wave of compassion filled his heart. It was unthinkable that Corinne, so young, so happy, so alive, would soon be no more than a small corpse shrivelled by frost . . . No! Too bad! Corinne must once more find the gentle world of valleys, even with her Jean-Pierre and marry him, be happy together and have many children! Anything but this cruel end! Now, what could he do?

How desperately difficult it was to materialise at such altitude, so high in the mountains . . . It required an effort and pain difficult to imagine, especially in a gale like this, but there was no other solution. At least it would spare Corinne from having to climb up again for the time being. Losing height might help her . . . Crapin moved off in the right direction, judging that at a distance of about ten metres he could be seen but not recognised. Suddenly, Jean-Pierre caught sight of him through the squalls.

'Another party, Corinne!' he cried. 'We'll get out together! . . . Wait for us!' he shouted to Crapin, but the latter went on slowly, signalling for them to follow.

Corinne seemed to have recovered some energy. She sighed with relief at knowing that they were not alone in that blizzard. Now she moved better, a little more quickly, no longer pausing at each step, yet how far they still had to go! How many hours and hours of effort and in such conditions! . . . Crapin too understood how hard it was to move at the limit of one's endurance, for to remain visible, to keep going at the right distance, neither too close nor too far, to wave reassuringly from time to time, he had to expend an energy which, with each step, seemed to be at the extremes of the possible.

In due course they had to ascend to the shoulder of Mont Maudit. Corinne was labouring desperately. It was a hard grind for everyone. The wind howled, whipping their faces with icy crystals. It seemed to be getting ever colder. Visibility was nil. Only Crapin, who had become familiar with these parts over the last few years, could find the way. Now and then Corinne fell to her knees in the snow, getting up again with difficulty. Jean-Pierre, by holding the rope between them very taut, gave her some encouragement, but he too was beginning to tire and Crapin was exhausted . . . They had by no means won through yet!

At last they reached the shoulder of Mont Maudit and Corinne collapsed against a rock. Frost and wind had swathed it in rime. Cagoules, over-trousers and axes were covered in ice. Corinne had a nose-bleed, Jean-Pierre attended to her, rubbed her numbed hands, made her drink, gave her sugar and chocolate, trying to instil some hope which he perhaps did not share . . .

A few metres from them, Crapin dematerialised and collapsed in the snow, saying to himself that he would never have the strength to start again and that all was lost.

'Are you better, Corinne?' asked Jean-Pierre. 'You're doing marvellously . . . Yes, you are! In such conditions, it's desperate going for everybody, you know . . . but we have covered a lot of ground . . . Now listen, it's still hard, but it's no longer dangerous. The worst is behind us. I don't know whether you even noticed it . . . Back there on that passage before the Brenva Col, after the bad weather finally caught us . ∶ . Did you realise that we were on a huge wind-slab?'

'I hate wind-slab,' replied Corinne. 'You heard about poor old Crapin's accident? . . .'

'Poor old Crapin!' She remembered him! And was sorry for him . . . Raymond's heart filled with warmth, tears rose to his eyes. Here! This was no time for emotion, just keep on going.

Straining to the utmost, Crapin rematerialised and risked shouting: 'Let's move!'

'Ah, there are the others!' Jean-Pierre remarked. 'Where did they get to? They're as elusive as ghosts . . . But the important thing is that they know where they are going. Perhaps they are a group from ENSA? Come on,

Corinne, quickly while we can still see the last one's anorak. Their tracks seem to vanish so fast! Not surprising in this blizzard!'

The way down to the great cwm separating them from Mont Blanc du Tacul was long and difficult. Fresh snow balled up under their boots. The slope was steep. Corinne often slipped and it was all that Jean-Pierre could do to hold her. He could have done with help from the other party he could just see ahead, but in such circumstances every group has to fight for its own survival. It was already kind enough of them to wait whenever a route finding problem arose.

Crapin dreaded an accident. It only needed Jean-Pierre to be careless in belaying for Corinne to start a fatal slide . . . But at last they reached the bergschrund. They had to rappel across it, leaving an ice-axe. The rope was frozen and the manoeuvre was slow. It was already three o'clock by the time they reached the bottom of the slope. The catastrophe now, thought Jean-Pierre, would be to lose their way and be caught by nightfall — death from cold, exhaustion and fear would be quick. Even so, they still had to stop to beat the ends of their boots and massage their hands threatened by frost-bite. The return of circulation made them moan with pain.

They started off again. The long, rising traverse to the shoulder of Mont Blanc du Tacul was crucifying. Crapin himself now sometimes fell . . . fell . . . got up . . . walked on. One step . . . then another . . . another . . . and then another, each a hard-won victory and still thousands more needed.

If only the storm would abate . . . If only visibility returned so the pair could find their own way . . . but no, there was no choice but to keep it up to the bitter end as the wind whistled and the snow fell . . . They'd never make it. It now seemed to Crapin that shreds of his ectoplasm were being torn from him by the squalls, pulled apart like images on a faulty television picture . . . Moving was nothing compared to the effort needed to keep his whole person assembled, together, visible at this altitude and in such conditions.

'We won't stop!' Jean-Pierre decided at the shoulder. 'We've got to reach the hut before nightfall. You're doing great, Corinne. It's not far now . . . Bear up!' . . . 'Let's hope the final slope isn't too avalanchy,' he muttered to himself.

It certainly was! However, Crapin decided to risk it and trust in Providence. All three of them had such difficulty, even in putting one foot in front of the other, that there was no question of trying to do anything more clever. He started down the slope and waved for them to follow. They floundered in the fresh snow, setting off mini-avalanches, but thank God, nothing more serious. Eventually, after wading through tons of powdery snow, they reached the ladder which had been fixed that year, to cross the gaping crevasse at the foot of the mountain. They had done it! Alone, Corinne and Jean-Pierre made their way to the Cosmiques Hut where they would find friendliness, warmth and a good plateful of soup! . . .

'Hey! I can't see the red anorak any more,' observed Jean-Pierre. 'Where did they get to? Presumably they went straight on to the Aiguille du Midi. Pity, I would have liked to thank them! . . . Anyhow, here's the hut! Corinne, we're safe now!'

Crapin collapsed on to the snow in a mass. He felt himself falling between great organs of ice, blindingly white. His ears rang like bells . . . no, like vast voices, voices which said to him:

'Raymond Crapin, you have fulfilled a major act of love. The Supreme Tribunal of Climbers Killed in the Mountains releases you from your punishment and summons you to join in the joys of the chosen . . .'

Translated by Daniel Roberts and John Wilkinson

THE PEST

Never had winter been so beautiful. The air was as keen as crystal and, in spite of the sun, the snow which had fallen heavily during the holidays remained thick, velvety, immaculate. Hoarfrost was already settling upon the bare branches. Overlooking the valley, the Aiguille du Glaive proudly stood in brilliant whiteness, while, higher still, snowy heights were ablaze against a pale sky where, soon, pure and distant, the first stars would shine.

On the path, the ice crackled under Achille Bletterans' boots. After a good day's work, he felt fit, satisfied and happy to be alive. Indeed, although he was in his fifties, he had remained strong and he could be proud of himself. He quickened his steps towards the farm, looking forward to the peaceful evening he had promised himself.

The farm was his 'thing', his victory. Still single, he had continued to live there since his mother died. Together, they had lived as in the old days, with cows in the cowshed and the byre full of sweet-scented hay. Trouble had started at the old woman's death, when the inheritance had had to be shared between seven brothers and sisters scattered in the valley and elsewhere. Leave the farm? Never! Fortunately, they had reached an agreement, and, by sacrificing all his savings, and by borrowing from the bank Achille had been able to pay off the rest of the family and keep the farm. And houses were more expensive in the valley than anywhere else, with no lack of tourists willing and able to cough up thousands for the humblest shack . . . So, an old farm, just imagine! With the date 1765 and the name of the Bletterans engraved on the main beam . . .

And he would have had to give up all that, go and live in one of those concrete rabbit-hutches which promoters were shoving up everywhere, walls like cardboard, and neighbours who would have kept him awake till God knows what time . . . No thanks! Now he had his own home, and never mind if the rates were a burden.

In the summer, Achille Bletterans worked as a guide, but, as he did not ski, he had to do something in the remaining nine or ten months. When his mother was alive, there was no problem; their needs were modest, they did a bit of work at home, they lived off the farm and the garden. But he had had to change all that to earn more and to pay his taxes. And because he was alone and sometimes away from home, he had to sell the cattle and now did odd-jobs here and there. At the moment he was working as a woodman, and it was a pleasure to be out of doors on these fine days of ice and sunshine.

For the housekeeping, one of his sisters who lived nearby, had agreed to come and tidy up during the day, and leave him some well-simmered stew on the stove. Perhaps things were even better than in his mother's day. She had become grumpy and insisted on running everything, as if Achille were still a child! But, for the last four years, he had been his own master; and, when the summer season was profitable, he furnished the house more to his taste. Away with the old stuff; on the other hand not the latest fashion, and certainly not the 'antiques' made for Parisians . . . no, just something clean, sensible and sturdy. Already the kitchen had been re-done with yellow tiles and cleverly designed white cupboards. There was also in the *séjour* as they say nowadays, a good woollen carpet, a wrought-iron table for the television, a comfortable armchair, English-style, with flowers on a red background. And in the bedroom, for good, relaxing nights, the superb beechwood bed with hand-carved designs and covers of deep-pink mohair — best quality. Yes, the house was welcoming now, and it was particularly pleasant to come home on a winter's evening . . .

There was some mail in the box: a copy of *Le Chasseur Français* and two letters. Achille Bletterans picked it all up, smiling under his moustache. After supper and before the film, he would read it, nice and cosy, sipping a small coffee with brandy.

But after dinner, his euphoria had somewhat evaporated! One of the letters was unimportant — just some advertising for an electric-drill. But the other! No need to say more, the other was from Yvonne Trugny! Ah, the bitch! He had nearly forgotten the creature, the 'bind', *la rûle*, as he called her in local dialect. A pain in the neck. And this was the one time of the year when he could forget her, for the memory of her pursued him months after the season and invaded him again as soon as spring came . . . Now peace was over, already!

Mlle Yvonne Trugny was Personnel Manager at the Ministry of Administrative Development. Achille knew no more than that about her work, but warmly pitied the colleagues and underlings who had to live with her during the eleven months she did not have to endure her, for Yvonne Trugny — 'The Trugny', as he liked to call her to himself — was a passionate climber, although age was reducing her capabilities more and more.

At first sight, she was a little prune of a woman; but only at first sight, for Achille knew to his cost how much she weighed when she was hanging at the end of a rope! In fact, her slimness was deceptive for she had broad hips and legs like gate-posts. She looked rather like an ant with her narrow chest, jet-black hair with only a touch of grey, dark eyes, faded features, thin lips shaded by a soupçon of moustache. One can't be responsible for one's physique, of course. But, at least, one is for one's behaviour and on holiday Mlle Trugny would behave like an adolescent. She simpered, she pretended to be silly and squeaked: 'But do call me Yvonne, Achille!' She had a shrill laugh . . . And that day when she had turned up with two little pigtails! 'Have you disguised yourself as radar?' Achille could not help asking. How furious she had been!

Memories flooded in . . . Those endless slogs up to the hut . . . Three hours, three hours and a half where two was usual . . . 'Let's stop, Achille!' . . . 'Achille, I want to put on my sunglasses!' . . . 'Achille, I'm thirsty!' . . . 'Achille, not so fast!' . . . 'Oh, the pretty flowers, Achille! I want to stop and pick flowers . . .' 'Oh, the pretty stone! Do look at the pretty stone, Achille!' All that for a break, of course, to pause for a while to ease the heavy breathing that tore the air behind him. It was sad, but why did she have to insist on carrying on?

And why, in mountain huts, play the little girl again? Or, worse still, act like a tomboy?

'The glacier's not that good today, is it?' she would broadcast all round in order to look like a mountaineer . . . And fussy! She had to have a corner bunk in the dormitory, and three blankets, and never mind if others had to go without. The soup was never hot enough. Her steak was too tough, the peas too big. The tisane took too long to come. The young were too noisy. The hut-keeper did not look after her properly.

'I am a veteran of the French Alpine Club,' she declared to whoever would listen, 'and I have the right to demand that . . .'

Ah, misery! She took sleeping-pills at night and snored. All right, it is true that she was not the only one in the hut, but in the morning! . . . She had to be shaken for hours before she would emerge, and then, God, what a scarecrow she looked! And the show was only starting. First she disappeared to the loo. After which she took hours to get ready, to lace her boots, getting it wrong, forgetting her gaiters, taking off her boots, putting them back on, rummaging in her basket, drinking her tea, nibbling at her bread.

'I can't swallow a thing at this time of day,' she would moan.

Yet how she did eat! And no sign of hurry, oh no! Then she would unpack her pots of cream and start greasing her snout . . . One cream for the eyes, one for her nose, one for her lips, and yet another . . .

'When will you stop smearing yourself with all this lard?' Achille had asked one day . . . 'It won't make you look younger, nor walk faster . . .'

Whew! She had been in such a bad temper that time, they had to give up the climb!

And the climbs themselves were something to write home about! One left half an hour after everyone else and never made up for lost time . . . Why did she always have to choose climbs beyond her ability? Sometimes she put herself down for a group which Achille was leading, and the whole group had to bear with the delays and the eternal: 'I'm an Alpine Club veteran, no one is going to teach me how to . . .' Really, she was a silly old bitch!

One had to admit that, usually, the other clients put up with her patiently. It was good of them. After all, Achille was paid to do it . . . while the others . . . Perhaps, after all, the amateurs were pleased to find someone more useless than themselves? So, one would hold out his hand to her, and another would push her bum, or steady her foot on a hold as Achille heaved on the rope like an ox . . .

'Keep it tight!' she would shout.

He would pull her up, there was nothing else he could do, and that even for simple little climbs.

On the way down, she always felt unwell: she had sore feet, sore knees, her thighs, her shoulders were all hurting. The more one lightened her rucksack the more she complained, whimpering as if to show that it was the least one could do for her . . .

All that changed as soon as she was back in the valley, showing off again, strutting past the Guides' Office telling everyone about her climbing adventures.

'On the ridge, I thought the wind would blow us away. Oh, and the chimney, a real IV! . . . Then I told Achille that he wasn't getting any younger . . . You don't mind, Achille, do you? . . . Yes, that's the fourth time I have done that traverse! . . . There's nothing left to do! . . . Ah, you were on the Aiguille des Névés. In good condition? . . . Oh, I'm not surprised, I have done it twice already, and the second time I saw the bergschrund it looked like nothing on earth . . . Yes, it's not bad, but I . . . Ah! You say the face is in condition again?' . . .

And so it went on, and on!

'Achille, I know where we'll climb next. When are you free? Achille! . . . Achille! . . .'

No, Mlle Trugny was not a gift! But she was a regular client. It's not easy to get rid of a good client. Discretely, Achille Bletterans had tried to pass her on to others.

'You free tomorrow? I've got two clients. You take Mlle Trugny with you, she wants to go to the Pointe Michel. She's done it three times already. There won't be any problem.'

But friends in the know didn't feel like going through that again . . .

So, they would fade together, she and he. When he could no longer do anything but take groups to the Grands Rognons, it would also be what she would be reduced to. Till the end of his days as a guide, every summer, he would be chained to Mlle Trugny . . .

But now there was worse! Tonight's letter!

'My dear Achille,' she announced, 'I am writing to give you some good news! I have always dreamed of taking a long holiday. My dream is going to come true and, thanks to a special leave, I will spend three months in the mountains this summer. I am counting on you, of course, and I am already collecting my modest savings (hoping you won't be too greedy!). My colleagues are envious and admire me when I tell them all I expect to achieve. Therefore, I am booking you this minute.

Expecting to find you in good form, as I shall be myself, I remain as one 'old' client to her faithful friend,

Yvonne Trugny

'Calamity!' sighed Achille, forgetting his brandy-coffee and the Western. 'Calamity!'

In vain he tried to reason with himself, and recalled his grandfather's frequent statement: *'Faut aller jusqu'à qu'on crevisse!'* One must go on till one dies!

You had to go on till you pushed up the daisies, and that was what would happen to him . . . For a long time he thought of that peasant wisdom, and felt stirred by the wind of revolt.

Couldn't it be she who'd . . .? 'Couldn't it be her?' he muttered.

Then he began to think. No, Miss Trugny would not die, at least, not by herself. She was healthy, and sport kept her in shape, perhaps not flatteringly, but in good shape. But who knows? A fall of rock, one of these days . . . Rocks fall . . . It happens. It happens only too often . . . And what about helping nature a bit . . . It was not an unpleasant thought anyway, and at least helped escape the prospect of those three months of purgatory . . .

Ethics, clearly, did not trouble Achille Bletterans, nor had films on television contributed much to develop them.

What do you do to commit crime? You kill the victim, right — as you do a sick animal. That's not the complicated part, but then you have to make the corpse disappear . . . Where? Down a glacier mill, maybe? Perhaps not. Up in the high mountains — much easier. An 'accident' can be arranged, and if it has been well carried out, you get out of it with full honours . . . Old rope can snap, or you can always say it was cut by a fall of rocks. Nobody would query it. Besides you would not be the first to lose a client that way . . . so stupidly. And he, Achille, had never had a serious accident. He had too good a reputation to be accused of negligence. Yes. But a good reputation is something precious; and you want to keep it intact . . . What to do, then? Obviously an accident could not happen when she was with someone else . . . So . . . Let's think . . . It does no harm just to think, and it doesn't cost anything . . . What would seem, say, like a stroke of bad luck? Without putting the guide's reputation into question? A malaise, of course! . . . A heart attack . . . That would not be too unlikely. They would only say: 'What bad luck! Poor Achille! An old client snuffing it while in his hands . . . His best client, too! More than twenty years they had climbed together!'

Daydreaming in this way, Achille Bletterans got used to this entrancing idea. He saw himself at the funeral, in his best suit and with a look of grief, shaking hands with friends who tapped him on the shoulder.

'Bad luck, really . . . It's obvious you were fond of her, you look all shattered.'

'She was my oldest client,' he would sigh. 'Ah, we do not count for much you know.'

True enough, we do not count for much! Especially in the mountains! . . . And then, Yvonne Trugny had no family . . . He might even save her from a sad old age . . . Gradually, as the years went by, she would feel less fit, doing a few climbs which could only tire her old bones. And later, on her own: illness . . . slow death in some home or hospital. Really, to do away with her would almost be a good deed! In any case . . . it would be good riddance!

A week later, he had made up his mind.

The question now was: how? Like all sportsmen, Achille Bletterans knew a little about first aid, and had some notion of the physiology of effort, drugs and heart strain . . . At the library, he consulted a medical encyclopaedia, had useful snippets of conversation with the chemist, and finally went to see a doctor about some alleged discomfort: breathlessness, tired by effort, his heart seeming to beat more slowly, his legs getting swollen in the evenings . . .

He voiced some prudent reservations about the prescription he obtained:

'But I am not really in the habit of taking pills and potions, doctor. Is it going to upset me, this stuff you're giving me? . . . I don't trust these things. In my opinion, the less you take, the fitter you are! . . . You're telling me that seven drops a day can do no harm, and that you're only giving me five . . . Well, in that case . . . For ten days . . . That'll be enough, I hope. If I don't feel well I will come back for more, but the old carcass is still going strong . . . In my opinion, it is just a small problem, and I am quite sure the old machine will get going again with this little shove you're giving it . . .

In fact, Achille did not return and showed every sign of recovered health. The incident was forgotten, but the visits to the chemist had helped him to acquire further information.

'Look at this stuff the doctor wants me to swallow, Roger! It's not going to do me any harm, is it? What does it do, exactly? Well, all right. He said a bottle, so give me a bottle then . . .'

In May, Achille Bletterans took his old car and gave himself two weeks holiday. He left the district for some place out of range of his local papers. It was only a precaution, for he wanted the odds to be in his favour.

He had perfected a fairly sure stratagem. Once a day, and in different places, he looked for a doctor to whom he repeated his story: 'Just my luck! And in my holidays, too! Such tiredness! Out of breath at the slightest effort! And my ankles, all swollen in the evening!' He'd had the same trouble that winter, and the doctor had given him some medicine which had really done him some good . . . What was it called? These medical terms! Ah, Digui, Di di . . . Could it be a name like that? Digitalin! That's right! Marvellous invention . . . Five drops a day, yes, doctor . . .'

He gave his real name. He had nothing to hide, and the number of visits wouldn't be known, of course, for he didn't intend to have the consultations and the medicines reimbursed by the Sécurité Sociale. It was rare for the doctor not to prescribe the suggested medicine, sometimes adding one or two from his own. Achille Bletterans made his purchases from local chemists, and in a shoe-box resting in the car boot the small white and green boxes of digitalin accumulated. Apart from the visits to doctors, it was an excellent trip, full of pleasures, good meals and visits to vineyards. Achille Bletterans came back in splendid form, feeling even cleverer than Arsène Lupin.

Years of repressed feelings made him consider the next steps as fair game. The most important thing, of course, was not to be caught — detective stories, of course, never taught anything else.

Mlle Yvonne Trugny arrived on the 15th June. She was worse than ever.

Achille wondered how he could have stood the summer without the prospect that sustained him. Three months of this! God! Meanwhile he had to see her every day in order to work out a programme of ascents. He took her climbing, for a bit of practice on ice, and when it really rained too much, invited her for a meal.

'You are a dear, this year, Achille,' she gushed. 'What are you hiding up your sleeve, eh? Come on, don't look so embarrassed, no one is going to doubt my virtue!'

She was always looking for him, hanging around. When they came down from a climb, if she had not seen him, that very evening, at the Guides' Office, she would track him to his home, and if he decided to relax and eat at the bistro, she would turn up in the morning, at coffee time . . .

'You weren't at home last night . . . What are you up to? A guide must have a regular routine during the season. And look at you, unshaven, buttons missing . . . And this sweater, full of holes . . . You can't have had it cleaned for a year! Marvellous! What will people think of me, going around with such a scarecrow? Really! A Swiss guide wouldn't present himself like this before his clients. It is a pity, really, that the Swiss franc is so high that one has to climb with peasants . . .'

As for choosing climbs, what a bind!

'You really must find me something new! Martial Tramelan always has new ideas for his clients . . . No! The Pic des Oiseaux I know every move by heart. By heart! No, the Aiguille de Pierre is too easy for me! No, the standard ascents are so boring! You must know my list of routes by now, surely! . . . You could hardly think I would be satisfied with such piddling little things . . . You're born and bred here, and it's me who has to do the thinking! It's me who is the guide! I want some climb worthy of me. You can't think of anything, of course! Right, so whether you like it or not, we'll go to the Hegesippe Simond Hut.'

So up they went again! How she showed off at the hut! And she wanted to be in charge of everything, in front of colleagues, in front of other clients . . .

'How many pegs? I am sure that won't be enough! . . . How many ice-screws? What! No ice-screws! . . . Don't protest, you never know when you might need some. Scared of the weight, I suppose? What rope have you taken? Why not the 11 mm? You have studied the route, I suppose.'

The route! Talk about the itinerary! She must spend the whole year learning the local guidebooks for the range by heart; and all the other books on selected climbs!

But much as she insisted on arguing about each pitch, she had no more sense of orientation than a slug. Nothing annoyed Achille more . . .

'Are you sure this is the way? I would have passed on the left . . . We are not lost, are we? If you had listened to me we wouldn't be groping around in the dark like this. Do you intend to take the 558 route or the 538a variant?'

'I don't bother with all that!' grumbled Achille. 'I just know where to pass, and, what's more, I can see where I'm going. That's enough!'

Silence, heavy with disdain, followed, until the wheedling voice started again.

'You seem to forget that the bergschrund usually goes on the right!'

Achille just wanted her to do one thing, look after herself, and leave the rest to him. She was going slower and slower, and became useless at the first difficulty.

'Are you sure you have the rope tight enough, Achille? Oh! . . . My rucksack is pulling me off-balance . . . I think I am going to fall . . . Achille, my fingers are giving out . . . I'll have to come down again . . . Achille, it can't be done . . . Achille, are you sure this is the right way? . . . It's too difficult to be the right way! Ah, at last, a hold . . . Achille, what is next?'

'Some inhuman grade one!'

'Oh, Achille, don't joke with mountains! . . . Oh, help! I'm coming off! . . . No . . . Yes! . . . My foot's slipping! It's much too difficult! You must have made a mistake . . . This is no joke . . . My legs are shaking, there you are, I'm off! No, I am not! . . . Aah! . . . I have never seen such a horrifying passage! No more holds . . . Achille, what can I do?'

'Climb!' sighed Achille.

Was she really happy climbing? It seemed unlikely. She certainly didn't get much satisfaction from her efforts. And it seemed that the scenery only pleased her on a photo, so you had to stop and look for her camera right at the bottom of her rucksack, putting it back for her and then do it all over again thirty metres further on because the view was better. Whereas that day when they were coming down from a Swiss summit in splendid weather, with mountains sparkling against the serene blue sky, her only thought seemed to be whether the CAF card would give her a reduction on the chairlift!

And once back down again! Sure, she paid for the climbs, but she certainly rubbed it in . . .

'Seven hundred and forty francs for three hundred metres? That's not peanuts! Agreed, you told me before going, but I thought you'd give me a small rebate . . . No? Well, for today I'll give you five hundred . . . and by cheque, all right? I don't see why you should cheat the taxman, on top of that . . . There you are. I hope you are satisfied.'

So it was without any scruple at all that Achille managed to make Mlle Trugny swallow, in jam, rillettes, coffee or in her soup, the ten drops of digitalin which he made her take daily. But she was tough, the old mule! At first, it looked as if it was giving her more guts! But, at last, the first signs of weakness! She was often out of breath and stopped frequently, with the corners of her mouth drooping, her eyes vacant, and with a look of disgust on her face. She looked as if she was seeing things, as they say, and Achille Bletterans would perhaps have deemed the game too cruel if Mlle Trugny's state was not combined with an extraordinary aggressiveness.

'No, I won't go this way! You're useless. It's enough for you to tell me that's the way for me to know it is wrong! You're useless! Now what? A storm? You're mad. There won't be any storm. Those clouds are harmless and I know what I am talking about. If it were stormy I'd have rheumatism . . . Would you be scared, by any chance? I decide whether we go on. After all, who's paying?'

And a little later:

'If you had really believed in that storm, you would have been more insistent . . . But you have so little authority! . . . We wouldn't have got soaked like this, not to mention all the risks we've had to take!'

He nearly gave up one day, when he saw her shaken with very unpleasant nausea. But, not satisfied this time to hassle her guide, she attacked his family.

'You are a boor,' she said sourly, when he wiped his moustache with the back of his hand. 'It's obvious your mother didn't bring you up properly.'

'My mother!' he exclaimed indignantly, 'She was a better woman than you are!' And he decided that Miss Trugny truly deserved her digitalin.

After her period of aggressiveness came one of depression.

'My legs won't carry me,' Yvonne Trugny stated. 'I feel sick, dizzy. Perhaps I should stop, go somewhere else . . .'

'Now that we have got this far,' answered Achille, as much for himself, 'we might as well go on. We must go on,' he added. 'Didn't you realise what it would be like? But we won't climb too high. We won't go above three thousand two hundred or three thousand five hundred. I'll carry the heavy stuff from your rucksack. We must go up again tomorrow, while the good weather lasts. The Flèches de Roc! There! How do you feel about a bit of climbing in the Flèches de Roc? It's not hard, not too far, and we can take our time. We can go up to the hut tomorrow, and the day after we can do one small summit, one or two, no more, and we'll come down nice and quietly.'

It really had to finish! It was already the end of July, and you could not go on like this forever. Not to mention that there were moments when Achille, sensing freedom so close, felt about to explode. And it would not have been very clever to let his friends, the hut-keeper or other climbers see how badly Mlle Trugny exasperated her guide. Nor must she go to a doctor who might take God knows what tests ... Truly, it really wasn't so easy to get rid of someone!

So, a couple of days later, in a whitening dawn, they set off to climb the Flèches de Roc. The place was deserted, which was a good thing ... The terrain was quite steep but easy. No need yet for a rope. Achille walked ahead, making sure of each step, careful not to knock off a rock. Yvonne Trugny followed, grumbling and making it clear she thought the climb badly chosen.

It was then the accident occurred. Did she suddenly feel faint? No one would ever know. Achille only heard the shout and turned round, his blood frozen in his veins. Mlle Trugny had fallen and was rolling down the scree overhanging a rocky wall. This was not the scenario Achille had worked out, and his professional conscience did not allow him even a moment's hesitation. He leapt down the slope, ran, nearly flew and pinned his client against a block on the fall-line. But then, suddenly, the falling scree caught him off-balance, and sent him sliding over the edge.

Fortunately, rescue came promptly. Two climbers leaving the hut had seen this sudden drama from afar. They told the hut-warden and as they climbed up to help, found Mlle Trugny in a state of shock, shaking but unscathed, and her guide lying a little further down, unconscious and with both legs broken. A helicopter soon removed the injured climbers.

When Achille came to, some while after a long operation, he had all the time in the world to philosophise on the difficulty men have in altering the path of fate. Mlle Trugny had left hospital after twenty-four hours, with bright eyes and a clear complexion, delighted at the prospect of recounting her adventure. As for Achille, he would have to put up with two months in bed, not counting physiotherapy, pain and exhaustion!

But, as soon as visits were allowed, he was not long in seeing the advantages of his situation. First of all, the Chief Guide came, on behalf of the others, to shake him warmly by the hand. Then, it was his friends' turn. Young ones, old ones, novices, the best. He was complimented, congratulated. He had risked his life for his client — good old Achille — in the pure guides' tradition!

They brought him the first articles about the accident and, as national news was a bit dull and the Middle East was calm, journalists were allowed to see him as soon as the surgeon would permit. They found him quite a character, with his salt-and-pepper moustache, his local accent, and the almost shy way he gave them the facts. He was photographed. They published his account of the accident below evocative titles: 'Guide sacrifices himself to save his lady client.' 'A guide straight from legend.' 'The simple courage of a Savoy peasant.' 'Heroism is not dead.'

Achille was quite overcome with each new article . . . And they were even promising him a medal!

Of course, Mlle Trugny knitted by his bedside for part of the day, making sure of receiving her due share of glory. Nor did she miss any opportunity to be interviewed as well.

'Marvellous! . . . He was marvellous! . . . I cannot recall exactly what happened. All I know I was falling helplessly towards the abyss . . . He never hesitated for a moment . . . He only listened to the call of duty! He leapt at the risk of his life! It is thanks to him that I am alive. I will never forget what he did . . . You know, we have been climbing together for twenty years . . .'

And so on, and so on . . . Achille listened to her purring away, perhaps not with much attention, but nevertheless, with a feeling of complete beatitude. And, of course, especially when they had visitors, she fussed round him, plumped up his pillows, made him drink, commented on his temperature-chart, even felt his pulse, pretended to scold him when he spoke too much, and wolfed half the goodies brought for him . . .

And, naturally, to cheer him up, she went on and on about the fine seasons they would share, in the years to come. She showed him lists of climbs, read him route descriptions in monotonous tones, and argued with him when he wanted to correct her way of doing a particular route. But it was clear that she admired him for having made her a woman for whom a man would not hesitate to risk his life.

And Achille felt that, thanks to her, he had acquired a new personality — had become such an interesting, courageous, even famous character. Mlle Trugny was in good form again, and he looked with affection at this precious being who owed everything to his heroism.

'You know,' he once confided to a colleague, 'that woman, I would have been sorry to lose her.'

'Naturally,' replied the other, somewhat puzzled at this statement of the obvious. 'Such an old client! Your best friend, in fact!'

Translated by Daniel and Geraldine Roberts

FOR WHOM THE HELICOPTER FLIES

*Never send to know for whom the helicopter flies.
It flies for thee.* (John Wilkinson)

Isabelle's mind was full of happy memories. She remembered mornings in the woods, the light slanting through the trees — paths carpeted with pine needles and seamed with tree roots. Clear streams tumbling down, swirling into deep pools where you could drink cool water from your cupped hands. Sometimes the shade was so thick that no plants could grow beneath the tall spruces. Sometimes there were sunny green glades where ragwort, cowparsley and briar roses flowered. And in the far distance, high up, ice and snow dazzled in the sunlight.

And tomorrow, all these wonders would be hers. Tomorrow! How wonderful! Into the scatter of cases went trousers and light dresses, a tartan swimsuit, a thick grey sweater. Isabelle smiled with pleasure as her fingers touched the familiar little roughness on the right-hand lock of the big suitcase. Everything would be ready by this evening when Luc came home. He would only need to put his gear in order: ropes, slings, pegs, friends and nuts stacked up in a corner of the room. And tomorrow at dawn, they'd be off.

And yet only a year earlier Isabelle had been gloomily contemplating a similar trip with very different feelings. A holiday away from the sea had seemed unthinkable, almost a punishment. Her godmother's letter had come like a shower of cold water.

'The operation has been successful,' it read, 'but the doctors tell me I cannot expect to be fully myself this summer, and that I would be unwise to spend my holiday alone, even in my beloved Chamonix. If by any chance Isabelle could spare a little of her time for my poor invalid self, she would be doing me a very great service. After all, she might find in our mountains some pleasures of which she is so far unaware . . .'

'No, damn it! No!' Isabelle had exclaimed. But there she had been, a few weeks later, sighing as she packed sweaters, boots, anoraks — and particularly books intended to while away the time over the holiday she had sacrificed.

Her forebodings proved correct, and for the first two weeks she was bored stiff. It rained a lot, it was cold, she had no friends, and although she did her best to seem cheerful for the old lady, who seemed to be improving every day, Isabelle found herself counting off the long summer days.

The only person at all young who came to the house she found quite exasperating. Pascal was a fanatical climber, and worse, he had a morbid taste for stories of mountain accidents, which he paraded for her entertainment.

'Eight hundred metres they fell! . . . Nothing left of them!'

'You're worrying Isabelle,' said the old lady, 'Why don't you tell us about some climbs that end all right?'

'But, Aunt Anna, accidents are part of mountaineering, too, you know. Look, in this morning's *Dauphiné*, six more dead . . .'

And then, one day, Pascal arrived together with Luc. They brought a new tale of woe, but this time Isabelle listened with a sympathetic ear.

'I've brought along a friend, Aunt Anna! Great bloke! Yes, Luc, you are! A natural climber! . . . The poor man has just broken an arm in a stone-fall on the North Face of the Mont Blanc de Cheilon. He was belaying, and held on even when he was hit by a rock . . . Otherwise they'd have fallen hundreds of metres and they'd have been buggered. Sorry, Aunt Anna . . . There'd already been two killed on Mont Blanc de Cheilon the week before and this would have made four. But now Luc's climbing season is all buggered up . . . Oh, sorry, Aunt Anna . . .'

Luc stayed to dinner and, as he came back often with Pascal, Isabelle began to take a new interest in him. The fine weather helped. They went for long walks together. Isabelle soon got to know the whole valley which she now saw with quite different eyes. They came home in the evenings with bags full of mushrooms or baskets of blueberries, with bunches of marguerites or scabious, with stories and laughter that echoed through the old house. The summer went happily by. The pink flowers of the willow-herb turned into stems of purplish pods, then into tufts of down which drifted away at the slightest breath of wind.

And at last there came a day when Luc and Isabelle escaped from Pascal and walked up to the source of the Arveyron. Every detail of that outing was etched in Isabelle's memory. The shafts of sunlight filtering through the branches of the fir trees. A criss-cross of light on an emerald mossy bank. A track as smooth as any in a park. The golden insects dancing their intricate ballet in the sunbeams. The clatter of a jay . . . They came to a remote and romantic spot, dominated by the Dru and the splendid rugged wall of the

Flammes de Pierre. Far away over the valley a low-lying mist heralded the onset of autumn. A light wind ruffled Isabelle's hair. Luc explained that in the last century the glacier had at this point formed a great arch of ice, but that as it retreated there had appeared the series of narrow gorges down which the Arveyron plunged into pools of green water and foaming waterfalls. And then he said nothing at all, except a bit later: 'We'll soon have to go our own ways . . . Unless of course . . .'

They were married that December. The year was a whirlwind of preparations, purchases, presents, invitations. They had to fit out a flatlet, work desperately hard to prepare the exams they had neglected. Sometimes in the evenings they got together with friends and inevitably the conversation turned to the mountains. Isabelle did not understand all this endless climbing talk, but it brought back happy memories of hours on the Col de Voza and the Col de Balme, the play of clouds and sunshine, the tops powdered with snow, and as she grew more familiar with the talk, she felt herself in harmony with it.

'Just a Grade V pitch, but a real thrutch — a smooth chimney full of verglas. No way we could wedge up it with sacks. We sweated like pigs and what with that and having to belay on one piton . . . Well! You couldn't afford to come off. Guy had just called, "Slack on red!" when there was a stone-fall. We were lucky, the rocks fell a few feet away, otherwise . . .'

'And, if not,' Pascal intervened, 'they'd have found you at the foot of the slabs, in the bergschrund. And that reminds me of Max's accident a couple of years ago. Yet, it had been a good day . . . Poor bloke — I really liked him!'

The start of the holidays was delightful. For the month of July, Luc and Isabelle had been lent a chalet in the upper part of Les Frasses. They mowed the lawn, weeded the garden, clipped the hedges, watered the geraniums . . . They went for walks again, waiting for Jacques, Luc's usual climbing partner, to arrive.

'You'll see,' Luc had said to his wife, 'We'll hardly be separated. There'll be the breaks between climbs and then there are all those bad weather days: I hope you'll get to love the mountains.'

It was quite true. She became aware of her growing love of the alpine world and could no longer imagine any other kind of holiday. Butterflies collected nectar in the meadows. Sparrows had made their nest under the eaves of a wooden barn and were feeding their cheeping nestlings. The chalet filled up with sheaves of lupins. Every evening they lit a wood fire and they ate their dinner around it, chatting and laughing, remembering all the things they had already enjoyed together and making plans for the future. One day they would buy their own chalet . . . Fill it with children's laughter.

Jacques arrived after a week. Luc was delighted to see him: a long spell of fine weather had just gone by and with nothing achieved. That evening Jacques dined in the chalet, and the talk was all of climbing.

'We'll go up to the hut tomorrow,' said Luc decisively.

'Come on, mate, let me get my breath,' Jacques protested. 'Here you've been resting for a whole week, and you're all tanned and fit! And here am I, just arrived, pale as a ghost, shagged out. Let me have a day to get my campsite organised and relax a bit. The weather forecast's good, there's no panic! How about a climb the day after tomorrow — the first téléphérique up the Aiguille du Midi? That'll give us a good start without getting up too early! Later we can tackle something more serious . . . How about the Seigneur Route on the Peigne? I don't think you've done it and neither have I . . .'

Luc explained to Isabelle — looking rather alarmed — that they'd only be away a very short time.

'The Peigne, that's the one above the Plan de l'Aiguille. You remember — it's nothing. Not too high, not too long, not too dangerous. We'll be home by the afternoon. You'll hardly have fixed dinner for two starving climbers before we're back! Go on . . . Smile!'

The next day but one, Luc got up early and disappeared without a sound. For Isabelle, the day was endless. She tried to read, tried to knit, tried to write postcards, went for a short walk, found it dull, went back to the chalet . . . At five o'clock she was still alone, her patience at an end. She would wait for the two men at the téléphérique station; if Jacques' car was not there, they'd have passed each other on the way and she'd come back to the chalet. But the car was still there. Isabelle parked her own car alongside and waited. The situation was becoming more interesting. Each téléphérique disgorged a little group of noisy tourists and climbers, their efforts showing in their faces. Isabelle felt proud to be waiting for one of them. She could see it now: he would pop up like the winning ticket in a lottery. He'd be surprised, delighted to be welcomed like this . . . They'd laugh together . . .

Time wore on. Isabelle went to the information desk to ask when the last car was due.

'It's on its way down now, Miss!'

Luc would arrive at any moment, and Isabelle waited with a delicious sense of anticipation. But the car came and the men were not in the group that got out. Isabelle went round the station, looked about and asked again.

'Don't panic, young lady!' was the answer she got. 'Your husband must have been delayed . . . He'll have missed the last car down. Happens every day! He'll walk down. Nothing serious . . . Just go home, he'll be there sooner than you think!'

The chalet seemed gloomy. Two hours went by. Isabelle found the loneliness unbearable and began to think the worst. The only person in the valley she could tell was Pascal . . . But could she stand the tales of accidents? At nine o'clock, she couldn't take it any longer; she grabbed the telephone and, sobbing, she poured out her fears: the long, the inexplicable delay.

Pascal was very good, even optimistic. Indeed he boosted her morale. Like the cable-car attendant, he seemed to find it all quite normal.

'Happens all the time . . . Don't fret . . . Anything could have happened . . . Not necessarily anything serious . . . No need to panic, I tell you . . . He could be here in five minutes. Just keep me posted . . . Don't hesitate to disturb me. Just call me as soon as he's back, or if you get bored!'

Isabelle set about waiting again. She called Pascal several times on the phone. By eleven o'clock she was in floods of tears.

'All right!' said Pascal, 'I'm not worried yet. But all the same, we'll do something. I'll telephone the Mountain Rescue to make sure they haven't had any accident reported to them, and I'll ask them to make a helicopter recce tomorrow morning, always assuming Jacques and Luc are still not back down. Now it's dark and there's nothing else to be done. Go to bed, there's a good girl. Take a sleeping-pill. I promise this is nothing out of the ordinary!'

Luc arrived about midnight. Isabelle threw herself into his arms, sobbing wildly.

'What on earth's the matter?' he asked. 'Has anything happened to you?'

'No. It's you. I thought you were dead . . .'

'. . . That I was dead? What a ridiculous idea! Do I look dead? . . . No! Come on! . . . But I am knackered! And I didn't expect to be welcomed home with a fit of hysterics!'

This remark unleashed another flood of tears from Isabelle. 'But you said you'd be back down by the afternoon! How was I to know? . . . All these stories of accidents! And the newspapers . . . By the way, Pascal has asked for the helicopter, for tomorrow morning . . . I was so frightened . . .'

'Oh, hell!' exclaimed Luc, grabbing the telephone . . . Then he realised, seeing his wife's distressed face, that it was all his own fault for not having explained things better. The poor girl simply didn't understand.

'It's just something that happens, darling Isabelle ... Sometimes you get held up ... We had a few unforeseen snags ... Above all, we lost hours helping a rope of three youngsters to get down. Absolutely knackered, they were, and inexperienced! ... If we hadn't looked after them, they'd have had to bivouac ... Here, take my hankie ... Watch it, it isn't very clean ... Normally, under those circumstances, we'd have spent the night at the Plan instead of pushing on down on foot in the dark ... It's for your sake we came back now ... But I didn't expect to find you in such a state ... Don't cry any more ... I'm alive and kicking ... I love you ... It's all over ...'

Three days of rest followed. Isabelle became slightly ashamed of her panic. The next time she would know how to behave as a real climber's wife should ...

The next time came soon enough, but on this occasion Luc took the necessary precautions.

'For this trip, I'll put you in the picture. It'll be a longer climb ... We're going to do the North Face of the Triolet. We'll be gone at least one night. I'll explain the route to you: we climb a steep wall above the Argentière glacier, and we'll come down by the *voie normale* to the Couvercle Hut and then by the Mer de Glace to the Montenvers. I shan't be able to telephone you from the Argentière Hut the first night, because there isn't any Argentière Hut! It's being rebuilt this summer and we'll have to bivouac. But when we get down, I'll call you from the Couvercle. Now you know what's involved. We may be fast. But you are beginning to understand how things are, one is sometimes overtaken by events, the face may be in bad condition ... If we have to pitch it all the way it'll take longer, you understand, and in that case we may be home late. Or we might even have to spend a second night at the Couvercle. Not very likely — but just so that you've been warned ... Just don't dwell on these accident stories! Pascal's a good bloke, but he does pile it on a bit ... And he ends by scaring himself ... Imagine what he must feel like at night in a hut, with all those emergencies buzzing round in his brain ... What a nightmare! There, you're laughing, that's better! I hope you'll still be laughing when we get back.'

This new departure was in fact much easier. Isabelle dined alone and spent the evening at the cinema; as she walked home under the stars she thought dreamily of Luc and fell asleep at once. Next morning was fine ...

All must be well on the mountain. She went for a swim in the pool. Waiting wasn't so bad after all, and she was surprised at how quickly she got used to it. She spent the rest of the afternoon making a peach tart which would do splendidly for the next day if they didn't eat it that evening. Isabelle had refused an invitation to dine with Aunt Anna, so as to be home if Luc turned up or phoned.

The evening was a bit dismal . . . There was no news of any kind. Isabelle ended by going up to bed, but it was some time before she fell asleep, thinking she heard noises on the ground floor, the click of the latch, the sound of a car engine, voices . . . But it wasn't Luc.

At nine o'clock in the morning on the third day, there was still nothing. Isabelle needed reassurance but hesitated to bother Pascal. She had made the acquaintance of the wife of a guide, who lived nearby. She went to ask her, as a neighbour, what could be the reasons for the delay, and luckily she caught the husband, packing his sack for a Mont Blanc trip.

'They're certainly a bit slow!' he reckoned, once she explained. 'But if you're worried, it's easy, just telephone the Couvercle Hut. Ask for the warden and tell him it's from me: we've known each other for years! He'll certainly let you know if they've been seen passing by, or if they're on their way down. It's no problem.'

But no . . . There were problems. Fear once more gripped Isabelle's heart. What could she say to the warden? And what, in heaven's name, might he tell her?

Eventually she rang Pascal. This time he was rather more surprised.

'North Face of the Triolet? Well, yes, they should have been here last night! Of course, all sorts of things can happen . . . But it's a good idea to ask the Couvercle . . . You daren't? Come on, don't get in such a state; I can hear the catch in your voice. OK, just hang on, I'll ring myself. I'll understand the answer better than you will . . .'

He rang back ten minutes later.

'Right, I've done it . . . Now, don't panic, Isabelle . . . I'm not quite sure what's happened, but just don't panic! . . . They haven't seen them yet at the Couvercle . . . And they weren't there last night either.'

There was a wail at the other end of the line.

'I told you not to get in a panic! They've probably had to bivouac . . . But something is a bit odd. A rope did the *voie normale* on the Triolet this morning, very early, and they're back already. I caught one of them on the phone. And it seems they didn't see anybody, not even any tracks coming off the North Face. Just a bit odd, I thought . . .'

'But what if they've fallen off the other side?' moaned Isabelle.

'Don't assume the worst, not just yet! They could have . . . well, I don't know . . . Gone very high up on the face and not been able to get over, and had to climb down again . . . I don't know . . . Or they might have had a slight accident which held them up . . . Just a bit of a problem . . . Nothing serious! Hang on, don't cry. I'll come round. I shouldn't have said anything. They'll be back any time. There'll be some explanation. Or else you'll have a call. I'm on my way, I'll be round in a minute. Don't cry like that.'

Pascal was actually more worried than be had been the previous time. They'd been slow, very slow . . . And it looked as if Luc and Jacques hadn't reached the top of the Triolet.

Isabelle was in a terrible state. She sat twisting her handkerchief between her fingers, and shaking her head continuously as if refusing to accept what he had said. Tears streamed down her face.

'I should never have let him go! I shouldn't have!' she sobbed.

'But you didn't know,' retorted Pascal, his arguments exhausted. 'What on earth can have happened? . . . Don't cry like that, it doesn't help . . . What a business! No, come on, don't look at me in that way! . . . All right, OK I'll call the helicopter.'

And a little later: 'They'll make a recce over the Argentière side at two o'clock . . . Now, calm down.'

Luc arrived back at ten to two and sized up the situation at a glance.

'Oh no! Not again!' he groaned.

While Pascal phoned to cancel the flight, Luc tried to calm down Isabelle, wracked with sobs. Then he began explaining things. Yes, they'd had some idiotic mishaps. Appalling conditions . . . Loose snow on ice for hundreds of feet. The way through the seracs had been bad . . . They'd got out of them at nightfall and had to bivouac a bit lower down, on the south side . . . A rope on the normal route? No, they hadn't seen it. They'd probably gone over the summit before they'd even woken up . . . Not surprising that the party hadn't seen any tracks, especially if they weren't looking out for them. The exit was all in ice and anyway there were several ways out. They'd just got down as quickly as possible. They'd been worn out after the day before and couldn't face going all the way up to the Couvercle just for a telephone call. All they wanted to do was get down as fast as they could . . .

As Pascal disappeared, Luc looked at Isabelle and shook his head.

'Well,' he said, 'you do make a fuss . . . Now, don't begin crying again.

Smile instead. I'm once more alive and kicking. I'm delighted to know you love me so much ... Very flattering, you know! I must be the most appreciated husband in the whole Chamonix Valley. But you've got to understand ... Mountain timetables aren't like railway timetables ... Is it clear this time? Well, there we are. Don't wipe your tears on my shoulder, please ... C'mon, cheer up ... And now I want that hot bath and the sleep I've been dreaming of for the last two days. Tonight we'll have dinner at the Dahu, to celebrate the North Face of the Triolet ... That'll be nice, won't it?'

Of course it was all right. In fact the affair soon became just a joke in climbing circles.

'Hallo, Isabelle? Want me to call the Mountain Rescue?' Pascal said every time she rang up.

It began to rain. They organised dinner parties to console themselves. And when the fine weather returned, Isabelle made sure she remembered her lesson.

Luc explained the next climb.

'This time, it's the Aiguille Verte by the Y Couloir. I daren't promise that we'll be back in good time. Above all, be careful — remember the chopper pilots' blood pressure! You will, won't you, Isabelle darling?'

He left home, reassured. Isabelle went down to Geneva to dine with a group of friends. This time she seemed completely at ease. And so she was ... She certainly spent a better night than Luc, who got up at some unearthly hour before she'd even gone to bed, to tackle the wearisome trudge up the glacier in the dark, and cross some particularly evil-looking bergschunds.

Isabelle woke late and lay lazing a bit; the weather looked fine after all, in spite of the slightly threatening cirrus clouds of the day before. Luc was in luck. If only she could find time before his return to do all the things she promised herself. First of all it was Saturday, the day of the nice little market. With her basket on her arm, full of housewifely good cheer, Isabelle went from stall to stall. A smile came to her lips as she remembered the anxiety that had harrowed her throughout the day of the trip to the Peigne. How long ago that seemed! She knew better now! Hello, Mirabel plums already!

The accident happened very early on the climb, quite unforeseeably. After all, it was freezing hard. But the loose stones suddenly swept down the fall-line of the couloir. Impossible to dodge. Luc and Jacques were moving together when they heard them . . . No time to find the least belay. They were both swept off, in a long punishing fall, jerked and tossed as the rope caught and freed. Luc didn't even know whether he had fallen into the bergschrund or into a crevasse lower down. If it was the bergschrund, it seemed a bit narrow, but terrifyingly deep. Fortunately, his sack had stopped him, caught over a blade of ice behind him. He was one mass of aches and pains. No sign at all of Jacques. The rope must have been cut by the stones. Jacques too must have finished up in the bergschrund or in a crevasse. And what sort of state would he be in? Luc had lost his ice-axe and one of his crampons. It was the sheerest chance that he'd kept his sack, that the waist-strap had held and that he was miraculously suspended on this blade of ice. With his remaining crampon, he tried to get a foothold on the opposite wall of the crevasse. There was an ominous tearing sound from the arm-strap of his sack . . . No! Better not budge . . . Not move at all . . . He was too precariously balanced. The sack couldn't hold forever . . . Luc had blood in his mouth. He was frozen . . . Mustn't get too cold, but then he couldn't move . . . Mustn't move. Just have to wait for help . . . But how long would Isabelle take to panic, this time round? . . . What had he said to her? . . . Nothing very clever, for sure? Ah yes, he'd joked about the chopper pilots' blood pressure . . . God! If only they knew! . . . How long before Isabelle called the helicopter? . . . How long?

Translated by Jane Taylor

LES FLAMMES DE PIERRE

Of all the evenings spent with my mountaineering friends, evenings that all seem forever memorable and yet which blur and slowly merge into the mists of memory, there is one that I believe I shall never forget. Maybe it sticks in my mind because of the bad weather that had descended on the valley that day, making the experience of being gathered for the pleasure of a good meal and shared friendship so much more valuable. Maybe it was because of the especially lively, warm and entertaining conversation. Maybe too because of the strange tale with which the dinner party ended . . . Whatever the reason, it will be a long time before I forget a single moment of that evening.

There were nine of us, I remember, and I can even recall where each of us sat around the table . . . There were Anne and John, our hosts, Rémi, Abigail, Claude, Jean, Robert, Clément and myself. I had never seen anything like the rain that was falling . . . but what rain! An eerie rain, whose sound had filled the air for hours as if the very sky were crashing earthwards in a downpour. So bad was it that we had left our cars on the upper road instead of taking the usual route down the short track that had now become a torrent. The sky was so dark that it seemed as if night had fallen earlier than usual and it was by the flashes of lightning that we reached the little chalet, now ringed by large pools of water.

One by one, we shook ourselves dry beneath the overhanging roof and left our umbrellas, anoraks and wellington boots against the old wooden bench.

'Come on in quickly!' we were urged.

It was like another world. The puddles, the overflowing gutters, the gusts of rain, all ceased to be anything but a phenomenon of the exterior, a distant presence of which only the sound reached us . . . A bright fire was burning in the little chimney-piece with its copper surround, the lamp-shades gave off a soft glow which merged into the shadows of the wood-panelling and the bronzed walnut ceiling. At the foot of the staircase, like a shower of delicate droplets, stood a large arrangement of lupins. One had only to sit down, revel in being there, well sheltered from the elements, and reach for a glass of the thirst-quenching and very British drink prepared by the master of the house — a curious mixture of some alcoholic base and lemonade in which floated thin slices of orange and cucumber and even fresh mint leaves . . . We began to talk about the bad weather, nibbling olives and pistachios . . . What luck Robert had been able to complete his route in time! . . . And that Claude had not gone up! . . . A couple of friends hadn't got back to the valley but they would certainly have made it to the hut for the night . . . But anyone caught out on the big routes would be having a grim time.

So it was that, once again, the conversation turned towards mountains and accidents . . . The sort of talk that often shocks laymen, whether intended to or not, but which provides a release: for there is a need to laugh at what threatens, to defy danger by exposing its workings, to break taboos with cheerful cynicism.

As we went to the table we were moving on to our own experiences of accidents. And as we cut the bread up into cubes for the fondue simmering in the kitchen, or a little later dipped our forks into the thick, creamy mixture which clung in long, drawn-out threads to the prongs, or filled our glasses with a delicious Pinot Gris de Neuchâtel, we recalled the most terrible moments of our mountaineering careers . . . The stories were all of crevasses, of avalanches, of falling rocks, bivouacs, white-outs, storms; and yet, oddly enough, they created an atmosphere of the most open and irrepressible gaiety.

I was sitting by the window, my back wedged in a corner of the wall, my feet resting on the foot-rail of the old polished walnut table and so I was the only person able to watch the raging universe outside. Filtering through the tall pines, the pale light cast by the roadside lamp sparkled in the shafts of rain beating on the ground. The noise of the downpour reached me like the distant roar of some ocean. Then, turning my gaze from the world outside, after a moment or two of abstraction, I would look at the little bunch of eglantine and the block of amethyst crystals on the window ledge and return to the tranquillity of the hearth, the mingled odours of fondue, methylated spirits and wine, the crackling of logs, the echoes and laughter of the conversation.

At dessert — it was, I remember, a chocolate mousse, light and creamy, served in a large white bowl — we turned to the most famous accidents in mountaineering history and recalled their various details. We could have spent the night thus occupied for the subject is inexhaustible . . . Or at any rate, we had not yet exhausted it when we left the table to go and sit by the fire on sheepskin rugs or on large bean-bags. There, drinking coffee or orange juice, we recalled in turn the great Breithorn accident, the disappearance of Mallory and Irvine on Everest, and naturally the Matterhorn catastrophe when after making the first ascent with Edward Whymper and the Taugwalders, four men, Hudson, Douglas, Hadow and the famous guide Michel Croz, had met their deaths in dramatic circumstances.

It was at that point that I noticed Clément Ripamonti biting his lip like someone longing to speak but hesitating. He had not said much until then and, it must be said, he was not really one of our group although we all knew him by sight and by reputation. He was seated opposite me at the table and several times I had noticed the way in which, from time to time, he appeared to lapse into a dream or rather withdraw into some inner reverie, then half open his mouth to say something when the conversation dropped and finally decide to remain silent . . . This time, however, he made up his mind.

'I myself,' he said, 'had a very curious experience. I have rarely talked about it because I'm not too sure what to make of it and once you've heard the story, you will be no more sure than I . . . I thought of mentioning it to you a moment ago and now, talking about the Matterhorn, I just can't get it out of my head . . .'

He fell silent for a moment and once more assumed that pensive air I had noticed during the course of the meal. We too remained silent, waiting for him to pick up the thread of his tale . . . The noise of the storm, which seemed fiercer still, filled the chalet and it was at that precise moment that there was a flash of lightning, followed by an ear-splitting roar of thunder. The lights blacked out. A little silvered bulb in the centre of a flower-shaped lamp burst with a sharp crack. There was no source of light other than the reddish glow of the fire and, for an instant, we froze, struck by the incident, banal in itself, which had occurred in an atmosphere of growing tension.

'That often happens when there's a storm,' said Abigail finally.

The spell was broken. We set to, sweeping up the splinters of broken bulb and lighting the candles. Anne, who loves stories, had not, however, forgotten the one Clément had begun.

'What were you going to tell us?' she asked.

And she went to unplug the lamps so that if the lights suddenly came back on again, he would not be interrupted a second time.

Clément resumed his story. He was seated on a small bench fixed at an angle to the fireplace and all the while he was speaking he did not take his eyes off the glowing embers, as if he were afraid of seeing a touch of mockery or disbelief on our faces . . .

'It was in the early days of my mountaineering career . . .' he began, 'My second season, in fact . . . I was nineteen, I was certainly good, but I lacked even the most basic experience . . . All I had was crazy self-confidence and beginner's luck . . . The first year, of course, I hadn't dared push myself too far, but the second was a real peak of achievement . . . I was good at rock climbing, much more athletic than most, and I didn't think about anything else. Snow, ice, the route — I trusted to my luck, certain that I'd already run the gamut of dangers that mountaineering could offer. August was drawing to a close and I still had masses of plans when I got an unpleasant surprise: a letter from my father. My holidays away from the family had already gone on far too long, and I was to return home to study for an exam I had to take in October . . . So, you see the set-up . . .

'As you can imagine, I wasn't too pleased to be interrupted like this! Not to mention the fact that I was beginning to make a name for myself as a little mountaineering hero and it's pretty embarrassing for a hero when his daddy summons him home . . .

'In short, I decided to carry on as if I hadn't yet received the letter and I planned one more route, something really spectacular!

'Along with François Malot — the chap who was later killed on the Capucin — I decided to attempt the Bonatti Pillar, the pinnacle of our mountaineering ambitions. Of course it was too much for us. What's more, as we were running out of time, we set off with a dubious weather forecast and without telling anyone for fear that they would try to stop us. Right from the start the route was dogged by bad omens . . . Instead of setting off from the Grands Montets, for financial reasons we went via Montenvers. I don't like being superstitious, but I was a bit shaken when we passed a covered stretcher, and my gloomy forebodings deepened when, at a stop on the way up the moraines that leads to the Rognon des Drus where we were to bivouac, my precious altimeter, an old model on whose glass I had painted my name in Indian ink, fell out of my sack and broke. When I held in my hand the splinters into which my name was now smashed, I felt a foolish tightening around the heart . . .

'But so what! We continued to the bivouac and in the early morning, under a red sky with its shepherd's warning, we ascended the Dru Couloir and attacked the route . . . We climbed like young cats, as fast as we could against the ever worsening weather. But, of course, it was the bad weather which won and we were under the 'Red Walls' when the first hailstones hit us.

'We might have been young and not very sensible but we were not mad and we immediately decided to retreat. In some ways, we were almost

relieved not to have to go on with an ascent that was right out of our league
. . . Although we were good rock-climbers, we were less expert in handling
abseils . . . The weather had rapidly turned nasty. The snow-laden wind and
the cold froze our feet and hands.

'By the time we got back down to the top of the great couloir, the light was
already fading. Hastily, taking the sort of risks which still make me shudder,
we set off down . . . and it was just a moment later that the air filled with the
crash of stone-fall. I don't know how we escaped being swept off, but when it
finished our rope had been cut in several places, my right hand was bruised
and swollen and François, who had been hit on the forehead by a rock, was
bleeding profusely and whimpering like a child.

'Descent was out of the question. It was lucky we were still able to climb
back up! Helping each other, driven by fear of staying there and falling rather
than by our own courage, we managed to find refuge on a sort of little col by
the Flammes de Pierre. We made makeshift dressings for our wounds in the
last of the light. François had lost his rucksack with the stove and the water-
bottle. After we had shared out my few spare clothes there was nothing left to
do but to sit there, miserable, frozen and soaked for the rest of the night. The
little bit of salami and the chocolate in my pack repelled us; we were simply
dying of thirst, but we had no more water and sucking snow chilled us so
much that we did not repeat the experience.

'I had let François, who was in a bad way, have the better place; he could
sit, even half lie down. With the two ends of rope still attached to our waists,
we managed more or less to tie ourselves on for the night. However, the
descent posed major problems even supposing we were strong enough for
it. No rope! And we did not dare go back into the Dru Couloir again. The
noise of falling stones or snow we could hear there at regular intervals
certainly did nothing to change our minds about that. Nor was there much
hope of crossing the Flammes de Pierre to reach the Charpoua Hut with no
rope. No one knew we were there . . . No one would risk coming up in this
storm . . . No one could be able to see us through the swirling cloud and snow
that surrounded us and would no doubt continue to do so for some time
too . . .'

Clément fell silent for a moment. I watched his thin, tanned profile,
silhouetted against the glow of a candle-flame. None of us dared break the
silence for fear that the narrator would be brought back to the present, and
cut short his tale. At last he went on.

'François had sunk into a sort of weary coma, punctuated by little moans

... As for me, I couldn't sleep ... I cradled my damaged hand in the hollow of my arm to warm it a bit, but I could feel it swelling and I was getting terrible shooting pains in it. The cold increased as the night went on. And above all, there was the anguish of knowing ourselves lost, with only a slim chance of pulling through, of both pulling through ... I regretted that I hadn't kept the lengths of rope we could have salvaged. Instead we had cut them off in the couloir to lighten our load and move quicker. They might have turned out useful. In any case it was too late ... I thought of my parents and of their despair ... Of the exam that I would never take. And then I dozed in a sort of troubled dream, haunted by various alpine disasters like those we've just been speaking of. That summer I had been lent Whymper's *Scrambles in the Alps* and I was just thinking of Michel Croz when suddenly I noticed that we were not alone on the col. Leaning against a rock, not far from the shelf on which I was half sitting, half crouching, was a stranger whom I initially took to be an Austrian. Why, I don't know — maybe it was because he was wearing a felt hat and a climbing jacket of a type no longer made here in France. When he spoke to me, however, I realised that he was French and that, judging by his Chamonix accent, he must be from the valley.

'"You have been extremely foolhardy," he admonished me dispassionately. "It's a waste of time, warning you youngsters. Might as well talk to a brick wall. It's not enough to be bold, young man, you also need to think!"

'"I realise that," I grumbled, thinking to myself that it was not a lecture I needed but a rope, and yet it never entered my head to ask the stranger if he could provide me with one.

'As he went on speaking to me, I observed him with some curiosity, making out his features in spite of the darkness without wondering how. He had a large moustache and a long squarish beard. Solidly built, with an open face and a jovial, fatherly expression, he vaguely reminded me of someone, but I did not know who. Then, naturally, with that sense of recognition which only happens in dreams, I suddenly realised that I was dealing with Michel Croz in person. It didn't seem in the least bit odd. He was lecturing me quite sharply, holding forth on anticipating risk in the mountains, on inevitable and on avoidable accidents ... I was half listening to him, but with a mien of respect.

'Slowly the col filled up with other mountaineers. It seemed to widen to take them. Nothing surprised me. At one point I recognised Whymper himself, next to me. He was annoyed. Shaking me by the elbow, he shouted some incomprehensible words. I should mention that my parents had made me learn German, Latin and Greek! . . . So I don't understand a word of English. But I still remember a phrase he kept repeating like a sort of refrain . . . something like "youceuléfoule".'

'Well of course,' John interrupted, 'It means "you silly fool"!'

'Anyway, I didn't understand, but he kept going on, still shaking me by the elbow . . . He even began to shake me harder and harder, and suddenly, I woke up . . . And there was François tugging at my elbow and saying that day was breaking and that the weather was still bad and, oh God, what were we going to do . . .'

All of us in the chalet, who had been listening enthralled, felt vaguely disappointed. So it was nothing but a dream, a bivouac nightmare, that Clément Ripamonti had wanted to tell us. Goodness knows what we had been expecting . . .

'And so how did you get back down?' asked Rémi, always practical.

'Well, . . . That's just it . . . When it was daylight I found a rope in the gully . . .'

Clément looked up at us, a glint of defiance in his eyes. Then he turned back to the fire and continued in a low voice.

'I swear that it hadn't been there the night before . . . The little col wasn't very wide and I had gone to great pains to fix the gear and settle François more or less safely. I can swear that if there had been a rope I would have seen it or touched it, I would have even knocked it off trying to make more space . . . But, in the morning there it was — a good long rope . . . Carefully coiled . . . A rope . . .'

His voice sank lower.

'Not a nylon rope like we have nowadays . . . A hemp rope . . .'

And then after another pause:

'So, of course, we were able to descend with no great difficulty. By that evening, we were back in the valley. Just as well, too — the bad weather lasted a week . . .'

'And the rope?' asked Robert.

'We had to abandon it on the last abseil,' explained Clément, 'It jammed . . .'

No one spoke. It was getting late and we noticed that the rain was now barely running off the shingle roof. Without saying a word we rose and got ready to leave, collecting anoraks, wellington boots and umbrellas from outside. Over the Aiguilles, the clouds were slowly breaking up and there was a gleam of moonlight. The tall black firs were dripping with the last of the rain. Splashing through the puddles, murmuring vague goodbyes, we went back to the cars. Headlights pierced into the darkness, engines sprang to life and everyone set off home.

Translated by Siobhān Anderson and Jane Taylor

THE STAR

As his finger touched the doorbell, Bertrand experienced a moment of uncertainty, unusual for him. This was the first step on the road to destiny: his destiny, and one he hoped would be fabulous. It was enough to unsettle the most resolute. He took a hold of himself, clenched his strong white teeth, drew in a deep breath, shut his eyes, savoured the moment, and then pressed the button with determination. A bell jangled on the landing.

Bertrand Pacôme was an ambitious young man. Not the ordinary sort of ambitious young man that dreams rather than acts or allows doubts, distractions, loves to divert him from his goals. No! Rather he was an ambitious type of the purest order, compared with whom Balzac's Rastignac would have looked positively naive. When Rastignac issued his famous challenge, 'It is you and me, now!' it was only to Paris. What Pacôme had in mind was the whole world. It had been the same from the earliest days of his youth. He saw himself as a conqueror ... Ruling the planet ... Nothing would be too good for him. But from the earliest age, too, he was careful: a good little boy, cuddling mummy and daddy, making himself liked by his teachers but managing to remain friends with the other boys, even willing to cede first place to stifle possible jealousy. He had known from the beginning that any job he could do, however mundane, might one day be useful. He therefore never stopped learning, in school and out — watching the plumber unblock a U-bend, the bus driver shift his gear-stick or the farmer set up an electric milking-machine. Later he studied humans with the same detachment as an entomologist might an ant: registering every facet of their individual behaviour, fascinated especially by anyone who 'looked good' on TV, continuously learning from them. When he was a child, this was still something instinctive rather than premeditated, but the habit grew over the years until it finally came to be calculated policy.

He had spent long hours weighing up success and failure, pondering the most cynical handbooks to achievement. He drew up his own simple guidelines: plan coolly, count only on yourself, seize every opportunity, take money wherever it can be found, be prepared, sacrifice immediate gratification when necessary, never be sentimental, have no moral scruples. But above all, give no hint of this: do not display ambition; show the greatest modesty and every sign of sincerity when the occasion demands it. Politics had totally convinced him that the most evil machinations can triumph so long as they are cloaked in completely opposite sentiments, words and ideologies.

During the year of his baccalaureate, Bertrand chatted at length with an old character who sometimes visited his grandparents. He was quite the opposite of Bertrand; that is to say he was completely unselfish, but in his way a genius. Old Klaren's passion was for psychology, mathematics and especially computer science which he saw as the future for mankind. It was, he said, the key to everything, the victory of science over the slough of sentiment, the triumph of logic over the mire of irrationality! Everything should stem from it.

'Look at all those failed marriages,' said Klaren, 'Why does it happen? Because everything is left to chance, unorganised. It's madness! Pair each man and each woman according to their dominant characteristics . . . and you'll soon see the result! A rejuvenated society, happy couples giving their best. Wouldn't you agree?'

'Well, yes!' Bertrand replied enthusiastically, thinking that he would probably find it quite useful to make a suitable marriage one day.

'And what a range of other possibilities for each of us! You, for instance! Your classmates! What are you going to do when you've finished school?'

The question was too pertinent: Bertrand could only sigh.

'Everyone — and I mean everyone,' the old man continued, 'has his ideal situation in life, his perfect vocation. As things are, you become a watchmaker like your dad or an insurance broker or take up politics when you reach forty . . . but on what criteria? Nothing but vague interests, vague family connections. Whereas, in any properly constituted society, everyone has his proper place, whatever it may be! Conductor, caretaker, tax-collector, actor, gangster, engine driver . . . Anything you like! Someone who thinks he'll muddle through life as a librarian would perhaps shine as a crane driver. The chap who . . .'

'What about me?' interrupted Bertrand, not interested in all these generalisations.

Old Klaren stared at him.

'Well, well,' he murmured. 'Ambitious, are you, young man?'

Bertrand hesitated no more than a second. He had never confided in anyone, but this time, he had the feeling that this was his chance. He decided to reveal himself, disguising his consuming inner tension with an air of smiling candour.

'I'm afraid so ... It's probably just my age. I want to succeed. Not just success, the top. But I don't feel that I have any particular vocation. I've worked hard at everything, I've tried to be good also at sport, to lead a balanced life, to control my feelings. I think I'm capable of doing anything but I don't know what. I need to find the field where the competition will be easiest to beat. Then it would be relatively simple to expand into new areas. But how to find it? I keep on wondering.'

'A classic case!' old Klaren replied, 'You interest me! I'm just developing a programme that will bring to fruition my last ten years of research. You'll get some idea of how sophisticated it is if I tell you that it even includes details like eye and hair colour, nail shape, dental structure and, of course, exam results and graphological samples ... Thousands of facts that are too often overlooked and which I believe may be linked to intellectual or psychological characteristics, certainly genetic ones. All this needs very delicate analysis, very delicate. And the results have to be fitted into the social structure of the time. I'll give you a piece of advice — take up Law, it will always stand you in good stead ... Work on the rest ... From time to time I'll contact you for information. In three or four years time my programme will be ready, I'll ask you for a few last details and you can be my first guinea pig. How about it?'

After an uneventful period of National Service, Bertrand Pacôme studied Law, followed by a no less profitable period at the élite *École des Sciences Politiques*. He increased his knowledge of music. He visited exhibitions and did some sketching. He mastered several foreign languages, read *Le Monde* every day, forced himself to follow a tedious physical training programme, working out at a gym three times a week, closely studied his diction, his appearance and his smile, cultivated friendships that looked as if they might be useful one day. It was, in fact, a preparation programme calculated and carried out with great thoroughness, but which left scarcely any room for soul-searching. Occasionally, however, Pacôme would be filled with a certain sense of aimlessness. He was still far from clear about the goal he was aiming at.

'I just hope the old man knows what he's up to,' he pondered, 'and that he doesn't go and have a heart attack on me before he finishes his programme ... I'm so lucky to have hold of him.'

The great moment finally arrived. Numerous questionnaires and a long interview with Klaren had defined all the parameters composing the personality of Bertrand Pacôme. A model of society was also ready. A Cray III super-computer had absorbed it all and was to deliver, with effortless efficiency, the perfect future for a human being. And it was to learn what his future might be that this young man was now calling on his mentor.

Scarcely had the doorbell stopped ringing when a heavy step approached.

'And not a moment too soon!' Pacôme thought to himself, registering at a glance the ravages the last months had effected . . . 'He's not going to make old bones! . . . Never mind. I've got what I wanted, that's the main thing.'

'How are you, old friend?' he said aloud. 'You're looking much better than when I last saw you . . . I hope you haven't been overdoing it for this experiment.'

'Well, I'm afraid I have,' sighed Klaren. 'I've worked like a slave, my lad — you can't know how . . . But I've got the answer. It surprised me at first, but now it appeals to me. Come and sit down a moment.'

Bertrand Pacôme followed him, experiencing simultaneously a feeling of turmoil and a rush of elation. He scarcely dared speak; raising his long brown lashes, he looked at Klaren questioningly.

The latter indulged himself in a bit of mischief, keeping him waiting for a few minutes before he finally began to speak.

'When we listed all your various talents in order to make a rough approximation of the answer,' he said, 'you never stressed that you were also quite good at mountaineering.' Bertrand was surprised by this unrelated digression.

'Mountaineering? . . . Yes . . . Why? . . . I did a bit of climbing two years ago, it's true. On principle I spend my holidays in a different place each year. Two years ago I rather wanted to get in with Professor La Reynie; he's got a chalet at Les Houches, near Chamonix. His son is a climbing fanatic, he tried to drag me into it. It was a good way of gaining access to the house as well as being great physical exercise; it built up reflexes, stamina, balance and self-control, but conditions were often unpleasant. In fact, I did some good routes with Gabriel La Reynie.'

'But you didn't carry on the following year?' asked Klaren.

'Certainly not! By that time I'd got in with the La Reynie family. Anyway Nicolas Delamare's daughter — he was still Minister — had invited me on a cruise and . . .'

'But there you are!' Klaren interrupted, 'Your mission in life! It's climbing.'

Bertrand Pacôme froze, incredulous. All that time wasted on a silly disappointment! The computer had made a mistake. After all that, they had ended up with a ridiculous malfunction.

'You're just as surprised as I was,' the old man remarked, 'but think about it a bit and you'll have to admit that it's really a stroke of genius. Cinema, pop-songs, literature, art, politics are already overcrowded. They're full of gifted people with an outstanding future. Just consider! Sailing has its great names. Climbing has had a few, all right, but they're not very well-known. Today, some have disappeared, others are no longer all that young or have difficulty keeping their names in front of the public. There's a great gap in the market. And that's where you fit in — the Ivan Lendl, the Alain Prost, the Gaza, the Kasparov of the climbing world.

Bertrand was torn. The old man had a point. But all the careers he'd worked for were slipping away — careers that would have called on all his social graces, all that culture he'd acquired so painfully. And what he was offered in exchange was the joyless prospect of carting around enormous sacks in an almost solitary effort . . . And all those noisy and overcrowded huts . . . And those endless conversations about the latest ice-axe or nut. A new and completely unproductive world . . . He pulled a sceptical face.

'A magnificent destiny!' Klaren insisted, 'Just think, it's a field where amateurism counts, even amongst professionals. Love of the mountains is the basis of a vocation . . . And of course that leaves the door open to every weakness, every error. Most mountaineers are too pure! Not you, though, because you will be ruled by reason . . . and just imagine! Obviously, to make your niche you'll have to get yourself known through climbing, but if you're clever, it will lead into the other activities that you've been considering. Books, lectures, photography, films, travel, business . . . not to mention political openings — it's happened before. With climbing as a starting point, anything's possible and . . .'

Bertrand Pacôme was thinking, weighing up, analysing. When he looked up his eyes were shining with dawning enthusiasm. That was it! He had his niche, and never would he have found it alone . . .

'Your programme — it's sheer genius!' he said with admiration.

The old man's face lit up with pleasure.

'What you need now,' he concluded, 'is a good manager.'

The following month Albert Klaren passed away — a stroke. Pacôme bent his principles to put off an appointment in order to go to the funeral. After all, the old gentleman had been an inventor of genius. It was a shame in a way that he had been unable to pursue such a promising line of research. But on the other hand, it was a relief that his amazing ideas should be buried with him and that no other new stars would be launched on to the market!

Meanwhile Bertrand Pacôme had had a lucky break; he'd found the man who was to be the second architect of his success. John Fitzgerald Bartlett had business all over Europe and the United States. He had launched washing-powders, snow-tyres, moisturising creams, underwear, long-life batteries, tanning lotions, chocolates, slimming machines, electronic calculators that played *The Ride of the Valkyries* while heating the teapot ... and he had occasionally launched personalities. He liked the business opportunity that was Bertrand Pacôme. He asked for forty-eight hours to think about it and make a few contacts, then gave a positive response, succinctly summing up how he envisaged the future.

'It's an excellent idea. Now we need some additional market research, and then we'll go on to a three-part sales strategy: one — find a product profile geared to public demand; two — evolve a career development plan, concentrating on the launch; three — put together a sponsoring consortium. They will of course remain in the background but their various brands will be subsequently linked to the product which, in the course of the progressive stages of the operation, will retain the totally natural appearance that will be one of his major assets.'

They soon started on the first stage of the operation. The profile study was entrusted to the famous advertising agency H & Q, whose founders, G.L. Hack and T.M. Quaintance, had established their reputation with the launch of Esperanza Bosca, the great film star of the 1990s, and with that of the no less memorable President Jack Barescut. The team of psychologists, semiologists, economists, creative artists and advertising and merchandis-ing experts conducted marketing surveys that tested the product on various target groups. The results surpassed all expectations; as old Klaren had expected, it turned out that the public were ready to accept the product Bertrand Pacôme, the climber, to project themselves on to him, to idolise him and therefore to buy him.

The characteristics that the product had to correspond to in order to best fulfil these expectations were then broken down as follows:

Name: It might have been necessary, for various reasons, to change the name of the future star so that it might correspond perfectly, semiotically to the image offered to the various target groups. A double-barrelled name could have put off the Left; a pseudo-regional one like Seamus O'Sean would not have provided a suitable brand-image, and something like Rock Hardy would have sounded like parody. However, when all the research had been completed, the name Bertrand Pacôme, although a touch too sophisticated for the product, could be kept, which was valuable for the air of authenticity required.

Physical appearance: Little to change. The only modification was a slight lightening of the hair colour. Its present fair chestnut would be changed to a hint of blonde intended to contrast tastefully with a permanent tan. The result would be obtained by discreet and subtle bleaching; a flask of hydrogen peroxide in a sportsman's bathroom would not arouse suspicion. The hairstyle itself would be dictated by yearly changes in fashion but for the time being, for the 'old' photos which would be dug out at a later date, it would aim at 'defiant adolescent' — his hair, that is to say, would be a bit longer than average and slightly tousled. The effect would be achieved by a light trim every month. That apart, his mouth was attractive, his teeth healthy, his nose straight, his complexion fresh and hands well-shaped. Eyes, china-blue with dark lashes, were perfect. The physique was supple and elegant; what strength he still lacked would be acquired in the course of the planned exercise regime.

Dress style: Simple, sporty, masculine outfits; emphasise his physical attributes. Key note — casual. Jeans, open-necked shirts, thick home-knitted wool sweaters, light leather jackets. There too, in the early stages, it was essential that the casual style be handled skilfully, maintaining a slightly scruffy but clean image. In town or on the mountain, his outfit should always include a touch of light blue to match his eyes.

Required behaviour: Key word — friendly. Pacôme was to make himself universally liked, in his close circle of friends and by passing acquaintances. He had to know how to listen, or at least give the impression of doing so, to be ready to help, settling a bill with what would appear to be his last penny, making gifts of his equipment in unforgettable bursts of friendship, always ready with a loan, always ready to give a hitch-hiker a lift . . . He had to know how to flatter discreetly with every appearance of sincerity, to convince the young he valued their advice, the old feel that they were still young, beautiful women that they were also intellectual, and the less attractive that they had an unsettling charm. For his part, he would be indefatigably modest, so encouraging others to establish his reputation without his assistance.

Ideological standpoints: The product would need a strong ideological content, but the ideology itself should remain nebulous and unrelated to specific doctrines. Working from this basic strategy, Bertrand Pacôme would show every sign of idealism. He would love the human race passionately, have total faith in its worth and each of his actions would stem from a healthy basic set of beliefs. A touch of ecological sympathy was desirable, provided that it was qualified by common sense. A dash of intellect would not be unbecoming, if accompanied by a romantic streak; it should not, however, provoke inner doubt or anguish. A hint of religion was desirable, so long as it did not commit him to any definable confession. Given all this, people would see him as a fighter, inspired only by his perfectionism; he would become involved only with those commercial brands whose quality he believed made them worthy of support. 'As a fine flower of the capitalist economy' — concluded the report — 'Bertrand Pacôme would offer an answer on a mythical level to basic human desires!'

Niche marketing: Detailed study of each market sector revealed the universal need for a Bertrand Pacôme; he should therefore respond to product aspiration for a range of different clientele. Children should make Bertrand Pacôme their hero, teenagers identify with him, young girls see in him the perfect fulfilment of their dreams, women, the man they should have met. As for the men, they should see in him a model they could still emulate. Mothers should see him as a child subject to terrible risk and, more generally, parents or grandparents should see him as the son they would have loved to have. As it would not be easy to appeal to all different generations, one solution would be provided by the relationship that Bertrand Pacôme would have with his own mother and father; they were not, of course, to be party to the secret. In effecting a great break in his life for the sake of an ideal, climbing, and in giving up the benefits of so much study, now 'redundant', the boy would have deeply disappointed his parents, and young people would respond to that. However, once he had caused this initial disappointment, Bertrand Pacôme would redeem himself in the eyes of the older generation by remaining close to his family in a way that would touch the hardest heart, speaking of his father with unmixed admiration ('I get it all from him') and displaying a deep tenderness for his mother ('Her love has seen me through my most difficult moments'). He would thus give off ambiguous signals, adolescent rebellion against adult conventions, recklessness, in contrast with delightfully reassuring family ties.

To all this would be added the myth of risk, appealing to all market-sectors and a source of endless pronouncements like 'To live is to take risks', 'I don't like danger, but I accept it', 'Some prefer an ordinary and sheltered life, but I prefer to live life intensely', 'I'm like everyone else: I'm afraid of death, but climbing is such a great adventure that it has taught me to accept risk-taking as a necessary part of all real human existence', etc . . . The danger element was also designed to arouse an unconscious tolerance in the few who would remain resistant to the Pacôme phenomena, and who would contemplate his violent end with a certain satisfaction.

Finally, a few minor advantages should be cultivated; the subtlest being humour, humour designed for a bored world. Bertrand Pacôme, it must be said, was somewhat lacking in that department. But the office would help out here, thinking up on his behalf a few epigrams, choice phrases and irresistible witticisms.

The overall profile thus being drawn up, the H & Q agency used the following winter as a season of varied and intensive training for Bertrand Pacôme in the United States. Under an assumed name and as a trainee in the world of showbusiness, he learnt how to take care of his complexion, balance his diet, breathe, walk, run, sit, go up and down stairs, smile frank smiles, light a cigarette and appear gauche but well-bred. He took courses in elocution, yoga, weight-lifting, golf, riding, skating, boxing and even parapsychology.

He was now ready to embark on the second phase of the operation. This was given over to intensive ski-touring and climbing under the guidance of a young Austrian guide with whom he struck up a warm friendship. The pair went all over the Austrian, Swiss and Italian Alps and got some well-known routes under their belts. Over a period of several months Bertrand Pacôme acquired solid experience and an almost professional technique on ice, snow, rock; he also became expert at rope-work and rescue techniques.

The rest of his life was mapped out, year by year, on an optimal career-curve to which the product was to adhere as closely as Nature would permit.

Meanwhile, J.F. Bartlett was recruiting the sponsors. As far as they were concerned, the business involved an element of risk: only one Bertrand Pacôme could be launched on to the market and despite all precautions he would remain vulnerable. Notwithstanding the risk, maybe even because of it, manufacturers liked the project. Small firms at first, then large businesses decided to back the product, supplying the invisible support necessary for his launch and hoping for considerable benefit from the subsequent advertising.

At the end of a few months, the list of sponsors stood as follows:

— Kitup: crampons and ice-axes.
— Fassdauben: skis.
— The Senior Scaler: sports shop.
— Carloman's: fashions.
— *Weekly Heights*: a monthly magazine.
— *Bad Weather*: a well-known alpine daily paper.
— Editions Fust et Schoeffer.
— Radio-Emosson: the pirate station.
— Bank of Chamonix & Katmandu Ltd.
— The pharmaceutical and health-product laboratory Dynagerm.
— The Neanderthal range of men's toiletries.

Two other companies had insisted on joining the venture — the gas pipeline firm, Sibérie, and the cat-litter producers, Cats' Ecstasy. The valid objection was raised that it would be difficult to link them to the product, but they were ready to pay and were therefore incorporated. Things had reached this stage, and the venture was beginning to assume considerable proportions when some particularly large-scale sponsors entered J.F. Bartlett's sights. After hard bargaining, he succeeded in winning their support also.

The first of these was a ski-resort scheduled to open in the next few years and which was to outshine anything so far built. Of an extremely ecological design, the resort — or rather, the three identical resorts of Cowpat 1800, Upper Cowpat and Cowpat Village — would sleep 50,000 and offer 120,000 metres of ski-lifts and 380 kilometres of pistes. Cowpat would follow the latest anti-pollution requirements in constructing its 30,000-space car-park in the flank of the mountain. The 25,000 cells of habitation were to be built of natural concrete and panelled, inside and out, with authentically aged plastic timber. In the restaurants, the cooking would be done over rustic hearths burning the station's own reprocessed rubbish. A fantastic traditional atmosphere would derive from three orthodox churches with bulbous bell-towers, bought in the USSR, dismantled piece by piece and then reconstructed in the centre of each of the three centres of Cowpat. Children would be able to visit a recreated model farm. Powerful machines would puff out genuine pine-scented air every half hour. Loud speakers would play Tyrolean songs. And, ultimate refinement (subtly justifying the station's name), real farm dung and liquid manure, flown in by plane directly from third world agricultural countries, would be spread each morning on the roads, where people would move around on foot or in sledges harnessed to blue reindeer, the product of genetic experimentation. The slopes would have names like 'Haystack', 'Glebe', 'Woodbine', 'Silage', 'Henbane', 'Slurry', 'Fleabane', 'Oats', 'Beetroot', 'Toadflax', 'Bugbane' — in short, it was a dream of patriarchal purity and simplicity, of rustic mountain wholesomeness. Every winter, Bertrand Pacôme was to ski at Cowpat and become the most startling of its brand images.

Although less spectacular, the second firm represented still greater capital input. The company was dedicated to the development of artificial winter and alpine sports facilities: ski-slopes, cross-country skiing and skating on plastic surfaces, toboggan runs on rails and, especially, most especially, climbing walls. Fashion was already moving in that direction. It only needed to be popularised, spread, democratised. Every municipality, whether or not it had recently laid out money for a swimming-pool, should henceforth make a point of finding the funds for its climbing wall, otherwise mayor and council would find themselves looking for new jobs after the next election. Every housing scheme would pride itself on its own wall. Every weekend cottage would offer its guests the use of its wall. In flats, however cramped, the use of cunning artificial holds would still offer a full range of delicate slabs, athletic chimneys, intricate traverse — everything that had until then been reserved for outdoor rock-climbers. The market was huge! The walls would be produced in every conceivable form: rustic stone, concrete, steel, plastic. Some would come in kits and could therefore grow with the finances and expertise of their happy owners. One extremely ingenious model would be made up of rotative cubes with each side, of a specific colour, corresponding to a specific level of climbing difficulty. One could thus choose everything from a blue wall, level I, for children, right up to a red wall, level VII, even level VIII, for seasoned climbers. Bertrand Pacôme himself would often practise on these 'Sproutup' walls and would unfailingly extol their astonishing qualities, 'I owe a good deal of my success to them,' he would confess, with no departure from the truth.

The system was set up. All that remained was to put it into action.

In mid-summer, Bertrand Pacôme made his 'official' entry into Chamonix behind the wheel of an old Citroën 2CV, painted canary yellow, covered with Green slogans and stuffed with climbing gear. The La Reynie family welcomed the return of the prodigal son with open arms and found him changed — for the better. Thanks to Gabriel, Bertrand was soon able to put his new skills to work and quickly infiltrated top French climbing circles, which from then on were to serve for his take-off.

Surely there is no need to rehearse every detail in the irresistible rise of Bertrand Pacôme? Suffice it to say that all went according to plan, and that Nature had the good manners not to throw any real obstacles in the way.

In the autumn, Bertrand sent his parents an affectionate but unexpected letter: — Carried away by his new passion, he was giving up his studies and intended from now on to live in the mountains where he would earn his living by the sweat of his brow. Monsieur Pacôme sighed, ranted and raved a little, but was secretly proud of the son whom he had considered until then as somewhat lacking in youthful folly. Madame Pacôme wept copiously and tried in vain to console herself by knitting warm thick sweaters.

Their offspring found a job for the winter as a ski-patroller. He experienced none of the doubts or worries that would ordinarily burden the existence of a young man making such a choice, for he had back-up. He had merely to go through the motions to finish, before long, as one of France's best climbers. If he did not become one of the leading lights of pure climbing, it didn't matter: an all-inclusive advertising campaign would make up for it.

Back in the city, other very talented climbers had to content themselves, for eleven out of the twelve months of the year, with nursing dreams of routes or expedition plans in the Underground; others lucky enough to be out in the mountains wasted precious time in café conversation, in front of the television or in bed. Whereas Bertrand Pacôme had only one aim in mind: methodical training! A cross-country run or ski each morning, a workout in the gym and some tough downhill skiing in the afternoon. The following summer, day after day, from the Oisans to the Dolomites, he did endless routes, wearing out even the most fanatical climbing partners. That season he qualified for the next stage of guide training.

At the same time he worked on the 'public relations' side of his programme. He helped, he supported, he assisted, he smiled ... Some people reproached themselves for finding this dedicated lad lacking in warmth, but attributed his reserve to a shyness that concealed a heart of gold. Before long, this carefully cultivated façade became second nature.

In fact, everything would have been perfect for Bertrand Pacôme if it had not been for those damned mountains ... Getting up at 1 a.m. in crowded huts where it was difficult to get hold of a mouthful of luke warm water for a drink before going out to tackle a daunting face. The glacial wind on the ridges that froze your very blood ... And the appalling screes where for hours on end you twisted your ankles ... And the rotten rock, where you couldn't be sure if the hold you had was going to come away in your hands, or if a loose block was going to fall, cutting short such a carefully planned career! ... And the insidious verglas making the cracks so lethally slippery ... And the capricious snow, now powdery so that you sunk in it up to your thighs, now crusted, now wind-slabbed, now soft, yellowish and treacherous, now half-melted into a slushy thin layer deceitfully concealing ice! As for the ice: blue, white, black, green or opaque with tiny bubbles, Bertrand Pacôme felt nothing but a profound hatred ... And the rock yet another penance, with its ever changing aspects, its intricate problems, the sack that jams, the rope that refuses to run. And then finally, just another summit, just another enthusiastic: 'Great, huh?' to a climbing-partner.

Nevertheless, as time went on, his progress became obvious. No climber yet had forced himself to the discipline of a Pacôme who trained for the mountain as a serious athlete trains for the Olympic Games. And it paid off! ... Aspirant guide ... ski-instructor ... guide. Pacôme soon found himself equipped with all those diplomas that the public find indispensable before putting their full confidence in a specialist. In addition, he had collected a wad of pages covered with personal impressions, descriptions of sunsets or north faces after a snowfall which would stand him in good stead when he wrote his first books. He had also learnt to take good photographs, and began to use a cine-camera skilfully.

So he moved on to phase two of the operation. Already, in spite of his apparent discretion, Pacôme seemed to have attracted journalists. It was he who had been singled out, in a major programme on snow, that first winter, as a representative ski-patroller, he who had been chosen for an illustrated article in a women's magazine to explain the life of a young climber who had given up all for his ideal. Again it was he who had been chosen by a radio station as their correspondent during the summer when a spell of bad weather had cut off a dozen climbers on exposed faces. But these were mere trifles designed to introduce the product's image. Now, it was time for the major, personal appearances.

The real launch was planned in three campaigns, to cover the three different phases of an alpine career as conceived by the media. True, it was difficult to introduce much novelty, but after all, the old tricks are the best. It was a computer that had selected them.

Campaign one consisted of the traditional route started in good weather but overtaken by a sudden storm — an adventure that experience had shown deeply affected Press and public alike.

Meteorological forecasts from a reliable long-range source would fix the date, at a stage when the Chamonix weather-station was still predicting sun and high pressure systems. It was to be an attempted first ascent, on a face sufficiently remote so that neither tourists nor journalists would be able to spend any bright spells searching with binoculars for the party in peril. Bertrand Pacôme's choice fell on the East Face of the Jorasses, little frequented and relatively little known, where the line of a new route, if not dazzling, would at least appear plausible in the eyes of the initiated. Moreover, the Jorasses were prestigious. Nobody would be able to accuse the young guide, who would have left Chamonix with a good weather forecast, of recklessness.

No sooner had the bad weather set in than great headlines splashed across the newspapers:

ALARM IN CHAMONIX
BERTRAND PACÔME STORMBOUND FOR THREE DAYS

In passing, it might be noted that there was also a party of Czechs in the range from whom there had been no news for five days, but this fact was of no interest to the papers. Accustomed as it was to the whims of the Press, the climbing world was not surprised. Seeing however that tension was rising around the Bertrand Pacôme affair, the Director of the National Guides' School and a lieutenant of the Alpine Police Squad issued reassuring statements on radio and television. It was certainly true that the weather was foul, that the helicopter could not take off and that a pair of friends who climbed to the foot of the route on the fifth day saw nothing and received no response to their calls, lost in the wind in any case.

After six days, everyone was getting genuinely anxious when the party returned, having completed the route. It transpired that Bertrand, whose fitness was proverbial, had been unwell just as they had begun on the ascent and that he and his friend, loaded with supplies, had decided to stay put until the next day. One day lost! They had then made good progress and bivouacked two-thirds of the way up the route, but being on an east face they had not seen the warning signs of bad weather coming in from the west and were caught out. Then Bertrand had suffered further spells of dizziness and vertigo which had immobilised them a further day and made slow going on the next. In short, nothing very epic. It was quite by chance that Bertrand had insisted they set out with a greater amount of equipment than usual! The two men had never been really worried but had been unable to signal the situation. Of course, by the end they had little left to eat, just billy cans of tea and soup . . . And they had had difficulty getting off the mountain. All quite straightforward, in fact . . .

The mountain itself had even made a bit of an effort, unleashing a small avalanche on the last day that forced the two heroes over the bergschrund rather faster than they would have liked. Pacôme's friend had sprained an ankle and he himself had had an unfortunate landing on the point of a crampon. He had bled a lot from just above his eyebrow and arrived in the Val d'Aoste with a dramatically wounded face. A swarm of reporters was on the spot and this triumphant return, after so tough a victory, hit the front pages of the papers, eclipsing a *coup d'état* in Central America, the taking of holy orders by a member of the Politburo and catastrophic floods in Qatar. The name of Bertrand Pacôme was thus firmly implanted in the public consciousness.

It was of course the following winter that his first book came out, almost entirely written by its author. *The Call of the Heights* was a great sell-out and was soon followed by *The Sky on the End of my Ice-Axe*, *Festive Summits* and *Voluptuous Faces*.

The young climber now made no secret of the fact that he considered Kitup equipment exceptionally solid and Fassdauben skis uniquely smooth, that he was dressed exclusively by Carloman's and that the healthy masculinity of Neanderthal men's toiletries were an indispensable part of his daily life.

Eighteen months after Operation Jorasses, the second part of the campaign swung into action. This time it was a more delicate business. Pacôme set off alone one day on skis, on a huge alpine crossing designed to take him from Nice to the Tyrol.

Nobody witnessed the departure which took place in January, at a time when there are very few people in the mountains. Neither did anyone witness the arrival, which took place within an incredibly short time. An account of this exceptional trek appeared in *Altitude Weekly* with details that failed fully to satisfy mountain-skiing experts. It was not long before a malicious tabloid dropped the bombshell — Bertrand Pacôme had not done the Mediterranean-Tyrol trek! The article even cast a doubt over his former achievements. There were violent clashes of opinion. Bertrand contented himself with shrugging his shoulders and refusing to make any statement. Proof against him flooded in; the timescale was too short, the photo illustrating the article had obviously been taken in the Pyrenees . . . besides, Bertrand himself, it seemed, had taken no photographs, nobody had seen him and he returned looking very pale-skinned, scarcely tanned by the sun and snow-glare . . .

In the face of such slander Pacôme became indignant and spoke up — and yes, he *had* been seen! And suddenly witnesses appeared — peasants he had spoken to, shopkeepers at whose stores he stocked up on fresh supplies, hikers who *could* produce photos of the lone climber. The view of the Pyrenees? A stupid error that had occurred during the page lay-out. The pale complexion? He had started to blister and wore a slitted handkerchief to protect his face, as the recently released photographs confirmed . . . It was a real *coup de théâtre*. The Press was full of the trek, of its remarkable completion time. There was mention of Zwingelstein, the great 1934 predecessor who, it was discovered, had been Pacôme's inspiration. The vile rag that had dared to cast doubt on a personality known for his honesty and purity was cuttingly condemned . . . Bertrand Pacôme, as a result of his exploit, of his discretion and of his idealism, was well on his way to becoming an idol.

From then on, he scheduled major lecture tours to strengthen his brand image, became the darling of Cowpat, generously supported Sproutup Walls' promotion efforts so that his fellows could share the same joys as he. Within two years his literary output had been translated into no fewer than twenty-seven languages.

The organisation of the third operation, which was to centre around a rescue, allowed a certain leeway. This operation was scarcely necessary any longer, but triggered by events it happened quite naturally one day and, in the full glare of the limelight, Pacôme appeared his usual sublimely brilliant, dedicated and modest persona. His reputation spread rapidly abroad where he regularly took part in official lecture-tours, showing films that he brought back from his distant expeditions. The Pacôme phenomenon became so major that he made a significant contribution to correcting France's balance of payments deficit.

All's well that ends well, you say? Not at all! An unforeseen grain of sand jammed the machine. There had already been warning signs which the sponsors — whose original investment had long since been more than covered — had not taken heed of . . . A few missed meetings, some moments of bad temper, the sudden breaking off of a lecture-tour . . . Pacôme seemed to be tired of frenzied crowds, to be feeling the need for solitude.

It all came to a head, however, one April morning at an occasion aimed at crowning the star. That day a somewhat novel Summit Conference was to be held, during which the Big Five were invited to participate in a friendly ski-descent of the Vallée Blanche. *Détente* at last! Bertrand Pacôme, with the help of some guide friends, was to watch over the turns and tumbles of the presidents. All the Press, all the radio and television stations were there, with more equipment than had ever been seen before, but no Bertrand Pacôme. He merely telegrammed his excuses, claiming to be stuck somewhere and nominating as his replacement another perfectly competent guide.

Later it emerged that he had gone off with two or three friends, that day, for a light-hearted ski-tour over the Tsanteleina ridges. Bertrand Pacôme had finished by falling in love with the mountains.

Translated by Siobhān Anderson and Jane Taylor

THE OTHER

There was once a Chamonix guide who possessed the power, unusual among the members of that honourable Company, of becoming two at will.

It had happened to him one day during childhood, but he had never boasted about it. The process was simple. He only had to say 'Fouchtra!', and there were two of him, which could be very convenient at times. One might object that *Fouchtra* is not a word known in magic circles, and only appears to be, or to have been, much used in the Auvergne. But it is hardly known to the natives of Chamonix, though if they tried it, who knows, they might find themselves endowed with Marcel Descharmoz's gift?

He had discovered this magical word by chance, one day off school when avoiding the chore of potato-lifting, an event to which his father had 'invited' him in no uncertain terms. He had vanished into the barn, in a deep hidey-hole made in the hay, near a gap between the boards which allowed enough light for the thrills of reading. Never mind about the spanking he would suffer in the evening. He would plead innocently, saying that he had forgotten, that he had gone out for a while, then had been detained ... detained by what? ... He'd see ... Anyway, the lecture which would ensue would not be too high a price to pay for an afternoon of peaceful happiness.

As it happened, his great friend Pierrot had just lent him a very promising book with the enticing title of *Choice Readings*. Equipped with this work, and with a generous helping of bread and jam acquired from the kitchen when his mother's back was turned, little Marcel snuggled deeper into the hay ... and his father's calls mixed with unflattering comments simply added a little spice to the venture.

The *Choice Readings* deserved their title, and had been compiled by a skilful master, each story being equally thrilling. Now, in one of them, an Auvergnat uttered: *Fouchtra!*.

The child found the expression delightful. It was the most entrancing word he had ever met. He read it carefully again several times, analysed it in its various parts, reflected on it and, finally, risked murmuring this wondrous word ...

'Fouchtra!'

The effect was instantaneous: he had become two. Another little Marcel was by his side, dressed like him, and glancing at what was left of the bread and jam. The two children were made to get on well. They shared the rest of the bread, finished the *Choice Readings*, conversed in low voices, stifled their giggles on hearing father and mother wondering where 'he' could have disappeared to.

But it was nearing supper-time. A reappearance was due, and Marcel knew he would be in even greater trouble if two of them turned up. So, he tried to become one again, and pronounced, several times, in a confident, authoritative or pleading voice:

'*Fouchtra!*'

To no avail . . . So he left Marcel No. 2 in the hay, promised to try and bring him some more bread and jam and a sweater, and climbed down, filled with disquiet.

At least the worry caused by the adventure saved him from more immediate problems, for he entered the kitchen with such a haggard look that his parents did not ask where he had been, but instead asked: 'What's wrong?' From then on it was easy. Marcel explained that he had felt ill all afternoon, sitting by a wood-pile near the shed. Yes, he had heard his parents call, but he had been unable to answer for the pain, here, and there . . . and there . . . He pointed to his knees, shoulders and chest . . . carefully avoiding his stomach, remembering a mistake which had once put him on to a very strict diet.

His parents' concern worried him, talking of taking him to the doctor, and noticing with some anxiety that even dinner had failed to bring back his usual healthy glow.

Marcel took the rest of his pudding to his double, with the promised sweater, and spent a dreadful night. It would not be easy to live and feed two on one ration, with the constant problem of hiding the other! He reflected deeply and finally thought he had a solution, which he carefully wrote down at first light.

In the morning, he slipped out to the barn, found his double and, not without some apprehension, uttered the reversed formula:

'*Arthcuof!*'

The result was as remarkable as his first experiment, and he was able to return to the farm in a state of oneness. His night's meditation had left him rather pale and, seeing his parents' worried looks, he quickly reassured them and offered to join his father on the potato field to make up for the previous day.

But he soon regretted this impulse of unconsidered altruism, the euphoric outcome of his success, and thought that he had been silly to miss such a good opportunity for a day off. But nothing could be done now. At lunch, however, he had a brilliant idea. There was just time to slip out to the barn, say *'Fouchtra!'* and send his double to the potato field, while he, himself, could relax peacefully in sweet-smelling hay . . .

Thus, without revealing to others a life anything out of the normal, Marcel spent a youth few children could have dreamt of. Almost everyday he uttered the magical *'Fouchtra!'* and sent his double to school, while he ran around the mountains like a chamois, picked wild strawberries or mushrooms, fished for trout, watched birds and marmots, climbed rocks, learned the signs of woods and sky, gaining experience which shaped him into a well-balanced and happy young man. In the evening, in the privacy of his room, he shared with his double his lessons and homework to speed up the task, then, with a powerful *'Arthcuof!'*, he became once more the unique Marcel Descharmoz about to share, with good appetite, his part of the familial supper.

When he was old enough to choose a profession, Marcel decided to become a mountain guide and skiing-instructor. His solitary expeditions had given him such a closeness to nature, so much strength and suppleness, and such sure footing, that he could not imagine anything else that could keep him in the clean air of his mountains. He also thought it wise to give up taking advantage of a gift which, now, would not only be useless, but might, on the contrary, put him in the very embarrassing situation of being seen 'double', — a threat which had worried him for years, but was becoming ever more disturbing. A child, to grown-up eyes, is always shrouded in some halo of mystery, by some strangeness and cunning which allows him to wriggle out of awkward situations. But Descharmoz realised that early adulthood was not an age of freedom, far from it, and that it was better to keep strictly to what others expected of you, which was confined to pretty narrow boundaries.

So Marcel passed through his various stages of training in his original form of oneness; the Company of Chamonix Guides, always open to the natives of the valley, welcomed him to its bosom and in a few years he acquired a healthy clientele, appreciative of his skills moulded by the two schools of nature and national education.

All went well until one day in July when Marcel, overworked, was faced with a difficult alternative. He could no longer satisfy demand. On the one hand, old Ratenelle, a pleasant and wealthy climber, was reminding him of his previous year's promise of a week's climbing in the Dolomites. On the other, there was the Michaille family, only there for a fortnight, whom he had also promised to satisfy, taking in turn the father who liked ice, the elder son who preferred difficult rock-climbs, and the daughters who would rather have long snowy ridges . . .

Having undertaken to satisfy everybody, Marcel realised that by failing to meet his obligations he risked losing a worthwhile part of his clientele. Temptation began to grow and took shape, when, having arranged to meet Mr Ratenelle the next day, Descharmoz saw the entire Michaille family arrive at the Guides' Office, and did not have the heart to disappoint them. He went home, worried. Had the formula lost its power?

'*Fouchtra!*' he cried as he stepped in.

'Ah!' It was still working! He was two again, and so could fulfil his engagements, although he would have to exercise caution not to be found out.

Thus it was that Marcel Descharmoz carried out, with Ratenelle, a week's climbing in the Dolomites, which soon turned to a fortnight while, at the same time, the Mont Blanc range was the scene of his other exploits. Everybody was happy and the financial result was equally satisfactory.

Although he had, at the start, vowed not to repeat this strategy, Descharmoz soon gave in to the temptation; and both in summer and winter, multiplied himself on climbs and ski-runs. Soon, too, his life became a true inferno, with the needs of an ever growing clientele leaving him no rest. Once, he even tried to quadruple himself, but in vain. The risk of being found out increased proportionately.

'It was on the 14th of July, I assure you, that I climbed the Couturier with Marcel,' a client insisted.

'But you're wrong. He was with me on the 14th, on the Gran Paradiso.'

'Don't insist,' Marcel would whisper to the one. 'He's not quite with it.'

'Don't argue with him,' he would then say to the other. 'He mixes everything up and hates being told he does.'

And there were also his colleagues whom he met on climbs and who might gossip together. Not to mention the hut log-books, in which clients are so fond of writing what they have done, with the guide's name. Even with places deliberately chosen well distanced from one another, those testimonies slowly built up a threatening dossier. One day, scandal would erupt . . . Marcel could not sleep because of it . . . Furthermore, he had to keep some highly complex accounts, declaring to the Guides' Office only one climb a day and then having to make sure that the other client did not go and settle his undeclared climb directly with the secretary! However one viewed the situation, it had become a gigantic trap. Already, Marcel felt that people looked at him askance, that they whispered behind his back . . . Or was he imagining things?

On the other hand, there were debts to settle for his chalet, for the car, the colour television, his modern kitchen, for the drawing-room with the leather upholstery, payments which one man alone could barely meet . . . It would be years before he could live normally again . . .

And that was not all! His double, obedient for so long, and delighted simply to be summoned into existence from time to time, was becoming more and more independent, even questioning the climbs allotted to him.

'Mont Blanc again! With those fools! I'd rather take your place and go to the Zmutt Ridge.'

'Will you shut up!' Marcel would exclaim. 'Otherwise, *Artc* . . .'

And the other would be quiet, but for how long? He knew that he was now indispensable.

Worse still, while Marcel was almost engaged to the Bionnay girl, his neighbours' youngest, his double was having a wild affair with one of the Michaille daughters. And rumours travel quickly in Chamonix! More quickly than events . . . There would certainly be talk already. It wouldn't be long before one of the other young women got wind of it.

It was with this state of affairs that Marcel, terrified, saw the new season looming, after a spring season during which he had exhausted himself with many Chamonix-Zermatts and in climbing in the Hoggar. Now, at home with the Other, he contemplated, with concern, the months to come. After prolonged thought, he made up his mind: he had to put a stop to all this before disaster happened. He had not mentioned his worries to his double, who was sipping a whisky and soda, probably daydreaming of little Michaille, and occasionally casting dirty looks at Marcel.

'*Arthcuof!*' shouted the latter, moving closer, as the spell did not work from a distance.

He found himself in the singular again, which felt much better. God knows of what the Other would have been capable. Living with him had become intolerably difficult. From now on, come what may, he would be only one forever. He would sell his flashy sports car, cut down on his lifestyle, take on as many expensive climbs as possible, reduce his clientele, starting by writing in a noncommittal way to the Michaille family about the coming season, which should see his marriage to Marie Françoise Bionnay ... Pauline Michaille would be furious, but then she was a bitch who did not deserve better ...

Thus, free from the Other, Marcel reshaped his life, gradually paid off his debts and, for the third time, enjoyed the delicious exquisiteness of everyday life. A little Marcelin had arrived to cheer a home which his father intended to keep well away from Auvergnat folklore ... The seasons followed one another peacefully, with snow covering hills and valleys, primroses and dandelions blooming afresh in the meadows, summer traffic jams, autumn forests adorned with golden larches ... All the gentleness of daily life drawn from the solid world of the ordinary, of its rational, commonplace coherence. Indeed, Marcel forgot that it could ever have been otherwise.

Until, that is, one fine August day, on the way up to the Couvercle Hut with old Ratenelle, who was moving so slowly that his guide had to daydream to keep his patience, he started thinking ... How strange those experiences had been ... What would have happened if he had not had the determination to put an end to his co-existence? Were there many other formulae, other ways which would allow him to cross the barrier between the real and foreign worlds?

The real world, at that precise moment, was heavy, and the following day bode even worse with the traverse of the Courtes which Ratenelle wanted to do, but had little chance of succeeding unless they climbed a great deal more quickly ...

The next day confirmed his pessimistic expectations. The approach march seemed endless. As for the ascent of the Col de la Tour des Courtes, best not talk about it! All the other ropes were already far ahead, or on their way down, while they were still staggering along the ridge. And when they reached the summit at last, it was so late that Marcel thought they should go back down the same way, immediately, instead of going on with the traverse. The sky was overcast and a sharp, cutting wind chilled them to the marrow; but, at least, it stopped the risk of avalanches which the sun might have caused at this time of day. However, on hearing of his decision, old Ratenelle protested grumpily, claiming that he was quite able to go on, and adding that, after all, it was he who was paying ... He was disagreeable in a way Marcel had never seen before ... It was his turn to get annoyed.

'I am in charge, Monsieur Ratenelle! And I do not intend to spend the whole day on this climb. And certainly not with the weather deteriorating. And ...forgive me for having to say it, but you are hardly moving. Here you are, sitting on your rucksack, a wreck. We are going down . . . Face up to it, for heaven's sake, you are no longer a young man!'

It was then that Ratenelle confessed:

'Precisely, Marcel . . . Listen to me . . . I didn't want to appear too sentimental, but this is an anniversary. I did this climb when I was eighteen years old . . . That was fifty years ago, the twenty-sixth of August, like today. It was my discovery of the mountains . . . And all my life since then . . . But you know about that . . . And now, here we are, at the top . . . The weather is not that bad . . . We can do this traverse . . . I'll manage . . . My first serious climb, and the last. Do you understand?'

The old man's begging eyes weakened Marcel. All right! They'd try, and they would succeed, even if it meant spending another night at the hut . . . To think that fifty short years could turn an enthusiastic teenager into a limp rag sunk on his rucksack, shrivelled with cold, exhausted and begging for his own martyrdom . . . Well, that was life!.

The traverse took a long time. He had to watch Ratenelle's every step, but had to admit that the old man was doing his best — an old child happy to relive memories at each halt . . .

'I remember, it was here that Jacques dropped his flask . . . Just when we were longing for a drink . . . Must admit that it was sunny then . . . Not like now . . .'

No, indeed it wasn't like now, the nearby summits were already shrouded in cloud. The slopes looked like grey cotton-wool. From dull skies swirled a few flakes, and the wind plucked grains of hardened snow from the ridges. Red rucksacks and ropes barely showed up against the grey monotony.

'What a shame there is no view,' regretted old Ratenelle at the next stop. 'It was wonderful! I almost feel that the mountains have changed. Ah! I am no longer eighteen!'

'Too true,' agreed Marcel. 'But come on now. We must move on.'

'Already?' sighed the old man '. . . just a moment longer.'

But it soon became clear that these first difficulties had been nothing but precursors. Near the Aiguille Qui Remue, Marcel saw his client grimace, rub his face with a shaking mitten, mumble some indistinct phrases, propping himself against a rock. His nostrils were pinched and his forehead moist in spite of the cold.

'I don't know what's the matter,' he murmured at last. 'It's like a vice round my chest. I am not well. You were right . . . I am exhausted.'

His trouble Marcel dared not consider; some sort of heart problem. He was a strong man and this was more than unfitness. After a while, Marcel helped him back on to his feet and tried to walk on with him, holding him by the arm . . . No use! The old man was falling over his feet, out of breath with the slightest effort. For sure, they were going to go down quicker than planned! And there was no one nearby to help. Nor was there any hope that the warden at the Couvercle could send out an SOS before the evening, nor that a helicopter would take off earlier than tomorrow, weather permitting, and Ratenelle, by then . . .

Marcel hesitated for a while before taking the only solution he could think of. True, he had vowed never to call the Other, but in such circumstances . . .

Only one word was needed . . . and the Other appeared, no more friendly than before . . . taking in the situation at a glance.

'So!' he grumbled, 'I am only wanted when you are in trouble, am I? Isn't it stupid to drag such incompetents up the mountains? A wreck! I wonder who is the more pathetic, he with his anniversary or you with your sentimentality. I will help you because I feel like making an appearance in the fresh air, but, after that, mate, we'll have to discuss my terms seriously . . .'

What did he mean? Marcel felt that now the Other would bring nothing but trouble. However, at that moment, he was invaluable, efficient, and enjoyed showing his skill. They had reached the Col des Cristaux, started the descent, and the Other helped Ratenelle while, above, Marcel belayed them, thinking that, at the right moment, near the hut, he would have to come closer in order to utter the inverted formula. Was it just chance that, during these manoeuvres, the Other always kept himself at a distance, at the end of the rope? . . . Otherwise he was perfect, except for a latent hostility that emanated from him, and the little sound which he uttered from time to time, as if clearing his throat:

'Arth . . . arth . . . arth . . . arth . . .'

Marcel felt a cold sweat when he realised it was the beginning of the formula. What would happen if the Other pronounced it? Would it be he, Marcel Descharmoz, who would disappear forever?

The Other, at that moment, had just got over the bergschrund with the old man. He raised his head, and Marcel saw an evil look in his eyes at the same moment as, from under his own foot, some stones, loosely held in place by the ice, gave way. It would have been easy enough to stop them by sticking his crampons into the slope, but he did not. He had no intention to harm, rather to distract the Other and leave him time to consider the situation.

The stones gathered speed picking up others in their wake.

'Watch out!' he yelled.

Too late! Hit on the head by a small bouncing rock, no bigger than a plum, the Other collapsed in the snow. In a flash Marcel rushed down the slope and sighed with relief, seeing that the Other was already coming to, that all seemed normal and that he, himself, felt nothing. As for Ratenelle, he was so dazed with exhaustion that he had not yet realised that he now had two guides . . .

They started off again. The slope was less steep, but there was still quite a distance before they reached the hut. Walking on either side of Ratenelle, whom they were almost carrying, Marcel and his double strove to arrive before nightfall. Marcel's professional pride had been shaken by the accident. How come he had not reacted by stopping the stones? Why had he not taken his helmet, even for this easy climb? He glanced at the Other: he had lost consciousness briefly, and was perhaps suffering from some brain trauma. But he did not seem affected by it and was bleeding from neither nose nor ear. And their lives were indeed independent, since he, himself, had not fainted.

The descent from the Col des Cristaux to the hut had never seemed so long as on that evening. Two hours later, in the grey dust, they were still twisting their ankles on the moraine. Suddenly, Marcel felt their small group collapse. His first thought was that Ratenelle had just died, but the old man was still there, turned in on himself, neither better nor worse than before, and it was the Other who was flat on his back, with a face as white as chalk, dilated pupils, and rigid in a kind of coma. The shock must have caused a clot, now reaching the brain . . . But what could Marcel do? Go to the hut and confess that he not only had a double, but a wounded double on top of it! Unthinkable! . . .

First, he had to get Ratenelle into safety for the night. The hut was not very far now, and he could reach it without help . . .

The hut-guardian welcomed them with relief.

'I was about to send out a search party,' he said. 'I was concerned . . . I say, your client, he doesn't look too good.'

'He felt unwell near the Aiguille qui Remue,' explained Marcel. 'What a worry it has been!'

'You must have had a hell of a problem getting him down!' . . .

'He wasn't alone,' muttered Ratenelle, who, sitting at one end of the bench, seemed to have recovered his wits. 'There were two of them all the time.'

To Marcel's relief, the hut-guardian raised his eyebrows and winked at him. If Ratenelle talked, people would think he had been hallucinating. But, now, Marcel had to go out again . . .

'Look after him,' he said to the guardian. 'Give him a bit of soup, put him to bed, and tomorrow you can ask for the helicopter to get him down. He'll be all right. But I must have lost my wallet on the moraine . . . I felt something slip as I got out my handkerchief. It must have dropped then. I must find it. I'll be back.'

The pretext seemed reasonable; so Marcel took his lamp and went out again, hurrying to the spot where the Other had fallen. When he saw him in the weak light of his headtorch, he realised at once the Other was dead. Marcel nearly uttered: '*Arthcuof!*'. But, who knew whether death might not take him at the same time as that immobile carcass? Nevertheless, the circumstances were such that he had to try. Once, twice, several times. Nothing happened. The spell no longer worked in this situation, and Marcel found himself facing the unbelievable problem of making his own body disappear. What to do? Tomorrow, somebody might come this way . . . But he must have time to think . . . So, Marcel dragged the corpse into a sort of scoop below a moraine block and began to cover it with stones, making sure that no bits of anorak or boots showed.

It was quite late when he returned to the hut.

'You took your time!' said the warden. 'You found the wallet, I trust?'

'No such luck!' grumbled Marcel. 'God, it makes me sick! I'll have to go back again!'

In spite of his tiredness, he spent the night working out a plan, feeling much like that earlier night, in his childhood, when he had eventually worked out the second formula. This time too he would have to find a solution. Once again in the morning, he thought he had discovered the answer. It had been decided to helicopter Ratenelle and himself down to the valley. The weather was changing for the worse and the rain battered the hut. No one would be wandering around the moraines in these conditions. So next day, or the day after, he would go back up to the Couvercle, on the excuse of looking for his wallet, and announce that he would be going straight back down again. In fact, he would wait for nightfall near the block. He would take the Other on his back in a mountain-rescue carrying pack — it would be devilishly heavy — and go down towards the Mer de Glace by the Pierre à Béranger to avoid the Egralets where there was always a risk of meeting someone. From there, he would go to the Moulins, those sorts of holes in the ice of fathomless depth by which the melt-water pours into the bowels of the glacier. Marcel would drop his double into one of them, where he would be forever lost, buried, crushed. It was by far the best solution, nearby crevasses not offering anything like the same security.

So, two days later, Descharmoz went back up to the Couvercle. He had rehearsed all the details of the operation in his mind so often that it seemed already done. He was confident it would succeed. As planned, he waited not far from the corpse, and at ten o'clock at night lifted it on to his back and started the descent. It was a weird team, one man carrying another, completely rigid, who looked like a twin-brother, through the masses of ice and moraine which divide the Talefre glacier and the Mer de Glace. A semi-fog hung around and formed an all pervading dankness. In the light of his headtorch Marcel sought the shortest way. The Other's body weighed heavily on his shoulders. He stopped often and allowed himself a mouthful from the whisky flask he had brought for the occasion. Towards the end, when he thought he would never be able to cover the last stretch, he began counting his steps, taking a swallow at each hundredth. A strange warmth, a joy, a kind of inebriation filled his being in spite of the crushing weight. At last, close to a *moulin*, whose roar he could hear, he dropped the Other and emptied the flask, knowing he had won. Elated with alcohol, he experienced a strange feeling of unreality, as well as an increased perception of every detail, of each stone encrusted in the ice, of each sound, close or distant in the mountain, and of the night coolness on his face . . . Finally, he made himself drag his double up to the *moulin* and, with a tremendous feeling of deliverance, tipped him into the abyss.

What a mad business, thought Marcel. Perhaps he should not have drunk so much, in order to do the job in a more orderly, more solemn fashion . . . Instead, he was laughing, alone on the glacier. He wanted to shout his adventure to the whole world. He was reliving every episode, from the surprise in the barn to this ultimate liberation. Now it was just a bad dream. And all because of one word, an absurd word . . .

'Fouchtra!' he shouted to every echo in the mountains.

He suddenly felt completely sober. The Other, or Another, had reappeared not far from him and was staring at him, threateningly . . .

Translated by Daniel Roberts and John Wilkinson

INTRUSION

The spaceship was approaching in rapid oscillations. It did not look like a flying saucer and still less a cigar, but rather — in so far as it is possible to compare the incomparable — an arborescent fern. Three interlaced vibrating antennae unwound themselves every few moments, one pointing towards the Earth's centre of gravity, the other towards the magnetic pole and the third towards Galaxy M64 of Berenice's Hair. Reaching a certain distance from the sun, it became enveloped in a purple glow, then proceeded to emit a sudden cloud of anti-photons rendering it totally invisible.

In any case, Alexis La Billaude had not seen it, being too absorbed in free-climbing down an unexpectedly smooth 'gendarme', traversing a loose gap and finally stancing, to secure his rope on a large block that at last offered a bit of security. Strange that the forecast should have promised good weather, for the sky was overcast, the sun nowhere to be seen and a bitter north wind whistled across the breach like air in an organ-pipe.

'Come on!' he shouted to his climbing partner, Didier. He settled himself a little more comfortably and let his glance wander over the sea of clouds that filled the valley. After all, it could well be that the weather was going to hold, cloudy lower down and clearing further up? In any case, they would know soon enough . . . Alexis La Billaude was not the worrying type . . .

The rope was still not moving. But all he had to do was wait. It would soon slacken and Alexis would see the red rucksack, the corduroy backside and Vibram soles of Didier Nozeroy appear at the top of the large 'gendarme'. He was taking his time! The worthy Didier must be answering a call of nature, these sort of things happen — to the intellectual as well as to others — taking off the sack, then putting it back on, it all takes time . . .

'Hurry up? I'm freezing!' he shouted, amiably enough, before returning to his contemplation of the sea of clouds.

And as a little later still, nothing appeared, he yelled out: 'Hey! What's happening? C'mon!'

'Get on with it!'

'Pull your finger out, Didier!'

'Hey! Are you all right? Oy!'

'Di-dier!'

The rope finally began to quiver but what appeared at the top of the gendarme was so horrible that Alexis, who was by no means a faint-hearted person, could not suppress a howl of terror. What was descending towards the gap was not the red sack and the familiar corduroy backside, but a sort of vaguely fluorescent yellow foam, a pulpy magma, fluffy, puffy and dripping, within which alternately gaped and closed air holes, pustules, pimples, alveoli, cankers and ventricles . . .

'I'm going nuts,' stammered Alexis . . . 'What's happening? . . . What on earth's going on? . . .'

Gripped by nausea, he shut his eyes for a moment. When he opened them again the yellow foam was approaching the gap, and, in one of its ventricles, Didier's boot made a sudden appearance. Alexis could not bear the sight of it, he rushed to seize it and attempted to grab his companion but the boot seemed to be no longer attached to a body and the decaying mess was so viscous to the touch that he let go almost immediately.

The yellow foam now almost filled the entire gap and its surface trembled like boiling lava. A more active area appeared in the top left-hand corner and, all of a sudden, burst with a great 'plop' to reveal a pustule in the form of a human mouth that said: 'Here-we-are!'

Alexis was paralysed with horror. He shut his eyes once more, finally he articulated 'Didier . . . What have you done with Didier?'

'Di-gest-ed!' was the reply, 'Di-gest-ed-for-sci-ence. We-space-pros-pect-ors-of-in-ter-sid-er-eal-space-must-di-gest-a-nat-ive-in-the-course-of-our-ex-plo-r-ations-in-or-der-to-as-sim-il-ate-the-lang-uage-and-then-make-con-tact-with-its-ho-mo-logue-to-learn-all-ab-out-his-plan-et-and-the-supreme-auth-or-ity-that-gov-erns-us-uses-our-sub-seq-uent-re-ports-to-dir-ect-op-er-ations . . . speak!'

'Didier!' moaned Alexis . . . 'Didi! . . . It can't be true! It's not possible! Hey! Didier. Answer me . . .'

'We-are-tel-ling-you . . .' the pustule replied . . .

Didier Nozeroy and Alexis La Billaude had set off that very same morning on a long ridge route that looked like being a magnificent one, four days planned high in the mountains, three bivouacs at altitude, far from the valley and all its complications . . . The plan was to climb the Flammes de Pierre, continue by the Drus and by the Sans Nom Ridge, reach the summit of the Aiguille Verte, traverse the Droites, the Courtes and to end up at the Triolet. The start had been promising, in the wild setting of the Flammes de Pierre, they had climbed without wasting time and with great efficiency, both in good physical shape and perfect harmony. Alexis was especially aware of this after all the problems he had had: his fall on the North Face of the Plan two years ago, miraculously halted before the final drop, followed by hours in the sun, with a fractured skull. Hospital, his friends looking at him sympathetically and asking each other as they left: 'Is he going to remain mad, do you think?'

'Mad? . . . He's not really mad . . . You have to bear in mind that even before he wasn't all there . . .'

'Even so, that laugh of his when he saw us coming . . .'

For to tell the truth, Alexis had never been considered as being blessed with a high intelligence quotient. He was a tall red-headed lad, strongly built with legs like tree trunks and great mits for hands, a huge jaw and a smaller forehead topped by close-cropped hair, in defiance of all fashion.

'Long hair. It would drain my brain!' he would say, laughing heartily.

People liked him for his spontaneity and his kindness and made fun of his naïvety, his unsubtle hints and his famous thundering laugh. His anger was explosive and his repentance sudden. He never had a steady job and, in the autumn, would take the first work that came along. Labourer, removal man, truck driver, cable-car attendant in turn, he asked but one thing: to be able to drop everything in June, to leave, put up his tent in the mountains and climb — a passion that he had acquired in a holiday camp when he was barely a teenager.

The previous summer — following the year of his accident — had been a difficult one. Alexis had arrived in Chamonix at the start of a long rainy spell. One evening in the cinema, he had heard some casual acquaintances who were sitting in the row in front and had not noticed his presence, speak of him as 'really batty now'. Leaning over the seats, he had set upon the originators of this malicious remark . . . The usherette had called the police and everyone had ended up at the police station . . . And a little later on in the season, Alexis had set off into the mountains with Raymond Grésin, a climber riddled with complexes, who worked off his frustrations all along the route, peppering his companion with jibes. In this instance too, the whole business ended unhappily . . .

And then the world had been set to rights with Didier Nozeroy's entry on to the scene. Yet never had a climbing partnership brought together two more disparate personalities: as cerebral as Alexis was muscular, as sociable as he was taciturn, as expansive as he was placid, Didier seethed with ideas, ambitions and knowledge. In the mountains he would plot his routes meticulously, study at length the possibilities of first ascents, consult weather charts, missing none of the pressure variations shown by altimeter, write up endless route notes on his return ... People watched ironically as they set off together and were astonished when they returned perfectly good friends. They complemented each other admirably and Alexis was touched beyond words by the thoughtfulness of Didier, who had let him lead on the first difficult passages, encouraged him, congratulated him, restored his confidence. No one could buck him up in the same way with his: 'Well done, old man! ... There aren't many climbers like you! ...'

That is why this season had begun so well, reuniting them once more in a climbing partnership. Didier was like a brother!

Didier ...

The exchange, from the yellow foam's point of view, had not been fruitful. There was nothing to be got from this idiot when questioned as to whether or not the inhabitants of his planet knew about the wheel, nuclear fusion, the Philosopher's Stone, interstellar navigation, telepathic irradiation or gravitational sublimation. These basic necessities were obviously the last things on his mind ... The simplest information had only been obtained with difficulty:

'What-were-you-do-ing?'

'Well, we were going up! We were going up the ridge of the Flammes de Pierre and then we were going to continue the ridge ...'

'What-for?'

'Well, nothing, of course! For pleasure ... To descend at the other end.'

'For-what-rea-son?'

'Well, none! ... No reason, I told you! ... Just to do it and then go back down ...'

'Were-you-ex-plor-ers?'

'Of course not. I'm telling you that no one gives a damn whether or not it serves any purpose ... There've been plenty of others who've been along here before us ... Are you thick or what? ... And now give me back Didier ...'

Then Alexis found himself alone, suddenly. He had just glimpsed a violet dazzle and a great whirlwind in the sky above him. All was as before, the pale sky, the sea of clouds covering the valley, the granite ridge ... But a length of orange nylon rope, frayed and melted, hung from his belt and Didier was no longer there . . .

Alexis had waited a long time, for hours probably, before abandoning all hope and finally considering his own fate. The descent looked bad because they had already gone high up the ridge and the twenty feet or so of rope that he had left was of scant help and soon had to be abandoned to reach the foot of an overhanging crack. Risking an accident a hundred times over, on smooth rounded slabs, in icy gullys, in loose chimneys, he bivouacked — numb with cold and despondency — on an uncomfortable ledge. Next morning Alexis finally reached the moraines, the glacier, the familiar paths of men.

He arrived at the campsite, his face puffed with fatigue.

'What? Back already!' exclaimed a neighbouring camper. 'Couldn't you do it? Where's Didier?'

'Dead!' stammered Alexis holding back his tears.

'Dead! Oh no! Where? How? . . . Sorry for asking, friend, but it's so terrible . . . Is there anything we can do? Should we call the rescue? . . . You're quite sure he's dead?'

'Oh yes I'm sure!' mumbled Alexis.

'Come on, in any case, we must do something! . . . Notify the police . . . I don't know . . . We'll come with you, come on then, let's go!'

'Grönnbchtillyorzdxortbkankdchmmustrrkolystkboung . . .,' sighed the yellow foam. 'Zgrummbloyddgzfrraikgdongjokch?'

'Bpchhtkroynk!' replied his flight companion amiably, absorbed in manoeuvring the spaceship . . .

As we fear, however, that the reader will not master all the common idioms of the Hair of Berenice, we will retranscribe here as faithful an interpretation as possible of the dialogue:

'Ex-plo-ration-of-space-is-the-ea-sy-part.   It-is-the-fil-ling-in-of-forms-af-ter-wards,' sighed the yellow foam. 'What-the-hell-am-I-to-put-in-my-re-port?' 'That's-not-my-pro-blem!' his crew-mate replied amiably, absorbed in manoeuvering the spaceship . . . 'You-'ve-ma-de-a-balls-of-it. You-sh-ould-have-di-ges-ted-the-o-ther-one . . .'

'They-ta-ste-aw-ful!' groaned the former. 'I-would-like-to-see-you-try . . . Dis-gust-ing! I-will-nev-er-for-get-it! To-di-gest-a-se-cond-one! We-must-com-pose-the-re-port-so-as-to-blur-the-facts . . . In-any-case-this-pla-net-is-ob-vious-ly-of-no-in-ter-est . . . Clim-bing-up-in-order-to-go-back-down . . . That-takes-the-bis-cuit!'

'Chief! Could you come here for a moment?' said Lieutenant Caramany tersely . . . 'There's a climber in my office who says his friend's been gobbled up by a Martian . . .'

Captain Estagel repressed a shudder. As if he did not already have enough on his plate with traffic accidents, climbing accidents, chalet burglaries, the Tour de France route, supermarket thefts, parking meter sabotages, sex scandals, drugs, Tunnel police . . .

'And here's yet another!' he grumbled . . . 'People watch too much television!'

And, with a grimace of disgust, he went into the next-door office.

'But I know this chap!' he exclaimed. 'We've already had dealings with him — last year . . . He's violent!'

In a flash the story became quite clear to him. Tempers quickly get heated at altitude . . . Yes, that was it, he and his companion must have quarrelled, come to blows, an accident happened and now this idiot was trying to concoct some rubbish to absolve himself from blame.

'What a fool!' the Captain thought. 'He could have come to see us with some straightforward story about a climbing accident and it would've been processed like a letter through the post, whereas this wild explanation . . .'

'Right. Let's start again!' he said drily. 'What were you telling Lieutenant Caramany?'

Alexis La Billaude sniffed with irritation. 'But as I've already told him . . .'

'No matter! Recommence!' interjected the Captain.

Long speeches were not La Billaude's forte, and still less when in the state of fatigue, emotion and grief that he was in today. He started again slowly:

'We were on the Flammes de Pierre Ridge . . . We wanted to do the Drus, the Sans Nom, the Verte and the whole caboodle including the Triolet . . . It was going well . . . I was leading . . . I had climbed a large gendarme, crossed a gap and belayed astride a small gendarme . . .'

He suddenly stopped, worried by a sense of incongruity.

'That's what they're called . . .' he explained with an anxious glance.

'I know! I know! I'm perfectly familiar with moutaineering terminology,' Captain Estagel said coldly. 'Continue!'

'I was sitting astride . . . a large block!' sighed La Billaude.

He stopped once again, satisfied with himself. It was what was known as a clever correction. Didier Nozeroy himself would not have found a better.

'Go on!' the Captain said again impatiently, unaware of the verbal effort of his interlocutor.

'I waited and waited . . . and then I saw coming . . . like a Martian . . .'

'A little green man?' the Captain asked sarcastically.

'Oh no! Not green ... yellow rather ... and not a little man ... more like vomit ... boiling vomit ... and inside I saw one of Didier's boots ...'

His voice caught in his throat. Captain Estagel looked at him with greater sympathy. After all, whatever might have happened, it could not be denied that this chap was genuinely upset. Maybe it was a real accident and sorrow had addled the survivor's brain. His mental state would have to be checked.

Bad weather had returned to the Mont Blanc massif and hampered the search for Didier Nozeroy's body. Jammed in an overhanging crack way off the proper route, a short length of orange rope, frayed and melted, went unnoticed by anyone and was gradually covered by a layer of ice.

Several light years away, a spaceship, shaped like an arborescent fern, travelled through space in search of inhabited worlds to subjugate ...

'Mountain rescue is the easy part. It's filling in of forms afterwards ...' sighed Lieutenant Caramany. 'What the hell am I going to put in my report?'

'That's not my problem!' his colleague replied amiably, absorbed in assembling the facts regarding the investigation of the planting of a plastic bomb on the motorway viaduct.

'Re-port-from-the-space-ship-B-G-Z-2-0-7-9-for-the-at-en-tion-of-the-Sup-reme-Auth-ority-of-Gal-axy-M64-of-the-Hair-of-Beren-ice.Noth-ing-of-note-to-rep-ort.Have-found-only-one-in-ha-bi-ted-pla-net.Di-gest-ed-one-in-divi-dual-and-est-abl-ish-ed-con-tact-with-his-ho-mo-logue.Lin-guis-tic-le-vel-in-ter-est-ing.Sci-enti-fic-le-vel-low.Ci-vil-isa-tion-and-ment-al-le-vel-zero.Found-them-pull-ing-up-the-heights-of-their-world-with-no-other-aim-than-that-of-go-ing-back-down-a-gain.Dec-ided-pop-ul-ation-use-less-our-plans,-con-tin-uing-ex-plor-ation-other-spa-ces.'

'Sound-de-ci-sion,' wired the Supreme Authority of Galaxy M64 of the Hair of Berenice, who then exclaimed to herself: 'In-cred-ible! Clim-bing-up-in-order-to-go-back-down.We-will-cert-ainly-have-to-rec-og-nise-one-day-the-fact-that-we-are-the-only-sen-sible-be-ings-in-the-uni-verse!'

'National Police Station

Preliminary Investigation Report.

Year nineteen hundred and ......, 15th July.

We, Estagel Philippe, Captain, head of the Chamonix Division; Caramany Dominique, Police Lieutenant, officers of the judicial police.

With respect to articles 16 to 19 and 75 of the Code of Criminal Procedure report on the following operations ...

On 8th July . . . at 16.20 hours, we were alerted by La Billaude Alexis, that a fatal accident had befallen his companion Nozeroy Didier on 7th July 19. . in the course of their ascent of the Flammes de Pierre Ridge. The accident occurred near the summit of the ridge, not far from the Aiguille du Dru in a rocky gap at an altitude of approximately 3,200 metres.

The search-parties led by the Alpine Police Squad comprising Lieutenant Saint-Féliu and police officers Fenestret and Alénya, dropped by the Civil Protection helicopter in this area in the late afternoon, and then again the following day, produced no result. Bad weather prevented further search. The body must have fallen into a couloir running down the ridge of the Flammes de Pierre and been lost in a bergschrund at the bottom. A rock-fall could have caused the accident and would have been responsible for the severing of the rope and the fall of the victim.

On the 8th July, and again on the 10th, we questioned La Billaude Alexis Charles Pierre, twenty-five years old, unskilled labourer, currently unemployed, residing at 176 Avenue Balthazar Bosca, 93240, Stains. The witness, very upset by the event, seems to have suffered various hallucinations following the accident, but we confirmed that he was not in a state of intoxication nor under the influence of drugs. He had already sustained a cranial injury two years ago following another climbing accident, as borne out by the enclosed hospital report. We had him examined by Dr Pothuau, psychiatrist at Annemasse Hospital, whose report is also enclosed, and who acknowledges the defendant's sincerity, but also notes a marked tendency to hallucinatory delirium following the above-mentioned cranial injury.

Missing person: Nozeroy Didier Philippe Amédée, born 6th April 19 . . . at 33110 — Le Bouscat, French national, engineer, resident at 95 Avenue du Pape Clément — 33200 — Caudéran . . .

Climbing has lost one of its most promising partnerships. Didier Nozeroy, having been officially declared missing, Alexis La Billaude — who has no idea that he saved Earth from the most terrible of catastrophes — has given up climbing for three reasons. He has lost the best of all climbing partners and knows that he will never find his equal. He would not be given the chance, in any case, for although he had been cleared by the investigation, he remains under a vague cloud of suspicion that discourages anyone from going on a route with him. Finally, it must be added, he is afraid of Martians.

Translated by Siobhān Anderson and John Wilkinson

THE BASKET

In every climber's life there are particularly painful moments, when one learns about an accident to an acquaintance, a friend, someone close. I've been through a number of them myself and been deeply affected since the victims are nearly always in their prime, bursting with vitality. More so than with any other death, their sudden disappearance leaves an impression of irreparable injustice.

The bad news may come in many ways, through a conversation, a letter, a phone call, a radio or television announcement, a newspaper article . . . but the shock is always the same, followed by the same absurd desire to hear the facts denied. Even worse is when the news terminates a period of uncertainty, and flickering hopes are finally dashed by the fatal outcome.

But the most intense experience of this kind I have ever been through was caused by a basket.

It was, of course, a hut basket, one of the lidless wicker baskets lined up on shelves in the main room of the hut and whose role in the life of a climber is privileged as well as humble, anonymous yet familiar. When a pair of climbers reaches a hut, their first concern is to get hold of an empty basket into which they can empty out food, clothing and climbing gear from their rucksacks. This allows them to find their breakfast things early in the morning when they get up, and to prepare the gear they need for leaving the hut: gaiters, anoraks, gloves, rope, harnesses, helmets. For one night, the basket contains all that is most precious for a person, belongings on which his very life may depend next day . . . And if it is planned to come back via the hut, the basket can be used to leave extra food and gear not actually needed on the climb.

I usually take my holiday in August, but that particular year I had to put it off for nearly a month, and so I took advantage of the long 14th of July weekend to escape from the city and spend four days in the Alps. Almost immediately I bumped into Julien Pillebois, one of my best friends but someone I don't see often enough since his moving to teach at a school in Valence. I immediately asked him if he planned to spend the summer in the valley as usual.

'No' he answered. 'I'm going to Greece! But in the meantime, I'm giving the mountains all I've got. Then I'll be off for the sun, the beaches, the ruins, shish-kebabs, Mediterranean wine . . . Some friends of mine have rented a boat. We're meeting in Marseilles on the morning of August 1st. Watch out! Between now and then, my list of routes will have got quite a bit longer!

It's easy to imagine my surprise, therefore, when, arriving at the Malafretaz Hut at the beginning of September with Martin Jouvençon and pulling out a basket, I saw in it pegs marked with a double mauve bar. That's how Pillebois marks his gear and I can't say why, but I immediately felt uneasy. The basket's remaining contents — packages of instant soup and orange drink, a chocolate bar, a gas stove cartridge — were quite anonymous, with the exception of a beige sweater which I vaguely remembered seeing Julien wear. As I indiscretely shuffled through the contents in the bottom of the basket, I came upon a guide-book which confirmed my suspicions — my friend's name was written inside the front cover.

As I said, an unpleasant feeling had taken hold of me without my being able to pin-point the reason. There might be a perfectly simple explanation! Julien hadn't gone to Greece and had continued his climbing season. What could be more straightforward? Anyway . . . I kept an eye out for him and looked up every time the door opened, a rare enough event for the Malafretaz Hut is little used. That evening we were only eight — four Scottish, two Spanish, and us two — the hut isn't guarded. Jouvençon had never met Pillebois. Once I'd told him how I'd taken down a basket whose contents belonged to someone I knew, someone who should have been in Greece, there seemed to be nothing much more to explain the vague feeling of unease that had come over me.

About eight o'clock in the evening everybody went to bed. Martin and I were at the end of the bunk. The Scottish climbers had opened the window and let in the cold night air. I regretted having taken only one blanket, I wasn't warm enough to fall asleep. One of the Spaniards snored . . . All sorts of ideas chased through my head, and I grew increasingly nervy, as the time passed without sleeping, of not being on form the next day, and also about Pillebois' absence. Suddenly a thought crossed my mind. Doubtless it had been developing unconsciously during the evening and was the source of my inexplicable uneasiness: mightn't the equipment have been there since July? . . . 'I'm giving it all I've got,' Julien had said, or something like that. If he'd had an accident? The more I thought about it, the more it seemed likely. No guardian to report that a party had failed to return. And the basket?

Someone would have had to know Pillebois like me to recognise his belongings at first glance ... In the valley, it would have been easy to suppose that he'd gone to Marseilles as planned ... And not seeing him arrive, his friends in Marseilles would have left without him, merely surprised that he hadn't called to let them know ... I drew a hand across my forehead and felt the perspiration. How could I find out? ... The answer came to me like a flash of light: the hut-book! Perhaps Pillebois had written something in it. I got up as quietly as possible and started towards the door. Trust me to have left my headtorch in my basket. I bumped into rucksacks, shoes, and must have woken up half the sleepers who grunted irritably. Eventually I reached the door, fumbled for the handle and slipped into the main room.

After I'd groped around to find my lighter and got the ceiling gas-lamp going, I began searching for the hut register, a large log-book covered in black cloth. It fell open at the page marked August lst of that year and I only had to turn back one page to find the entry I was looking for: 28th July, 19. ., Julien Pillebois, Valence, GHM, departure solo for Mont Revel North Face.

My worst suspicions were confirmed. I passed a long moment, numbed by my discovery ... Julien! His smile, his *joie de vivre*, his passionate enthusiasm for everything he did ... I could see the sparkle in his eyes and the funny frown he made just before breaking into a laugh ... I could hear the sound of his voice ... The sun ... The Mediterranean wine ... Poor Julien, he'd never got to see Greece ... And I was undoubtedly the first to know. Otherwise the belongings in the basket would have been taken back down ... He didn't write often and his family would not have been surprised by not hearing from him ... Poor, poor Julien!

Thus I pondered sadly as I sat with my head in my hands before that page of the hut-book. I finally shook myself. In spite of everything, I had to think about getting some sleep and doubtless carrying on with doing the route as planned with my partner. After a month there was no hope of rescuing Julien, and as for the rest, the next evening was early enough to alert the police ...

So I decided to go back to bed, and after turning out the lamp, braved again and just as clumsily the mine-field of the dormitory floor, then slid into my place. Still sleep would not come. It was past midnight. I was thinking of Julien, of our last conversation. Emotion choked me. How stupid to die in this way, so young, for what was really nothing ... Fatigue finally got the upper hand and I must have dozed off for a while. A sound woke me. I began thinking of Julien again, turning over the terrible business in my mind. I gave up trying to get back to sleep and decided to pass the remaining hour — it was two o'clock and we were to get up at three — by returning to the main room and making myself a cup of coffee. This time not only did I stumble over the scattered gear, but I caught my foot in a loop of rope and noisily regained my balance. Multilingual mutterings warned me, as though it were necessary, that my nocturnal prowlings were increasingly unpopular.

With renewed precaution I approached the door. A ray of light shone beneath it, but exhausted as I was, it didn't strike me as being unusual. I passed quickly through into the main room, closed the latch, turned around and barely managed to stifle a scream.

Straight in front of me, gaunt and pale in the dim light stood Julien Pillebois.

— 'You! Julien! You! Thank God!,' I stuttered foolishly. Julien's partner must have found my words singularly stupid and he slyly winked at my friend and tapped his index finger unpleasantly against his temple.

As for Julien, he seemed completely indifferent to my outpourings of friendship.

— 'Do you know many climbers,' he said somewhat drily, 'who finish the traverse of the Aiguilles Marboz before nightfall? When did you expect us to arrive, for afternoon tea?'

— 'But Greece?' I started tentatively.

— 'What about Greece? I spent three weeks there as planned, then I came back. What's the matter? You're absolutely livid!'

I didn't dare explain . . . All those silly suppositions . . . The basket . . . The hut book . . . The climb on the 28th of July . . . Wild imaginings, that was all! But I felt unfairly treated by someone on whom I'd just spent so much emotion. It was hard to regain my composure.

— 'Listen,' I announced as the two men crunched some biscuits before going to bed, 'in honour of your traverse of the Aiguilles Marboz, you're invited to have dinner anywhere you like when we're all back down!'

I got the impression that I may have risen a bit in the esteem of Julien's partner though my sanity remained a questionable affair. As for Julien, his face puckered into that funny frown I'd thought of earlier, his eyes sparkled . . . and I joined in when he burst into laughter.

Translated by Linda Collinge and John Wilkinson

LIBERATION!

A parable (from an idea by Alfred Sauvy)

Having gained some knowledge of geology, hydrology and glaciology, mankind imagined — in its usual way — that it knew all, or almost all, about the mountains. In this, mankind was much mistaken. For the mountains were not just heaps of rock, formed by orogenesis in primeval times and covered by glaciers or eternal snows. The whole point about the mountains was that they had minds, or . . . how can I put it? . . . they had souls; each had its vital spark, its own individual spirit. The rest was only for show.

Nor was science alone in error. Folk wisdom, so-called, was equally wide of the mark in coining proverbs to the effect that mountains never meet. As a matter of fact, mountains do meet, or at least they used to meet at the time when this story begins. They did not actually shift their great masses of rock and ice about the place, of course, but their minds frequently met in agreeable social gatherings, usually held on some high plateau or lofty peak. Here they would talk, hold discussions, even gossip, about anything and everything: the weather, erosion, last winter's snows, glaciation, how best to avoid getting badly cracked by the frost . . .

'You should just see my bergschrund these days!' remarked one of them. 'It would hold the entire Jetoula Ridge!'

'Amazing!' replied another. 'Bergschrunds are gaping particularly wide this year, and that's a fact. I'm going through a most unusual experience myself! Believe it or not, my North Ridge, which is always covered with snow, is completely bare at the moment . . .'

'You don't say!' exclaimed the first. 'Listen, everyone, have you heard what's happened to the Piz Bernina?'

And so on, and so forth. They talked about the chamois which had leaped a supposedly insuperable precipice. They chuckled over the shapes of the marmots' burrows. They told each other when the jackdaws' eggs were about to hatch. They exchanged news of the flights of butterflies and the migration of swallows. They waxed sentimental over the moss-campion with its pretty little tufted clumps, sprinkled with pink flowers, which could cling to the rock even at the highest altitudes.

No, there was never any shortage of subjects of conversation! And anyway they were all fond of each other, and it was so nice to meet . . .

When humans arrived in the high alpine valleys they were welcomed with the customary goodwill of the mountains, who viewed them with kindness and amusement. To think that large as they were, they were far less bold than hares or marmots! They dared not come too close! They distrusted everything above the altitude at which their cattle could graze! They even claimed that the mountains were accursed places! Accursed! The finest works in all Creation!

Men entrenched themselves as best they could in their smoke-filled huts and forbade their children to go wandering off towards the moraines. Consequently, you could observe them only from a distance, but they were interesting all the same, and sometimes good for a laugh.

Then, gradually, they became less timid. Of course there had already been some exceptions, but the exception, as they say, only proves the rule. These exceptions had included that oddity of a Carthaginian general who crossed the Alps with his army and his enormous elephants! And Antoine de Ville, who took it into his head to scale Mont Aiguille, no less! And Gessner, who went up Mount Pilatus just for fun, to see what went on at the top of it!

But now men in general were getting bolder. They hunted chamois. They even climbed really high and scraped your crust looking for crystal caves. The damage was not too bad; the frost did worse! And they took only such a tiny part of your hidden treasures, those billions of amethyst and quartz crystals sealed for all eternity into the shadowy sides of the needles of rock. All these new departures, therefore, were regarded as good entertainment.

Then men became more and more enterprising. The Buet and Mont Vélan found they had been climbed before they knew it. It took them a little time to adjust to the fact, but then they became rather proud of it, announcing that it was a great privilege for them, the adventure had enriched them, it was to be hoped that all other mountains would benefit from the same experience — and meanwhile, they set up as experts on all questions concerning humanity.

'It tickles!' Mont Vélan confided to his closest friends.

The notion that they might be conquered was still amusing some mountains and causing anxiety to others when that character Saussure turned up, bent on climbing everywhere with his measuring instruments. How he made them laugh! But then he and his friends seemed to be setting their sights on Mont Blanc . . .

'They'll get you yet!' Mont Blanc's friends told him.

'No, they won't!' he said. 'It's impossible! Not even a chamois has ever reached my summit. You lot are out of your minds! After all, I'm the highest!'

But Mont Blanc was conquered after all! Not just once, but again and again! Everyone seemed to want to climb him simply because he *was* the highest. That was a funny idea if you like! The chamois had never discriminated in such an illogical way. They climbed for pleasure at their own sweet will. It was far from clear what pleasure men got out of it. They sweated, panted, gasped, groaned and swore in their efforts to reach the top, and once they were up they seemed to be in a tremendous hurry to get down again!

Mont Blanc never became as reconciled to being climbed as the Buet and Mont Vélan. To avoid losing face, so to speak, he agreed with the others that it was a normal and indeed an interesting experience, but he never sounded very enthusiastic, and it was suspected that certain fatal avalanches which fell from his flanks were not due solely to thaws or poor cohesion between the seracs of glaciers.

And the ascents went on. More and more humans came to the mountains every year. They anchored little huts to the islands of rock among the snow and ice. They obviously felt it was a great thing to climb a peak no one else had ever scaled before, even if the peak in question was not as high, handsome and strong as its neighbours. Once they used to count the mountains they had climbed; soon they were counting those they had not. Only a few little peaks, far away on remote ridges and with nothing to draw them to the attention of climbers, escaped the common fate. One of these exceptions was Gendarme 3037, who put on great airs over his own virginity.

'Unsullied as I am . . .' Gendarme 3037 was always saying.

'All right, all right, we know!' said the other mountains.

In fact the first disagreements between the mountains arose over humans, since it was difficult not to take sides in the matter. There were rifts; interminable discussions began and were actually fostered by human ways of thinking, sophistry, prejudices and acrimony.

Some mountains remained well disposed to men, and went to some lengths to provide them with good weather. They held their rockfalls and avalanches back, they closed up their crevasses, they made their spangled snows shine in the sunlight and moonlight. Some of them even occasionally pushed handholds or footholds out a little way at the crucial moment.

Others, however, took a diametrically opposite attitude and wei
downright hostile. The imaginative reader will easily guess what dama
might ensue. These mountains had dreaded the 'first time' from the sta
and defended their approaches fiercely. Everyone knows, to mention b
one case, of the tragedies that occurred on the Matterhorn. With all dt
respect for the facts, it must be reported that in the face of general indignatic
some mountains — for instance the Eiger, the Aiguille Verte and the Aiguil
du Requin — began keeping a tally of their deaths and even, it has to I
confessed, competed with each other! This was frowned upon, but they to
no notice.

'Eight at a go! Good ones too!' one mountain announced.

'That's not what counts,' retorted another mountain. 'That's just a on
off. The seasonal total is what matters!'

And thus, day by day, each mountain forged itself a personality and
doctrine which it meant to enforce at any price. The 'hawks' were opposed
the 'doves', and in the long run the latter became just as difficult to deal wi
not to say dangerous, as the former.

'We must be available to everyone,' they explained, endlessly. 'The or
mountaineering that counts today is mountaineering for the masses. Let
have no more of that odious élitism whereby only a chosen few were once a
to enjoy the icy air of our peaks! In the name of individual liberties and tl
democratic equality which will allow the climbing masses to rule society so
day, we must encourage the assertive struggle which will lead to justice a
brotherhood! We want to be available to everyone, and accordingly we call
the permanent construction of new huts, new cable-cars, new lifts, new trac
new roads, and non-stop free helicopter flights. We shall struggle to ens
that everything possible is done to allow human beings, all human bein
even those who would never have thought of it, even those who don't want
to climb us *en masse* in a great popular movement!'

'You must be joking!' interrupted Gendarme 3037. 'Allow me to tell y
unsullied as I have always remained —'

'Here we go again!' said the Yatagan, cuttingly.

A small group formed, with the aim of restoring harmony. Its princi
members were such saintly souls as the Doigt de Dieu, the Père Eternel,
Aiguille du Saint Esprit, the Vierge, the Gran Paradiso and the Petit Para
the Col de l'Ange, the Brèche de Chérubins, the Cardinal, the Evêq
the Nonne, the Mönch, the Capucin, the Enfant de Choeur and the Péleri

No one will be surprised to hear that their fiercest, indeed their most cussed opponents included the Aiguilles du Diable, the Mont Maudit and the Roc du Soufre.

Yet again, human activity made its influence felt: once a cross or a statue of the Virgin had been set up on such peaks as the Matterhorn, the Dru, the Grépon, Mont Blanc du Tacul or the Dent du Géant, their original characters changed and they became complex creatures torn between natural aggression and piety, the latter being often of a very edifying nature.

Few remained neutral, and soon the only mountains left in that category were the Agneaux, the Col du Bonhomme and the Aiguille du Tricot, whose placid temperaments still resisted all impassioned argument.

I could go on forever about the different personalities that emerged where once all was loving friendship and sweet reason. The Col du Geant took advantage of his size to bully the Petit Capucin. The Grand Flambeau made inflammatory remarks about the Chandelle. The Guêpe said stinging things to the Mouche. The Dôme du Goûter tabled a claim to the Pain de Sucre and the Brioche. The Peigne threatened Tête Rousse with a good dressing-down, while Mont Tondu had a close shave in his argument with the Rasoir. The Deux Aigles each had an eagle eye on ownership of the Bec d'Oiseau. The Dames Anglaises pursed their lips up in a very ladylike way when they encountered the Aiguille du Pissoir. There was open war between the Roi de Siam and the République. The Couturier cut up rough when only his claim to own the Ciseaux was allowed, and extended the thread of his argument to claiming every needle of rock in the Alps! The Râteau raked up an old grievance against the Aiguille du Jardin, and the Clocher and Minaret were forever ringing the changes in their disputes. The Echiquier made a play for the Domino. The Epée, the Coup de Sabre and the Yatagan were at daggers drawn. In short, it was goodbye to the happy days of the past!

When the mountains met, there was no more of the friendly atmosphere of old times. Animated proposals, fierce opposition and acid exchanges were the order of the day.

Some of the more progressive spirits suggested that meetings could no longer be held in the old, traditional way: informally, without rhyme or reason. That viewpoint seemed so obvious that it was immediately adopted, with a semblance of general reconciliation. Agendas were drawn up, elections were held, there were chairmountains, advisory meetings, general meetings, commissions and enquiries, plans and planning officers, delegations, study centres, research institutes, conferences, action committees, liaison reports, congresses, seminars and symposiums.

There was also talk of organisation, of new forms of collective encounters, concrete actions, a common strategy, objectives, co-ordination, appeals, ways and means, procedures, development and priorities.

And things went on no better than before.

Matters had reached this point when the world of humanity was shaken by the riots that came to be known as 'the events' of May 1968, and although mankind emerged relatively easily from that particular phase of its growing pains, the effect on the mountains went far deeper. Invaded the following summer by hundreds of students and lecturers endlessly discussing the affair, they echoed and re-echoed to the sound of fanatical debate which fuelled further interminable arguments.

In fact, like those great dinosaurs which failed to survive modifications of their environment to which dragonflies adapted with ease, the high peaks were unable to solve problems easily surmounted by puny men.

The wind of debate blew more fiercely than the föhn moaning among the great pines, or the north wind swirling up powdery snow on the ridges. Overcome by a vast discontentment, the mountains began questioning the most firmly established of values. The sun, the snow and the clouds were criticised in a manner no one would even have dreamed of a few years earlier.

However, it was the Aiguilles Rouges who really saw red and kindled the torch of revolution. Until now they had been reasonably happy with their modest role on the lower side of the Chamonix valley. But now the low altitudes, aesthetic mediocrity and lack of glaciers to which they had always resigned themselves suddenly struck them as intolerable. In the most violent of terms, they demanded equality for all mountains, aspiring to put an end to what they described as the imperialism and triumphalism of the big peaks.

The Becs Rouges, the Cheval Rouge, the Pointe des Boeufs Rouges, the Rouges du Dolent, the Sentinelle Rouge and the Zinal Rothorn soon joined them in a great movement of revolutionary solidarity. At a private meeting, arranged with the utmost mysterious secrecy to show how important the matter was, they decided to launch the struggle for the Revolution. The question was, who were they revolting against? Some thought the Roi de Siam and the Reine de l'Echiquier would be suitable targets, but they lacked a certain something because of their modest dimensions. Declaring war on

Mont Blanc or all mountains above the four-thousand-metre mark seemed a nobler aim — an aim, as one might say, more suited to the aspirations of the oppressed mountainous masses — but the Sentinelle Rouge, whose personal interests were involved, flatly refused to have Mont Blanc dragged into it. It was therefore decided that they would simply prepare the offensive, and decide who it was to be against later.

The situation thus came to the attention of the Aiguille Sans Nom, who had always felt rather embarrassed by his anonymity in the company of other mountains. He lacked that sense of identity which a name confers, and had therefore recently conceived a dull resentment, which he was unable to express, when circumstances made him an outright anarchist. The business was bound up with the personal development of a young man of good background who had failed in his studies, and followed Bakunin's example by having recourse to a profound scorn for society in general and the examinations it sets in particular. He had taken a couple of like-minded companions to the mountains with him, and as he had deliberately neglected to listen to the weather forecasts, and bad weather had taken a violent hand in things, the three daring young men found themselves snowbound for three days and four nights on the top of the Aiguille Sans Nom, owing their survival only to a highly efficient rescue organisation which they deplored on principle, although not to the point of refusing its services.

'All's Well That Ends Well', said the newspaper headlines – or alternatively, 'No Lasting Effects on Young Climbers' Imprudence'. But there had indeed been lasting effects from it! For three days and four nights the Aiguille Sans Nom had been saturated in the theories of Bakunin, ideas which struck him as wholly in accord with his own musings. From then on he fervently promoted the organisation of disorder, and he soon enlisted the support of his girlfriend L'Innominata, not to mention the aid of the Tour Noir, the Tête Noire and the Aiguille Noire de Peuterey.

'We will not follow any beaten track!' they announced. 'We are revolutionaries in the truest sense of the word, and we will crush all revolutionaries who are not as truly revolutionary as us! And seeing that we oppose violence we shall not hesitate to resort to all forms of violence to overthrow such violence as we encounter elsewhere! We also oppose all hierarchy! Now, what do we see in mountain society today? We see that we all stand at different altitudes! There lies the source of the trouble! No mountain must be higher than any other mountain, and the supporters of the *status quo* cut no ice with us! Down with the fascism of the technocrats, we say! Conceit and vanity is at the root of those fools' morality! And that's not all, either! We're sick and tired of the ridiculous ideas now current about the existence of the Doigt de Dieu. No such Finger of God exists, period. The belief that there is a peak 3974 metres high called the Doigt de Dieu on the ridge of the Meije, east of the Grand Pic and west of the eastern Meije, is nothing but a delusion zealously fostered and disseminated by those most affected. Anyone who believes in it is mentally sick. What's more, Bakunin said that if the Doigt de Dieu did exist it would have to be destroyed, but it doesn't exist anyway, so that makes matters simpler! Up with anarchy! Our order will usher in the day of total disorder!'

But as the anarchist mountains could never agree to stay away from the mountain meetings at the same time, no one ever took their movement very seriously.

However, a party did form in opposition to the Reds and the Blacks, a party promoting strict discipline. Its members were not numerous, but they made a great deal of noise, and the passion they displayed merely aggravated everyone else's discontent. The most active and militant members of this group could soon be identified as the Coup de Sabre, the Grand Gendarme, the Yatagan, the Epée des Périades, the Casque, the Brèche du Carabinier, the Col des Chasseurs, the Aiguilles Dorées and the Écrins.

'Heads must roll!' they proclaimed. 'Once we've chopped off a few of their peaks, and sent a few more off to muck about in the bergschrunds, things will improve! We've had enough of those Reds and Blacks infesting our altitudes! Yes, infesting, that's the word, and let's not fight shy of it! Besides, there's no other way to describe their nauseating presence and equally nauseating ideas. Long ago Mount Ararat showed culpable laxity by letting himself appear in all colours of the rainbow, ready to welcome God knows who! And this sort of thing is still going on! We don't like colour, and what's happening at this very moment under the skies of Savoy isn't calculated to make us like it any better! Things are going from bad to worse. Why, we've even heard from a reliable source that the Aiguilles Rouges are cooking up something really explosive! The only trouble is that the policies they proclaim, determined and revolutionary as they believe them to be, are not what you might call new, and we have not lost our memories. Remember piling Pelion on Ossa? A total failure, right? Conceit and vanity is at the root of those fools' morality! Well, we say no to all that! A good rock-fall and we shall breathe more easily all the way from Briançon to Innsbruck!'

Nor was that all: a little later a movement formed claiming to represent ecological values, and comprising the Aiguille du Jardin, the Tête du Grand Bois, the Pointe du Grand Pré, the Dôme de Chasseforêt, the Aiguille du Fruit, the Oreilles de Lapin, the Cornes de Chamois, the Pointes des Chevrettes, the Grands Mulets and the Papillons Arête: plant and animal lovers to a mountain.

This group campaigned against almost everything: obviously it opposed the driving of pegs and wooden wedges into fissures, but it was also against glaciation, deglaciation, evaporation, fusion, crystallisation, and most of all it was against erosion.

'When,' it demanded, 'when will there be an end to the appalling scandal of erosion? Erosion has to be prevented! Official reports show that the phenomena of erosion are of major significance in a number of sloping sectors, and the situation calls for immediate anti-erosive action, even if our means remain limited and we cannot be absolutely certain of the efficacy of the results. As an interim measure, accordingly, we have decided to induce the marmots to replace gravel on the slopes. This will be a slow process, of course, but all the more reason to start on it at once. Marmots well disposed to our cause must be recruited, and if we can get enough of them together and concentrate our efforts on a single slope at a time, the labour may not be so Herculean as it might appear. We have therefore decided to operate *en masse*. We meet at 6 a.m. on Saturday, 11 July, at the bottom of the Col de la Bûche, which will be our first testing ground. That date does, unfortunately, coincide with the great annual feast day of the marmots, but you are hereby invited to persuade any marmots who may not wish to join in the festivities to take part in Operation Gravel on the Col de la Bûche. If the results looks promising enough, Operation Gravel Mark Two may be envisaged at a later date . . . Support us! Make sure our aims are widely known! And spread our slogan: No to Erosion Power!'

At the same time, the ideas of certain lady mountaineers who considered themselves liberated had not fallen on deaf ears, and the Dames Anglaises, the Femme du Midi, Pointe Isabelle, Pointe Carmen, Pointe Nini, Pointe Marguerite-Micheline, the Pic de la Vieille Femme, the Minettes and the Jungfrau might be seen protesting angrily against all mankind, and all mountainkind too. They set up as a collective, but let there be no misunderstanding: collective ascents were anathema to them.

'Our bodies are ours!' they shrilly announced. 'No one has the right to trample all over us! We must raise our consciousness until we have rid ourselves of the sense of alienation into which man's desire has plunged us! The whole thing is ridiculous! We're treated as nothing but climbing-objects! All they want is to admire our faces, flanks and shoulders! They want to mount us! They want to conquer us — little do they care for the vertiginous depths of our minds! We will no longer tolerate being gang-banged every summer by mountaineers bent on imposing their terrorist, Fascist will on us! We won't tolerate their language either. We demand reforms there too! We want the proverb about the mountain labouring and bringing forth a mouse abolished, because we don't want to bring anything forth, not even a mouse, nothing! We alone matter! Our bodies are ours! Ours! Ours! Ours!'

'Personally,' Gendarme 3037 commented one day when he happened to be in the vicinity, 'I can tell you, unsullied as I am . . .'

'Shut up!' cried the ladies. 'Nonsense!'

In the end there was a tendency for everyone to go round in circles. And then one day, during the 28th session of the 33rd Congress of the Alpine Party, the Cheval Rouge rose to deliver a magisterial speech which electrified his audience.

'The whole thing is scandalous!' he began. 'We have had enough of mankind's odious imperialism! We demand the liberation of the granite masses!'

'And the schist masses!' someone shouted.

'And the limestone masses!'

'We demand,' the speaker continued, 'the liberation of the granite, schist, limestone, sandstone and all other masses!'

'Hear, hear!' shouted everyone.

'And to that end,' he went on, 'we must put a stop to our shameful colonialist exploitation by mankind! We must cast off the yoke of slavery that has oppressed us! Who benefits by the cableways built on our flanks? Mankind! Who gets the vile profits from the rack-and-pinion railways driven into our crusts? Mankind! Whose are the capitalist interests of the hotel centres built in our flesh itself? They are the interests of mankind! There is no way of escaping this hell but to do away with all the parasitic encrustations, all the dictatorial, repressive structures, which have reduced us for too long to the role of pariahs! We are sick of the conditions imposed on us! Fed to the back teeth! Fed to the very summit, in fact! Our patience is at an end!'

'Hear, hear!'

'Only popular mobilisation and mass revolutionary co-ordination will enable us to struggle against the aggressive bourgeois junta which has exploited us until today! Down with the imperialists! Smash the whole outfit! Comrades, our common interests must unite us in the struggle against human aggression and the profit-making classes in an avenging and militant mass offensive!'

'Hear, hear!' cried the mountains.

And since despite his warlike terminology — struggle, combat, offensive, mobilisation and so on — what the Cheval Rouge actually envisaged was a beautiful future of peace, concord, progress, liberty and happiness, almost all the mountains, even those which had once welcomed mankind, fell into line and were carried away on a great tide of opinion which seemed to be opening up a new era in the thousands of years of the alpine massif's existence.

This was how the Alpine Liberation Front, or ALF, came into being. And this time its aims were clear: to get rid of men, whose fragile little bones and soft flesh were so easily destroyed that the venture was not very risky, and all the more enjoyable for that.

The mountains made a slow start, unaccustomed as they still were to organised violence. For several seasons it was just a matter of crevasses gaping wider than usual when climbers were rash, or particularly slow; of more stones falling than usual; of slabs of snow coming adrift more frequently.

The humans could not make it out. 'Sequence of Alpine Accidents', said the newspaper headlines, 'Unprecedented Run of Disasters at Chamonix', 'Series of Tragedies in the Oberland', 'Should Access to Mountaineering be Limited?' Men tried to find reasons, spoke of the meteorological conditions, the inexperience of many young climbers, the increasing pressures of competition. In fact many explanations were found . . . but not the right one!

Winter brought avalanches falling lower and more violently than usual. Chalets, houses and apartment buildings were carried away, at first from the less secure sites, then from places which were supposed to be well out of the range of any danger. People sought to identify those responsible. Town councils, local government and administration and sometimes even national governments were implicated. New laws were passed. Plans for land development were revised. With more common sense than might have been expected, people blamed themselves rather than others for their misfortunes, and consequently managed to limit the damage.

But meanwhile the mountains had taken a liking to violence. They wanted more of it, and they wanted it to be worse. They had acquired a taste for destruction, and they nurtured murderous rage within themselves. One day, for instance, a handsome red nylon rope was traversing the Ciseaux, and for no particular reason the Fou cried, 'Dare you to cut it!'

Whereupon the Ciseaux closed abruptly, destroying not only the rope but the people on it, and causing itself to collapse as well.

The Caïman and the Crocodile started snapping up any mountaineers who came within their reach. The Droites stood so straight and upright that the Cornuau-Davaille turned into a vast overhang (explained by the geologists as the result of 'tectonic movement'). Almost everywhere fissures opened up, sending pegs and wedges clattering to the bottom of the rock-wall below. Mont Pourri, the Grande Ruine and the Aiguille de l'Eboulement became masses of shifting, sliding stones. And mountaineers got into the way of distrusting cracks, crevasses and bergschrunds as though it were a natural phenomenon the way their edges suddenly gaped wide whilst leader and second were on either side of a gap.

Rivalries arose. You were now regarded as lukewarm, and soon as 'suspect', if you had chalked up an inadequate number of violent deaths. The Fou, issuing a unilateral declaration of independence, went so far as to say that he personally was declaring war on the suspect mountains, and periodically sent rockfalls rolling down his flanks at them in all directions. The struggle against mankind continued and intensified. 'Shifting terrain' carried away Pylon P4 of the Grands Montets cable-car, which the locals had always distrusted anyway. Then there was a small earth tremor which destroyed the tower-blocks and domes of Chamonix: as no right-minded human being could regret them, this was not considered a huge success in high places. More successful was the great fall of the Taconnaz glacier, cutting the valley in half between the Houches and the Bossons. Subsequently, accidents multiplied apace.

By the time the law of the 3rd July banning mountaineering was passed, only a very few particularly fanatical enthusiasts were affected: most mountaineers had long since switched to canoeing or sailboarding. To give but one example, the French Alpine Club had no more than twenty-seven active members — not counting, of course, the one thousand seven hundred and ninety-two members of its Administrative Council, who managed eight hundred and sixty-three unsupervised mountain huts. *Mountaineering* magazine had long since changed its name to *Aquatics and Water Sports*.

The reader may be feeling some concern for the fate of the Chamonix guides, who had to be born in Chamonix to belong to their exclusive Company. They were all right: they had already emigrated to Wales, and unless you were a founder member you now had to be a native of Llanberis to join. However, to show how flexible its rules were the Company quoted the case of a young climber born in Llanfairpwllgwyngyll who had managed to gain admission, and had been a member for nearly two years.

Eventually mankind abandoned the high alpine valleys entirely. For a while the disastrous failure of certain building societies made news, but then people turned to other concerns.

By now, however, the mountains could not stop. Faced with this situation, they turned upon each other with invectives of a violence hitherto unknown among them.

'It's your fault, you lot!' howled the Fou. 'You're just lukewarm! They cleared out before we'd destroyed them all! Happy now, are you? You can be proud of yourselves!'

'You've got it all wrong!' shouted his neighbour, the Aiguille de Blaitiere. 'It's idiots like you who hastened their departure by doing too much. If you'd only listened to me . . .'

Whereupon the Fou unleashed a murderous cannonade of rocks. Furious at having several hits scored on him, the Grépon shook so hard that he toppled the Aiguille de la République into the Mer de Glace. The Chaîne des Ecclésiastiques tried in vain to murmur soothing words.

'Who will rid me of these turbulent peaks?' cried the Verte, and with a titanic effort she uprooted the Dru and brought it crashing down on the Ecclésiastiques. This was the signal for general plutonic upheaval. In a fit of infectious fury, the mountains cast off all restraint, some attacking the last remaining vestiges left by the passing of mankind, some turning directly on their neighbours. It was a scene of unbelievable chaos, a thunderous falling of rocks, a downpour of stones, a bombardment of ice, an apocalypse.

When the monstrous, distant din which had shaken the Alps finally died away, and men returned to see what had happened, they could hardly believe their eyes: there were no mountains left! In the fury of their rival claims and internal conflicts, they had succeeded only in destroying themselves. Now, instead of the emerald-green alpine pastures, the deep forests of larches and the tumbling mountain streams, instead of the tall needles of red granite and the sparkling white glaciers, there was nothing to be seen but a great plateau of black and sinister scree, from which, however, there still jutted the pinnacle of the Père Eternel, its rock soaring skyward like the symbol of one last hope.

Translated by Anthea Bell